Sugarfiend

by Caroline Burau

For Best Friends.
And in memory of Tim.

ACKNOWLEDGEMENTS

On the subject of best friends, I actually have way more of them than I deserve. There is Jim, who cheers me, encourages me, loves me endlessly, and stands by patiently with donuts, coffee and technical support.

There is Julie, who lent her spirit for this book, but whose spirit is more resilient than I could ever adequately describe.

There is Kellie, who supports, reads, and sometimes drops my rough drafts into the bath tub.

There is Marie, my sister by something more than blood.

I love you all dearly.

January something, somewhere in the Caribbean.

It's karaoke night here on the SS Sugar Shock and I'm absolutely *killing*. I'm a star, a queen! A legend in my own mind.

Loretta Lynn never struck me as someone who would know exactly how many calories there are in one M&M (seven the in plain, twelve or so in the peanut), but if this song I'm singing at top volume is any indication, the woman does know heartbreak. Heartbreak and lyin' and cheatin'. Therefore, I could absolutely be wrong about the M&Ms.

I've been wrong before.

Like when I thought James was something more than just a thirteenth-stepping chubby-chaser. Or like when I thought Bill was worthy of even touching the hem of my size-14 potato sack. Or like when I thought I could ever, for even one minute, abstain from sugar without eventually going batshit crazy.

As I round the corner from the verse to the chorus, I try to get a read on my audience. Suddenly, I experience one of those moments where one's initial feeling of triumph gives way to the possibility that I actually have toilet paper stuck to my shoe or asparagus in my teeth, if I ever ate asparagus. Or that everyone in this place is completely on to the fact that I am in the middle of *batshit crazy.*

Women like you are a dime a dozen, you can buy 'em anywhere.

For you to get to him, I'd have to move over, and I'm gonna stand right here.

The waitress with the pretzel-stick thighs looks pensive. My twin bunkmates Rhonda and Roxanne look bored and worried, respectively. But, that's how they always look. There's nothing much to read in Rhonda's face that couldn't be found in ten minutes of any given episode of *The Jersey Shore*, but Roxanne's face is really saying something. It's saying, I think, that this journey I'm on was doomed from the start. It's saying that whatever I boarded this ship to do I've long since overdone and that what's needed now is a little restraint. What's needed here is better judgment. Moderation, for crying out loud!

But I don't do moderation. I'm an all-or-nothing girl.

That's how the hell I got here on a week-long Caribbean cruise, spending money I don't have for this trip that was only ever going to sustain my insane decadence for seven days and six nights. My goal, which really is an anti-goal, was to drop all my self-imposed limits, throw up my hands, and just let my addictions take me wherever they would. My goal, when I quit my job, my life and my apartment in Minnesota, was not to have one.

But this isn't quite how I pictured it. Not even twenty-percent as glamorous as I'd hoped. This is what happens when you get your brand new copy of *Eat, Pray, Love* and never get past *Eat*. This is what happens when self-help meets self-loathing. This is Cinderella without a Fairy Godmother, without so much as a pumpkin. This is that little Hobbit dude without his entourage of hot elves on horses. I have no direction, and nobody to tell me where I'm not going. At some point on a personal journey, growth is highly recommended, but in my case, clearly not achievable.

It's easy to see why. When you're a bottomless pit, you're never happy. You just throw stuff down the hole and listen to the echo of it hitting the walls on the way down. You sleep with the wrong guys and you eat stale cake just for the frosting, and you sing Loretta Lynn songs even though you really have *no earthly right*.

It'll be over my dead body, so get out while you can.

'Cause you ain't woman enough to take my man!

I finish Loretta's song with an exaggerated flourish, and the karaoke DJ, a Samoan, super-tan Rosanne Barr, takes the microphone from my hand before the steel guitar is even done playing or the last lyrics have disappeared from the blue screen.

"Thank you for all of that," she says abruptly. "Now for Jenny to sing *I Will Survive.* Jenny? Get on up to here!"

Roxanne gives me her best supportive-mother clap. Rhonda appears to be dozing. Briefly, I reflect on how it feels to have truly, in just about every meaningful way, worn out my welcome.

It's not as satisfying as I'd hoped.

Chapter 1

Five weeks earlier. New Year's Day … to be exact.

Last month's copy of Glamour Mag says people who journal about what they eat and how they feel about it tend to lose more weight and keep it off. The issue also features "Fifty things to do with your breasts."

Today's journal entry is easy because I only ate one thing: an entire pan of peanut butter chocolate frosted cereal bars. Oh, and roughly three glasses of skim milk. I know. That's kind of a lot. I'm missing a self control chip. I'm the Forrest Gump of sugar.

If my life was a box of chocolates, it would be one of those sampler boxes with the flavor guides under the lid. Maple nut. Strawberry cream. Turtle. But here's the thing: In my box, I check the flavor guide, I pick my chocolate, I take a bite, and nothing. Chalk. Chocolate covered chalk.

So I pick another one. Supposed to be a Caramel something. I take a bite. Blast! Chalk. I take another. Chalk. And another. Three guesses as to what I get. Yet I'm surprised every single time.

Anyone else would take the stupid thing back to CVS for a refund. Anyone else would know that no normal person buys herself a box of chocolates to begin with. Only lovers and nursing home patients get chocolates . . . as gifts. Single twenty-somethings aren't supposed to buy themselves chocolates.

Anyway, hope springs eternal, so I just try and try and try every last candy until I'm so full of chocolate-covered chalk I can barely breathe. Too full to even get up and write a sternly-worded letter to Whitman's.

That's my life in a yellow box with cross-stitching.

So it is no surprise that I would find myself here, semi-conscious on the kitchen floor, barely capable of holding pen to paper, and brought to the brink of insanity by a nine by thirteen pan of Special K bars.

I blame this one on a blues musician.

When James asked me to the New Year's Eve party, it was after about a ten-day stretch of not knowing whether we were on or off, coming or going, friends? Friends with benefits? I'm one of those girls who needs to know.

When I asked him where he'd been, he said he'd gotten a gig on a Casino Boat last minute over the holidays, which is complete bullshit because this is the frozen tundra, not St. Louis, so of course some parts of me were wanting to tell him to go flog himself. But those parts never actually show themselves when he's around. Instead the parts of me that want to show him all my naughty parts take over and next thing I know I'm trying to starve myself right in the middle of the holiday season because the only "Little" Black Dress I own is a size twelvish and I'm a size fourteenish this week (originally scheduled for size sixteenish starting January.)

It's not easy to lose a dress size in a little over a week, especially since I got sober, but it can be done. Therefore, for the sake of love, or something which resembles love if viewed in poor lighting, I went ahead and did it.

Because I knew it would only be for nine days, I made Denise Austin my new best friend and did my own little modified Slim-Fast/Lean Cuisine diet. It went a little something like this: One delicious shake for breakfast, one delicious shake for lunch, nausea and headaches all day until dinnertime. At five o'clock, I would at last snarf down a frozen 300-calorie box of some kind of noodles with some kind of sauce. By this point anything I ate tasted like Baked Ziti at the Lexington. For dessert, an apple. Around day three, when my crap began coming out feeling like small live porcupines, I added a couple of

Metamucil wafers to my regimen. (I wouldn't want to end up in the ER, diagnosed with Flaming Slim-Fast Ass.)

New Year's Eve found me nine pounds lighter, one dress size happier, and trying to decide between the black pumps and the black knee-boots. Let me tell you, I was hungry as hell, but high as a kite on that old familiar feeling of *newly skinny*. My roommate, Gloria, said the knee boots made me look easy.

I said, "Really? I've been shitting pinecones for a week just to get ready for one lousy date. I think I took a left past easy about ten blocks ago, my sister."

Gloria snorted. "Trust me, it's the pumps. Plus, I want to wear your boots to work."

When I picked up James last night (his license is suspended for DWI), he barely seemed to notice the dress or the way my hips fit in it or how I curled my hair or that he was in the car with a friggin' member of the female gender, for that matter.

Instead, he paused for a long time, put his seatbelt on, and said, "My sponsor says I should be honest with you. That I owe you an amend."

Here we go. Twelve-step people, man. You should be required to apply for a permit if you want to carry a Big Book.

"In all honesty," he said, "I've been seeing someone special."

Did you copy that so far? New mystery girl: special. Me? Other-than special. Thirty-percent less special than the leading brands. Practically special-free. I definitely should've worn the knee boots.

She's special, all right. He met her at their psychiatrist's office in the lobby. She's a recovering bulimic, anorexic and alcoholic. Hmm. A triple threat. This makes me want to ask how far along she is with that anorexia bit, so I know just how skinny I can expect her to be, but I don't. She's a former model. For who, and of what? I wanted to ask. Vogue? Lingerie? Mills Fleet Farm? What kind of hotness are we dealing with here?

I didn't get much info because the moment we got to the party, James went missing. I mean, his segue to missing was slick enough. He checked my coat in the hotel lobby, presented our pre-paid tickets to the girl in the tuxedo shirt at the door, procured me a Diet Coke with ice, then made a beeline for some guy he "goes to a Monday night meeting with" and *poof* he was one gone alcoholic.

I didn't bother chasing after him. I may be desperate enough to starve myself for nine days for one lousy date, but I don't run in four-inch platforms. That's insanity. Besides, if she's like, *Victoria's Secret* hot, I surely don't want to know.

I'd never been to a "sober" party before, but one thing's for sure: dry drunks really know how to eat. When you've joined a group of people who don't ever plan to drink again (one tick-tock, God-awful day at a time, that is), they tend to have a lot of money to spend that used to go to other recreational activities . . . and they tend to get a little ambitious with the food.

And I'm totally okay with that.

So there I was, stranded, dumped, rejected, and burning with the hunger of ten-thousand fasts. And there it was: the buffet that would make it all go away. Okay, I wasn't exactly stranded since I drove. But upwards of fifteen dollars had been spent to get me into this place, and not eating the food offerings would be a major waste, and well, I just wasn't raised that way.

I looked right; I looked left. No James. I imagined him off in a suite somewhere making out with Miss Someone Special Purge Girl. I took a chilled white plate. I didn't know a soul at this shindig, though I'd been to many meetings since treatment. It would be just like eating alone, only in full hair and makeup.

"Hi! I'm Gregory," chirped a friendly, unfamiliar voice from behind the soup station. "Are you new to the program?"

I sized up Friendly Gregory. On just about any other night, attention from a member of the opposite sex might be enough to abort my mission. The mission, of course, was to eat myself into a frenzy, stuff my purse full of rolls and mints, then get the hell out of there. But I knew right away I could have no romantic intentions toward a man who would walk right up to me and start talking without any prior torture or dance of cool avoidance. Gregory seemed straightforward, honest, and respectful. Snore.

As we loaded our plates with beef roast, creamy salads, and cheesy potatoes, he prattled on and on about his new sober life and how high he was on it and something nonsensical about being a "little boy whistling in the dark."

"What's your drug of choice?" I heard him say after a minute. Sober people ask each other that kind of thing *all the time.* It's how we size each other up. "Alcohol" is an old classic, of course, hinting at the idea that you still might have some money or property that you didn't lose in your using days, but you probably take the bus to work due to the DUI situation. "Pot" reveals you may be deeply immature, yet a great person to have at parties. "Meth" says you're living in your parents' basement and working at Starbucks. "Oxycontin" means you're pretty well set up, but one good back injury away from losing your private practice.

We say we're "cross-addicted" when we don't have time to say that we're addicted to drugs *and* alcohol, or alcohol *and* gambling or drug *and* spending . . . you get the picture. Someone who admits to being "cross-addicted" is usually insanely complicated, knows it, and uses it routinely to pick up members of the opposite sex as they file out of the Al-anon meeting across the hall.

I handed Gregory my dinner plate so I could properly take advantage of the dessert table. He took it without even hesitating. I love alcoholics who are also codependent. I mean, I'm not attracted to them, but they make great friends, and if you relapse, they can always be counted on to hold your hair during the vomiting stage.

"Cheesecake is my drug of choice," I said, popping a chocolate petit-four into my mouth, straight from the table. "And these. And those. And a little bit of that."

"Ha! Yeah, I really like sweets, too." Gregory guffawed. "And coffee. I can't live without my coffee."

"Coffee!" I exclaimed. "That's what mamma needs." I put one last brownie on my insultingly-small dessert plate and turned toward a round table with several large coffee urns and neatly stacked white coffee cups.

"You want coffee?" I asked Gregory, who, thanks to me, had run out of hands to get his own.

"Here," he said politely. "Why don't you take your plates back, go find a table and I'll meet you there with the coffee? I mean, can I sit with you?"

I paused. It wasn't ideal for a binge: an audience, I mean. Oh, what the hell. I nodded my approval slowly, then turned to look for a remote table where the sounds of a buzz-saw wouldn't startle the rest of the guests too much.

Just as I had spotted such a table, and had started walking, I felt a familiar hand on the small of my back.

"There you are!" As if he'd been looking *all over* for me.

"James!" I sighed. *Shit.*

"Hungry?" James sized up my plates, each stacked to capacity.

I looked behind James for his mystery model holding a plate with one lima bean on it, but saw nobody.

"No . . ." I stuttered. "I'm holding these for a friend."

And right on cue, Gregory arrived, balancing our coffee and his own plate and smiling a classic 12-step smile that says *I keep a Post-It of the Serenity Prayer on my bathroom mirror!*

"Uh huh," James said. "Anyway, Es, I just wanted you to know that you don't have to bring me home tonight if you don't want to."

16

"Really, why?" God in heaven, musicians are horseshit liars. Blues musicians, doubly so.

"I, uh, ran into some old friends who are staying here, so, I'll just crash here, you know, or not, but either way I can catch a cab later."

"Of *course* you can."

"I'm Gregory," Gregory said, high on sobriety. "I'd shake your hand, but . . ."

"It's cool," James said, still looking at me with about a quarter-cup of concern.

"Okay." It was all I could think to say.

"Enjoy your dinner." James pecked me on the cheek. "Happy New Year." He was gone before I could remind him about how I was holding all that food for a friend. A very, very hungry, depressed and lonely friend whose life is beyond pathetic.

When we at last reached our table, I grabbed a fork and dug the hell in. Gregory timidly unrolled his utensils from their neat, white cloth napkin.

"You ever been on a cruise?" he asked awkwardly. "If you like buffets, you'd love cruises. Enough food to choke a horse. I just got back from one."

I never got that expression, but I've also never seen a choking horse.

"Oh yeah?" I said, taking a second between bites to breathe. "You do look rather sun-kissed."

"Yeah," Gregory said hesitantly, popping a small piece of bread stick into his mouth. "Uh, I can see you're in a lot of pain."

"What? No, I'm awesome! Healthy as a horse." Since we're on the subject of horses...

"You're not. Would you like to talk about what just happened?"

Oh, *hell* no.

I put my fork down. This would not do.

Greg straightened up like somebody ready to receive. He crossed the fingers of both hands like a priest in his confessional. I took the napkin off of my size twelvish dress and set it on the table.

It's not that I wasn't still hungry. I was *so* hungry. I was a swirling tornado pointing down into a sucking abdominal wall -- a gaping, needy abyss. But I had to get out of there. Gregory was going to ruin my buzz with all his program talk.

"Excuse me just a sec," I said, gesturing toward the restroom.

Sorry, Gregory. It's not your fault.

One of my drugs of choice just dumped me for a Victoria's Secret model.

***

Dick Clark, you inspiring bastard. There you go, rocking America's New Year's Eve, even though you're something like 109 years old, post-stroke, one side of your mouth chasing the other side around like a wounded puppy, and nobody actually able to understand a word you say including your co-host, the irrepressible, knock-kneed, candy-apple-lipped Taylor Swift. No matter. It's basically the same thing every year, anyway. You go, Dick. You go on and do that thing you do, whatever the hell it actually is.

God, I'm a bitter woman. Dick Clark is an American institution. Taylor Swift is the songwriter of at least a quarter of a generation. It's just that I have no desire to ring in the New Year with them. I had such high hopes for this night, this first New Year's Eve since getting sober nine months ago, this big-ass drinking holiday, during which James' love was going to take away the sting of giving up booze and drugs, which at this moment I don't actually miss . . .

Why don't I? Why don't I want to drink?

Probably because of my super-stable rock-solid sobriety and superb mental health. Yeah. That's why.

***

When I picked up the first Special K bar and poured the first glass of milk, it felt good. It felt right, and I was justified.

If you're not familiar with the Special K bar then let me school you. Special K bars are like rice crispy bars in that they are named for a dry, flavorless cereal, which if eaten with milk equals just a few empty carbs and some protein, and could even be somebody's idea of a diet-conscious type of food. For Special K bars, one takes said dry cereal, adds it to about three pounds of butter, three cups of corn syrup, and in this case, a whole bag of caramel chips, melts it all together over medium heat, spreads it into a 9 x 13 pan, then covers it with chocolate frosting from a can.

The Special K cereal is in there for the crunch-factor, probably, but mostly because without the Special K, one might as well just take a stick of butter, dip it like a French fry into a vat of caramel, and call it dessert.

When I picked up that first Special K bar, I was actually hungry. And, okay, just a smidge upset. Dick Clark was smiling his half-smile at me like he knew this would be my evening all along. Taylor Swift and her little size 4 white pea-coat shrugged condescendingly. Right at that moment, she was writing a song for me in her curly-haired little dome called, "Estelle Eats Alone On Hip Holidays" (strumma strumma strumma) and already thinking about making it a duet with Kid Rock.

Effing James and his effing amends. Special K Bar Number One went down fast. Like a twig in a wood-chipper fast. As I was lacking in protein, I noted that *milk* is high in protein and basically drank the first glass in one long guuuuuuhlp.

Effing models. Effing therapists offices.

19

Bar number two barely registered.

If I'd been in the appreciating mode, I would have noticed that number two, like number one, was a little salty and very sweet, crunchy, creamy, warm. A culinary triumph, really. Bravo, Gloria.

I poured another glass of protein and wondered for a moment how many bars I could eat before Gloria would take notice and ask me just what the hell happened.

Effing Gloria. Why isn't she here? Why aren't we on this binge together, therefore justifying its very existence and exonerating us both from any actual wrongdoing?

Bar three was nothin' but net. I slowed down on the milk a little. Denise Austin says it's possible to have too much protein. I think that DVD's around here somewhere . .

Bar four.

Bar five.

Effing Gregory and his treatment high.

Bar six could've been a chocolate covered Brillo pad for all I knew.

More milk.

I was only going to have the one. Okay, that's a lie. But I didn't plan on – I *never* plan on -- eating until there's an economy car in my stomach. It's no wonder I can't find a decent man. I'm not right in the head, that's why. I'm an addict out of control.

A fiend.

Size fourteen going on size 40.

Okay, I figured, still in the denial stage of this particular blow-out, *All is not lost.* I calculated just exactly how many calories I consumed, so that I could make up for this most egregious lapse in judgment by eating fewer calories for the rest of the week. If there are 500 calories in one piece, then what we have here is . . . just multiply that by six . . . okay I mean fourteen pieces . . . okay 3,000 calories.

Therefore, if I ate only 1200 calories each day for the next seven days, I can make it all go away.

Or, if I work out a couple extra hours every day for the next week.

Or I could take up bulimia . . . but just as a part-time thing.

Or I could cut off one of my arms and lose twenty pounds instantly. Wonder how much for a leg.

Or I could stop doing this. I could just stop.

Hah! Stop.

On the up side, at least for this one precious moment, I felt that if I ever so much as looked at another sweet, sugary thing, I'd explode into a million jagged shards. I was incapacitated. Sugar shocked, I fell asleep on the couch with the TV on like a drunken bum.

Bea would later remind me that it could be worse because I didn't relapse on drugs or alcohol. Just eat less next time, she'd say. Bea is my AA sponsor, and she has weighed 123 pounds (give or take five pounds, she always adds) for her entire adult life, which in my book makes her an alien life form. Bea keeps Reese's Peanut Butter Cups in her bread box and eats maybe one or two a week. What kind of shit is that? Bea is immune to the pull of sugar, and therefore cannot be trusted.

***

When I woke to the sound of Sesame tipping over half a glass of milk on my coffee table, the digital VCR clock read 8:04. Jack would be expecting me to work by 9. Gloria got off at 7, so . . . maybe she had to stay late.

When I moved to Minneapolis after treatment, I thought it would be the beginning of a different kind of life from the pathetic, drugged-out existence I'd had in St. Paul. Everyone told me how progressive Minneapolis was. Sober clubs. Posh coffee shops. Vintage clothes. Sober clubs: meat-markets with near-beer. Posh coffee shops: What's so wrong with asking for whipped cream and caramel drizzle on my house blend? Vintage clothes: Plenty of cool frocks to be had, if you're a size Depression.

Every night I drive the freeway from the north end of the city to the south end, wondering where everyone's going and whether I'm late for there, wherever it is. I stare up at the high-rises, wondering if all the people behind the lighted windows are as baffled as I am about the simplest things. What am I doing? Am I too young? Am I too old? Too fat? Am I wrong? Am I right? Am I lovable? Am I here? Is this thing on?

See why I need a boyfriend? Chicks with boyfriends are too busy worrying about their next great date outfit to get all "what does it mean" about everything all the time. Chicks with boyfriends eat Special K with milk and Splenda, the way it's supposed to be eaten, and they never, ever, kiss their TV screens on New Year's Eve.

As I watched Sesame make milk-prints across my coffee table, I noticed VCR clock had jumped to 8:24. Getting up from the couch was no picnic, but losing my job because I ate too much might make it seem as if I had some sort of *food issue.* I wondered if this was what it feels like to be one of those drug smugglers who swallows like twenty sacks of hashish or whatever so they can get it from place to place undetected.

I showered, scrunched my hair a bit, and donned some black Gap sweats. New sweatpants are a sugarfiend's best friend because they make you look like you haven't given up on your looks completely, yet they don't judge you. They don't tell you your stomach's bloated, they just tie all nice and loosely wherever you want them to.

I cleaned up the puddle of milk on the coffee table and left Gloria a note by the half-ravaged pan of Special K bars.

"Some friends came over and we had a few too many. Hope you don't mind. They were so good!"

"Denial," Bea would tell me later as if she herself wrote it, "is not a river in Egypt."

I wrapped myself into a nice long unbelted wool coat, put on my "I'm a normal working girl who gets a healthy balance of protein and greens" face, and headed out the door into the Happy New Year.

Chapter 2

It's hard to get anything past Jack; he's a sensitive type of guy. He says because he's paralyzed from the neck down that all of his other senses are heightened: sight, taste, and smell especially. He can smell a pot-smoker a mile away. He can tell if a woman is menstruating just by being in the same room.

Man.

Of course when I showed up for work all gorked with Special K Remorse, he could tell like always that something was amiss. But he didn't hassle me. He just let me move kinda *slow*. We popped in his *Hotel California* CD and I got all weepy when we got to *The Sad Café*. He just grabbed a Kleenex in his curly old hand and passed it to me.

Lately, Jack's the best friend I've got. Picture Bruce Willis during his *Moonlighting* days, but with blond hair and a sleek, black electric wheelchair. For the last eight months, I've seen him every day, twice a day. I'm his only employee. Sometimes I wish he had more people working for him, so I could get some time off (to do *what*, I don't exactly know). Whenever I ask about the others who used to work for him, he just says, *Oh, this one has bad B.O.*, or *that guy drinks all my coffee*. Nobody's good enough. It's okay, I guess. I don't mind getting paid for twelve hours a day, seven days a week. Keeping a wardrobe in five different sizes does get somewhat expensive.

Sundays and holidays are nice and easy because he doesn't have to wear a shirt and tie like he does during the week when he works as a programmer for some insurance company. Sundays and holidays mean just jeans and T-shirts, which are loose and easy to put on him. And he doesn't have to be anywhere on time.

Every day, before getting him into his shower chair, I exercise Jack's stiff, pale legs to keep the blood circulating. As I pump them up and down and back and forth, I try not to stare at the Playboy centerfolds that cover his bedroom walls from floor to ceiling. Of course the harder you try not to look at something, the more you end up looking at it, and pretty soon it's just a vicious, fake-boobed, Brazilian-waxed cycle.

It took me a long time to get used to Miss January, Miss February, and all the other 110-pound months of the year, with their glossy skin, impossibly tiny naked bellies and perfect areolas. If you look at them long enough, though, they start getting rather cartoonish and silly, like the whole Kardashian family, or Michele Bachmann. Still, they're always there to remind me that I already ate more calories before 9 a.m. than they have all week. And they're always, always smiling as though it's perfectly normal to be wearing nothing but half a bustier and a pair of reading glasses while checking out books at the Old Miss library.

Jack says he just likes having the centerfolds handy in case he wants to read the articles on the back. This makes me want to draw mustaches and black eyes on every last one of them while he sits there helpless to stop me.

When we're done with physical therapy, I shower him, dress him, and spray him with cologne. When he's all settled into his wheelchair, I make breakfast. Strawberry waffles when the berries are in season, Eggos when they're not. I didn't eat breakfast this morning, of course. Black coffee, no Sweet 'n Low today. Jack takes his coffee black too, with an extra long straw. We sipped in silence, but for the Eagles in the background. Jack's a good friend.

I gathered up his dirty clothes for weekly laundry, set up his coffee so he could reach it without help, rolled him a joint, and lit a candle for him to light it off of. It's not as hard as you'd think . . . being a recovering addict and rolling joints for someone else. He's not doing it to get stoned. Without cannabis, Jack's body is one big muscle spasm twenty-four hours a day. Too bad he has to purchase these essential meds from a freelance "sidewalk artist" named *Pez.*

Before I loaded everything up for the Laundromat, he gave me a hug. He shrugged helplessly.

"Talked to Bea lately?"

"Good idea," I mumbled. "See you tonight."

Chapter 3

Jack

In my dreams, I can still walk.

I hike to the top of the cliff and look down on the Mississippi. The sun wraps around my long hair and lights me from behind like a rock star on stage in front of thousands. There are no spine-breaking rocks at the bottom, just infinite blue water. My college buddies egg me on, tell me which dive to do this time. A gaggle of girls in bikinis and tube tops giggle and swoon. They can't believe I'm going to jump again.

In my dreams, I fear nothing!

Sometimes, Estelle is one of the girls on the cliff with me. She never wants me to jump; in fact she always looks ready to vomit. But she is outnumbered. I ask her to join me. She backs away and tells me I'm crazy. We could play that game all day and I know she'll never jump. The me watching the dream knows it, but the me in the dream pulling on her just keeps trying and trying to get her. Get her to jump. Get her to be with me anywhere. She just laughs. She never jumps, but she looks killer in that tube top.

Finally, I jump, but never hit the water.

I just fall and fall.

Then I wake up.

When I open my eyes, Estelle's always there, but I'm not a tan, cock-sure college co-ed anymore. I'm a long skinny crippled dude with atrophied, pointed feet and curled hands. I'm a man who can't get out of his bed or piss without help. And I'm naked.

We say very little in the morning hours, and it's comfortable. We tune the radio to a talk show that alternately expounds on the news of the day and spins bands like Jethro Tull and Steely Dan. Estelle hops up on the bed for my physical therapy. She pushes on my stubborn feet and bends my legs. She lifts them in and out, up and down.

When she pulls me out of bed for my shower, it is a series of hugging and tugging. We interlock arms to slide me over, she tugs my ass to the end of the bed. I put my arms up and around her to sit up. She locks my knees in hers, we embrace again, then she swings me in one final move and I am seated in a shower chair.

We shower; she gets about as wet as I do. I'll admit to a few staged spasms here and there. She's almost never got a bra on under her T-shirt. I think you get the picture.

She dries me. I'm fussy about this. If she doesn't dry me well, I pay later. If I correct her too much, she gets a look. Tough. When it comes to my skin, I'm like a soldier in a war. My body, my wheelchair, my clothes, everything that touches me is at war with my skin. I have to keep it perfect and without agitation. People think that being a quad means you can't feel anything, like your body becomes a chunk of dried beef that does nothing more than hold your head up. But it's not true. Instead, my body is like a baby that I have to watch every second or it will stick a finger in the electrical socket and fry me, or roll over in two inches of water and silently suffocate. My body can always find new ways to fail me, kill me. I can feel pain, but I might not know where it's coming from until it's too late. I can still break bones, but I can't heal them.

After my shower, Estelle puts me back onto the bed the same way she got me out, dries me some more. Now it's time to deal with the issue of my penis. If you'd have told me at age nineteen that some hired chic would be messing around with my lower half every single morning for the rest of my life, I'd have done cartwheels. But I could never have imagined this. Now my dick is part of a health-care routine. It's a caution, another on a long checklist of my body parts that must remain clean, dry, unblemished and properly handled. It's no picnic. Dozens, maybe a hundred or more different people, women and men, have handled me down there. They handle it not like an instrument of power or pleasure, but like a dead fish to be wrapped. They handle it like a wound that needs bandaging. They inspect this, comment on that.

Estelle carefully slides a condom catheter over my penis. This is basically a thick condom with a tube that attaches to a leg bag, which straps to my leg and collects my piss. In order for the condom to roll on properly, I have to be erect. That never seems to be a problem in the morning.

Sometimes, Estelle gets embarrassed at this point, and I have to admit I'm glad. I'm still a man, anyway. I'm entitled to a little bit of a reaction every so often. That's what it's there for. It's not an inanimate object. It lives. I live.

In fact, it's the only part of me that's the same as it was before the accident. There are divots in my head from the metallic halo that held it steady the first two months after the accident. On my neck are surgical scars. My chest and shoulders, once thick and muscular, are now pale and flat. My arms are bent and atrophied, my fingers, only strong enough to bring a cigarette to my lips or tap the keys on a keyboard. My legs, of course, useless. My feet, calloused and pointed.

My dick, absent any brace or apparatus, just rises and rests, rises and rests like it always did. It is oblivious to the state of its counterparts or that it sits right in the center of a unit that everyone says is "paralyzed."

Though I try not to think about it, I know that someday, my plumbing will get too old and lazy for the condom, and some nurse will insert the long plastic tube of an internal catheter. Then my crippling will be complete.

Estelle goes quietly through the motions of hooking the condom to a tube, which attaches to a bag on my leg. That's how it gets done. All day long I collect my piss in a bag, so I can bring it home and make her empty it.

Then she dresses me. More tugging, pulling, these socks, those pants, careful with my sack!, straighten my waistline. Again, she clamps her knees around mine, we lock our arms around each other's necks, and she swivels me into my electric ride. She sprays cologne on my neck, my oxford dress shirt goes on, my tie. Then my tie comes off because she tied it crooked. Then it goes back on.

She examines me in the mirror, straitens my tie, smoothes down a kink with her hand. She checks her own image too. Her hair is frizzy and matted; her eyes are tired. She regards herself like someone who has woken to find a flooded basement, or cat puke on the rug. Her self-loathing is her guilty pleasure, next to binging. She thinks I don't know. Why do chicks do that to themselves? Blows my mind.

I check the mirror one last time and take us both in. I'm not some lanky college boy with strong lean legs anymore, and there are no more cliffs for me to jump off. But I'm the crippled computer geek, closet romantic who hugs her four times every morning without fail. And she is the beautiful, disheveled, sour-breathed maiden who handles my junk every single damn day.

We pretend that it is unremarkable, all this touching. We sip our morning coffee and take in the weather channel like two old marrieds. We eat waffles. Then I go off to work and try not to think about her arms around my neck, her bare feet in my shower.

Chapter 4

Food journal. Why didn't I think of that?

Let's call it FJ for short. The nutritionist who told me to write this food journal says I don't have an eating disorder, but I have disordered eating. I didn't have the heart to tell her about last month's Glamour. *I have a feeling she was giving me her A Game.*

Despite the Special K debacle, I got up Monday, got Jack out the door to work, then proceeded to eat like seven or possibly ten strawberry waffles. That can't be normal. I couldn't stop shoving, chewing, chewing, chewing. More. More. More.

So I called my HMO, who transferred me to someone, who made an appointment. I took the bus; downtown driving scares me.   I had some time to kill before my appointment, so I stopped for sliders at the WC.

Which is a real pisser because I'd forgotten about the fact that when you go to the clinic, they make you get on a scale no matter what you're there for, even if it's like a bloody nose or a broken pinky toe. So, I made the nurse wait while I took off my shoes, my coat, my hat, my sweatshirt, my belt, and my headband. I also took some change out of my pocket, but stopped short of removing my earrings.

The nutritionist was maybe five years older than me, and could've even gone to my same suburban high school, but probably made "better life choices" (as Bea would say) to get this far in her chosen career. She gestured toward a cushioned chair that was angled to her desk, and she flashed me a reassuring a smile that instantly told me she had already decided not to be surprised by anything I was about to tell her.

"Estelle, what brings you here?"

I wanted to say "the bus," but instinctively knew she'd also decided not to find me funny.

"Um, I think I have an eating problem."

"How so?"

"Cravings run my life. Sugar. I can't stop thinking about it. Sometimes I eat all the time. Sometimes I diet. I want to be skinny, but you'd never guess it because I'm always just trying to figure out ways to stuff myself."

She appeared unmoved, so I continued.

"On New Year's Eve, I ate half a pan of Special K bars. You know the ones, like butter, sugar, Special K."

"Um hmm. What else do you like?"

"Cake. Donuts. If men tasted like cake and donuts, I'd probably work harder at being skinny so I could have more of them. I like men and cake and donuts."

She smiled a smile that felt more like a pat on the head. I recognized the look from treatment. It's what happens when I free-think and shut off my filter, and it almost always happens when I'm sitting in a cushy chair, at an angle, with a clinician of some sort.

"I think you're very typical," she said finally.

"That kind of hurts," I said frankly. It really did.

"I mean that I see a lot of women like you," she said. "Now, I have a series of questions to ask you so I can make some recommendations."

"Okay," I said, ready to blow her socks off.

"Do you eat breakfast?"

Seriously?

Twenty minutes later, I was back on the bus, free again to roam among the masses, an addict set loose on a city of delis, pancake houses, and bakeries.

Fuck! I was agitated. I ached to start a fight with the bus driver, who hadn't said "hello" back to me when I got on. The bus rolled past Mickey's Diner. *I should have stopped for pancakes*. Hunger and disappointment boiled in my belly.

How could she leave me to my own devices? The last time I asked for help, admitted to being addicted to booze and whatnot, they put me in a 30-day program, and I was whisked away, and it was awful, but comfortable. The food was good, and there was plenty of it. I wanted another 30-day program for my eating insanity. I wanted someone to tell me I'm not normal, that I have to go away and be coddled and nurtured, and in 30 days, or 60 or even 90 days, I can pop out brand new like a slimy little baby with toned thighs and a six-pack.

I want someone to make me fix it. I mean, tie me down. Save me from myself, my mouth, my hands, my stomach.

But I don't have disease, she said, just disorder.

What does that mean?

What do you do with disorder? Call 911? Help me, please, I'm disordered.

I wonder if my nutritionist's got it too. I mean, I sized her up and she looks pretty normal. But then, so do I until I start talking. I wonder if she goes to Cub Foods every day after eating a sensible lunch, buys three cookies from the bakery, a slice of deli cheesecake, and a box of Oreos, then takes them home and washes them down with a glass of skim milk (You know, because there are just too many calories in two percent). I wonder if she keeps gummy worms under her bed, or hides Hershey Kisses from her kids. I wonder.

Did she at least *used* to have disorder? Couldn't she have just told me if she had? Miss Perfect Nutrition? Miss tweed suit with the square buttons and the perfect lip liner?

Disordered eating. Gawd. It's so *middle of the road*.

I wish I had the guts to just go ahead and get super-fat. So fat that Jack wouldn't look at me the way he sometimes does with his beautiful long blond eyelashes and his shriveled hands under his chin. So fat that I could say James never calls me because I'm so fat, and not because of some Bulimic model, who is just so *complicated.*

So fat that I could go audition for one of those shows where they put you on national television and humiliate the fat out of you. Yeah! I should get super-fat, go on The Biggest Loser, and let Jillian Michaels stand on my back while I do pushups, then later thank her for saving my life with her precious, trademark cruelty.

But if I can't achieve super-fatness, then I wish I could be one of those super-models who live on cigarettes and spinach salads with fat-free dressing. Then like once a week I could eat a whole loaf of bread and then barf it up because my parents got divorced when I was ten, which they, in fact, did not.

Instead, I reside in diet purgatory. Instead, I wake up every morning knowing every bite I eat must again be voted on by the deranged, demented committee in my head. This committee has no clear goals or objectives except to keep me completely in the dark about what dress size I will be from one week to the next and to make sure I feel just a little bit hungry twenty-four hours a day, no matter what I eat or how much of it.

Oh, why must I be just one binge shy of an honest disorder?

Do I need to try harder?

And if so, in what direction?

So, anyway, Miss Perfect Buttons gave me a book called *When Food Is Love.*

Whatever.

Perhaps it should be called *I ate half of Minneapolis without puking yesterday, and all I got was this lousy book.*

Chapter 5

I feel like I've reached some sort of bottom. A sugar bottom? It's been twenty-four hours since I had any sugar. But the day is young.

I talked to Bea. She said "Go to a meeting." She always says "Go to a meeting." She also always says:

Easy does it.

One day at a time.

God never gives us more than we can handle.

The only meeting you're ever late for is your first one.

But she said something new this time. She seemed kind of flustered; she said, "Why don't you stop when you're full?" I had no answer. She said that I should try Overeater's Anonymous.

Shit.

I'm a drunk; I'm a druggie. Now I'm an Overeater? There's a twelve-step group for everything. I've been at meetings where it takes people three minutes each just to identify themselves. "Hi, I'm so and so, and I'm chemically dependent, alcoholic, a recovering bulimic, a shopaholic, a gaming addict . . ."

All I've ever heard about OA is that they practice "abstinence." Abstain from what? Sugar? Food? Can't be food. Everybody has to eat.

Abstain from sugar? Must be sugar. Can't be sugar. Must be water. Or perhaps oxygen.

I went to an AA meeting instead.

The Maplewood Alano Club is a two-story house owned by the adjacent church. I talked Gloria into going there once, but usually, I go alone or with Bea.

I went to my usual mid-morning meeting, which I can attend between mornings with Jack and afternoons – eating and working out. The meetings start with everyone in the main hall, men and women, praying the serenity prayer and making announcements about potlucks and softball tournaments. Sometimes I get hit on at this point, which I like. Recently, I've begun a little bit of a stare-fest with a brown-haired Metro Mobility driver, who, as far as I can tell, has a decent handle on the sober life. He drives a Mitsubishi Eclipse and wears khakis every day. Definitely more *preppy* than anyone I had ever dated. Perhaps the perfect thing for a sugar-free lifestyle.

After announcements, everyone headed to their respective groups. I took one last look at Mr. Preppy and headed to the women's meeting.

Nice pants.

I think his name was Leo. I figure Leo and I could join a health club together, and get completely buff. His love and concern would keep me skinny. We would find a two-bedroom apartment, we would adopt a second cat, a buddy for Sesame, and we would live attractively ever after.

By the time it was my turn to talk, I realized I hadn't listened to a word anyone said.

Shit. What step are we on? Can it be that I'm too scattered . . . for AA?

I'm Estelle, I'm an alcoholic," And a drug addict, and a sugar fiend, and sometimes I talk to my Denise Austin DVDs.

"Hi, Estelle," spoke a room full of women who had been talking about the seventh step and its impact on their lives.

"I, uh, struggle with people places and things that are out of my control," I glanced up at the group, finding a friendly-faced, pony-tailed lesbian named Tony to focus on. "I'm sober, but I'm just nuts. I'm nuts."

A number of um-hums and sighs of acknowledgement emanated from the group.

"And … I think I'm going to try an Overeater's Anonymous meeting today later. I just feel like maybe that's what I should do. You know what they say. If nothing changes, nothing changes, right?"

Enthusiastic head-bobbing all around. Atta girl. Good for you.

Oh my God. Does that mean they think I'm fat?

Tony hugged me after the meeting. I get along well with lesbians, generally, and especially gay men. I think it's that angsty, unstable *Judy Garland* thing I've got going. Anyway, when I got back out to the parking lot, Leo's ride was gone. As often happens after listening to a bunch of women spill their guts out, I was hungry again, this time for something sweet and cakey. I headed to the gas station to buy some cupcakes and half a gallon of skim milk.

AA made me want to eat. Not eating made me want to eat. Eating made me want to eat. Maybe Bea was on to something.

I pointed my car toward Jack's place. I figured I could use his computer to find an OA meeting. Plus, I could eat my cupcakes in peace without wondering what's going on with Gloria or Sesame trying to steal my milk.

***

"Estelle?"

"Mmmmph."

"Wake up, Es." Jack paused. "Or don't. I mean, are you sick or something?"

"What? No. Sweetie. Hi." *Just your basic Hostess Hangover, that's all.*

Jack had managed to open the front door, make his way through it, close it, and maneuver his sport jacket off -- all normally my job. I rolled off his old brown sectional and straightened my baggy jeans a bit.

"How was work?" He seemed tired; I gently loosened his tie and pulled it over his head.

"Hey! You know. It's a wheelchair world, after all."

"Fuckin' A, dude. My thoughts exactly."

"You hungry?"

"I, uh, had a snack a little while ago, so I'll just make something for you," I muttered.

"How 'bout a pork chop and a baked potato?"

"How about a black eye and a fat lip?"

"Woman! I will punch you in the clit."

"Bring it, Beeyatch!" I said, then ambled off to the kitchen to make his meal.

Jack ate in silence while I sipped some milk.

"I'm, uh, going to a meeting tonight," I said finally. "But I'll be back at nine for nighty-night time."

"I thought you always did those during the day," Jack said, stabbing a pre-cut piece of meat.

"I did. I do. This is an Overeater's Anonymous meeting."

Jack just blinked.

"I need you to just nod and say 'okay' like I'm not a total freak," I said, defeated. "And like everybody you know is as jacked up as I am."

"Okay, beautiful." Jack smiled. "You show those overeaters how it's *done.*"

Chapter 6

Gloria

I hate keeping things from her. She's my best friend. I don't know why I do this to myself. Get a good thing going, then shoot it all to hell.

If I tell her what's going on with me, she'll just try to get me to another one of those sad-ass meetings she's always at. Or get a sponsor. Isn't a sponsor someone who's supposed to give you money? "And now, a word from our sponsor?" I don't need advice. Still trying to recover from all the swell advice I got in treatment.

Estelle always took the whole Twelve-Step thing so much more seriously than I could. All those meetings. All that coffee and commiserating. I never got the point.

Estelle was the only girl even close to my age in treatment. She looked like she belonged there even less than I did. Her teeth were a little brown, but she had nice clothes and a new haircut, and she was plain, but pretty. She had all the ghetto guys hitting on her, and then all the middle-aged white chicks telling her they'd spilled more than she's ever drank. Maybe so, but I saw her thumbnails up close, all burnt. I know what's what.

In between groups, we talked for hours over Kool cigarettes and decaf coffee. Seems like our using stories were almost the same, except she grew up a lot more sheltered than I did, so everything I did was just the slightest bit more messed up than anything she'd done.

She slept around a little, but I'd had two kids by the time I was twenty. She smoked a lot of crack, but I've smoked more, and for longer, and I've forged more checks. My mom's a drama-queen speed-freak working on her third divorce, and my

41

dad has cirrhosis of the liver. Estelle's parents are just Catholic.

We both had boyfriends in treatment, of course. I started sleeping with this mulatto pot-dealer named Tyrone, and Estelle met an out-of-work blues guitarist named James. Tyrone was just something to do; somebody to keep the other weirdoes from hitting on me. But Estelle got all wrapped up in James. And he got all wrapped up in her . . . for about five minutes. By the time he got his thirty-day chip, he was already calling his ex-girlfriend on the pay phone between groups and thanking Estelle for "being such a good friend" during his "difficult adjustment period."

On the other hand, sometimes that girl just begs to get dumped on. Poor old Estelle. I'll never forget her standing there with her thirty-day pin, all suede pumps and mopey eyes. Should have been so proud of herself for 30 straight days of sobriety; instead, she's just standing there with that "everybody leaves me" look on her face.

That night, we went to Red Lobster, just the two of us, to celebrate our freedom. We didn't drink, but man, I never seen anybody who could binge as hard as me until I met Estelle.

We'd eaten our share of Doritos and box cake in treatment, but when I watched her eat five biscuits, thirty fried shrimp, one baked potato, and one Mount Chocolate Sundae all by herself, I knew this was the beginning of a beautiful friendship.

That night, we shared all our dirty little food secrets. I used to eat whole sticks of butter in the middle of the night when my parents were sleeping. Estelle once drank a whole jar of honey after being dumped by the drummer for Austin Healey.

We went back to her parents' house and stayed up for hours eating their leftover Halloween candy and sharing euphoric recall of fish-bowl-sized margaritas and grocery-shopping on acid.

We talked about when we used to fit into size 30 Guess Jeans without sucking anything in or busting anything out.

We cried about my son and daughter, both adopted and living in separate and unknown suburban towns with other families.

We kept each other sober.

That was then. We're still sober, I guess, but we're not on the same road. Poor old Estelle is going to get left behind again. It's not about her, though she'd never believe it. I don't even know what it is *about.*

I saw him again last night, but I'm not in love. I'm just doing what comes naturally. Ruining everything.

Chapter 7

Day 1: Sugar Free?

Just for today, I am committing myself

Just for today, I commit to a plan of abstinence from sugar. I can see now that sugar has become an addiction for me, just like my drugs and alcohol. I'm reading the OA literature pamphlets, I'm eating a lot of carrots (natural sugars), and I'm doing my daily Inner Harvest meditations. So, I commit to eat only foods with . . . well . . . which don't have sugar. I guess what I'm promising is to NOT do something, instead of to DO something.

The OA meeting was just what I expected. It was just like AA, only a little fatter. Church bible study room. Tiny chairs. Baby Jesus drawings all over the place. A whole room full of Baby Jesus drawings laughing at all the fat chicks in tiny chairs. I could relate to everything I heard, what I was able to concentrate on. The cupcakes still had me a little buzzed.

They talked about "abstinence." Abstinence involves refraining from the great joys of my life: sugar, fatty foods, and compulsive eating.

They said "Try it for just one day. Aren't you sick and tired of being sick and tired?"

Yeah, but . . .

They said the definition of insanity is doing the same thing over and over and expecting different results. Denise Austin's perfect tennis shoes bounced and bounced on my temples with the eternal dance of the desperate. What am I without insanity? Repetition is all I know. *Just four more, three more, two more, one more.* Denise Austin insisted. *Good! Just fifty-three sets to go!*

45

One day at a time, right? What have I got to lose? Wait until Gloria gets a load of this no sugar business. She's going to freak.

I cleaned out all foods that contain sugar from my kitchen, my backpack, my glove box, my purse, my flute case, and the shoebox underneath my bed, which left me a bag of apples and a veggie burger from some bygone diet. I'll have to go grocery shopping after work. Gloria eats junk food by the bucket-load, which could be a bit of a problem. But she's not a sugar fiend like me. She just eats sticks of butter. Not sure what that's called.

Anyway . . .

Day one without sugar wasn't too bad. I made Jack his strawberry waffles for breakfast without any problem. Jack thinks I'm crazy, by the way. When I got syrup on my finger, I wiped it with a wet towel instead of licking it.

Then I said a prayer:

God, grant me the serenity to accept the foods I cannot eat, the courage to eat the three or four things that taste halfway decent, and the wisdom to put salad dressing on everything else.

I'm hungry.

Nothing to eat in my backpack or my purse.

Oh, yeah. And just for the record, I ate three eggs with cheese for breakfast, a ham sandwich and twenty saltines for lunch. Beef stroganoff with Jack for dinner. A handful of saltine crumbs after I helped Jack to bed.

I was a little shaky with him in the shower. Sugar withdrawals, I suppose. I can never get his ball-sack to sit right in the shower chair. The shampoo slipped off onto the floor, and it made an ominous thud. I said, "What was that?" and Jack said, "My scrotum."

We laughed. Oh, the hi-jinks.

Still hungry.

Always hungry.

I have to find something new to do in the afternoons when I'm waiting for Jack to get back from work. I used to watch "General Hospital" and make cookies. Or I'd keep the TV off and make cookies and eat cookie dough. I'll have to find something else. Certainly, "General Hospital" is not something one can watch without some kind of stimulant.

Note to self: find something to do that doesn't involve sugar.

Cross-stitch?

Hang-gliding?

Taxidermy?

Anyway, the coffee at OA was good. Plenty of Sweet n Low was provided, of course.

Some of those women have been without sugar for years. Years. I can't think about that or I won't get anywhere. But they aren't super skinny, and this bothers me. I mean, don't get me wrong, serenity and spiritual growth are swell, but I want skinny. I could live without the growth if I could just get the body.

Skinny people are always talking about how being skinny doesn't guarantee happiness. But they're just saying that because they're trying to maintain the monopoly. If everybody was skinny, it wouldn't be any big deal. In fact, we'd probably return to the days when heavy women were rare and thereby considered beautiful, like unicorns. Then people like Denise Austin would be considered the sick ones, and they would be made to attend twelve-step meetings and admit they were addicted and that their healthy eating habits had ruined their lives.

That would totally rock.

Chapter 8

Day 2. Sugar Free for realsies:

With the time I've saved not shoving sugar into every possible orifice, I've been able to read the entire first chapter of Potatoes, Not Prozac, *another gift from my nutritionist. According to this, people like me are considered "sugar sensitive" because eating sugar gives us an "emotional boost."*

So, sugar gets me high?

Next thing I know, I'm reading about brain chemistry and neurons and receptors and whatnot and I'm reminded why I dropped out of nursing school. I don't need a book to tell me I'm addicted to sugar. And I don't need a 300-page answer to one simple question. What should I do if I'm addicted to sugar?

Stop eating sugar.

Simple.

So, I guess what I'm going through today is more Sugar Withdrawal. I'm edgy. I'm cranky. I'm plain old pissed. Mood swings and headaches are also symptoms of sugar addiction; so sayeth the Potato book.

Gloria finally showed her face, and I kind of bit it off. She looked tired. She asked about her Effing Damn Special K Bars. When I told her about all of my cool friends who had come over and eaten them, she just shrugged and proceeded to scoop herself half a gallon of ice cream for breakfast. I cringed. Her blond, permed hair seemed kind of matted on one side, like she'd spent the night with her head down on the counter. She'd worn flannel pajama bottoms to work. Yellow and blue with little duckies wearing sunglasses and smiling.

It's a little early in my game to start judging what she's eating, or anything else, but I was. I so very was. I was mad at her ice cream, her pajama pants, her ability to not care that I was mad.

Among the fun things I said during that conversation were the following:

"Where the hell have you been?"

"Do they really let you dress like that?"

And . . .

"Let me get you a shovel for that ice cream."

Then, in the middle of the rather astute inventory I was taking of her entire life, she ran to the bathroom and threw up. What the hell? Maybe she's becoming the bulimic we have both always aspired to be.

I told her about this new Sugar Free thing I'm doing and she just stared at me and my shitty attitude with this so *how's that working out for ya?* Look on her face.

I said, "A little support on this would be just ducky." I couldn't help it. The ducks on her pants were really speaking to me.

She reached into her purse and threw me one of those gas station sugar packets. "You should probably keep that handy," she said.

"Some support!" I railed.

"In case of mental breakdown, just tear and eat," she said cautiously. "I'm going to bed now." Then she backed away slowly and retreated to her room.

Then I emptied her ice cream into the tub. Edy's Cookies 'n Cream.

I don't know. I feel like I could have handled that better.

***

Day 3

I admit, I'm just making this shit up as I go along.

The nice ladies in Overeaters Anonymous didn't specifically tell me I can't have sugar. They didn't have to. I'm a Sugar-holic and an alcoholic and a drug addict, and when I start I can't stop. That's the way it is. I can't eat sugar.

Bea likes to say "Remember the KISS principle: Keep It Simple, Stupid." And it's oh, so simple, indeed. And so hard.

For the purposes of reading labels, I've decided that I won't eat anything with "sugar" in the first five ingredients on the list. According to The Potato Lady, I also need to watch out for "covert" sugars lurking around corners and in dark alleyways called "high fructose corn syrup," "malt barley," and "maltodextrin." Even raisins are a covert sugar. (I never trusted those little bastards with their dark sunglasses and their incessant finger-snapping.)

By that definition, there's sugar in Wheat Chex. There's sugar in peanut butter. There's sugar in spaghetti sauce. Spaghetti sauce!

I called mom to tell her my news, like I'd gotten a new job or maybe won $500 in scratch-offs. "No sugar?" she said. "I'm not sure how I'm going to explain this to your dad. Do you have a minute? He's going to have some questions."

Giving up drugs and alcohol was such a *cakewalk* compared to giving up sugar. If I don't go to bars and I don't hang out in back alleys, I don't have to think about booze and cocaine. Easy. When it comes to bars, Bea says, *If you hang around the barber shop long enough, sooner or later, you'll get your hair cut.* But with sugar, the whole world is a barber shop. Candy dishes at the doctor's office. Chocolate bars at the hardware store. Don't even get me started on gas stations.

Grocery shopping is like a part-time job now. Walking the aisles used to be so exciting! Now it takes me three and a half hours to buy two bags' worth with all the label-reading. It's kind of a treasure hunt. What is there to enjoy that doesn't have sugar? Where's Waldo?

And then there's the cost of all this gingko-biloba health-food crap I'm buying. For the money I spent on three organic kiwi fruits, I could've bought myself a 9 by 9 marble sheet cake with butter-cream frosting, colored balloons, and plenty of space to hand-write the words, "Somebody Please Shoot Me" in green frosting.

But it's not all bad. This new obsession is like an anti-obsession. It keeps my mind busy. Sure as hell doesn't give me time to fret about how much I wish James would call, for example. Nor do I have time to wish Gloria would come out of her room every so often and gab with me, you know? We could eat Triscuits and non-fat cheese and talk about all the sex I'm not having. It would be almost like the old days.

Bea says Gloria's *depressed.* She says it like if you could read Gloria's label, "depressed" would be all of the top five ingredients. I've been talking to Bea every day while Jack's off at work. Bea says Gloria's addiction is going to catch up with her because she doesn't go to meetings. I picture a life-sized crack pipe with white leggings and Converse sneakers chasing Gloria down the alley behind our house.

The first time I saw Gloria was in the lecture hall at Riverplace Treatment Center. The topic was "Letting Go." She scowled like a pit bull. She didn't seem to be *letting go* of anything, or making any immediate plans to. I knew from high school that any girl who looked like that was either gonna break my nose and run off laughing with my Nike high tops, or become my best friend.

Gloria was an Amazon Lita Ford. She was all three of Charlie's Angels. She wore the straight-legged, stone washed jeans and leather suede boots of a woman who could find her way around a thrift store, but the black eye-liner and pink gloss of someone who shoplifted only the best that Carson Pirie Scott had to offer. She was a *Nice n Easy* blond with dark, neglected roots, and she wore her hair long and layered, like a woman who had accepted the end of the Farrah Fawcett era, but was just half a can of Aqua Net away from welcoming it back.

She was court-ordered, and she was cool. We wore the same size, which was every size possible from about 10 up to 18. She borrowed my favorite jeans without asking, and my Nike high-tops. But I didn't mind, and even if I had, I wouldn't have had the seeds to say so.

After a couple of days skipping group and sneaking off to Broadway Burger for Oreo malts, it was obvious that Gloria's hard shell was just there to cover a gooey center. She loved cats. She loved the color pink.

She asked me what my story was. I'd been in treatment two weeks and nobody had actually asked me anything about myself yet. It was such a relief. I mean, I didn't really have one, but that wasn't the point.

She was my first friend after getting sober, so I've always just wanted to protect her like a fragile little kitten . . . a fragile little kitten who smokes Camels without the filter and once punched the drummer for *Alice in Chains* in the teeth and swiped his stocking cap.

Anyway, that was then. What's with all this *Gloria worship* anyway? Maybe Gloria's not the only one who's changing. Maybe I'm changing too. Growing, and hopefully shrinking.

At my Monday morning women's meeting, Ginger told me I looked too skinny. Betty commented on the way my jeans hung to my hips, even with a belt. I knew all this worry was just their way of letting me know what a babe I was becoming. After the meeting, I went out for coffee and everyone guffawed at my control, my will power, my decaf herbal tea and my bowl of muskmelon. Let me tell you, that's a high no yellow cake could give me. Power over processed sugar!

Tawanda! Or something.

Chapter 9

Day 7 . . . One Whole Week!

Standing atop the Sugar Mountain, and looking utterly kick-ass in my new sports-tank and hiking boots.

Dearest, life-affirming, sugar journal,

I've lost six pounds. Yesterday, I went three hours without once thinking about sugar. I took a walk, and a dump-truck driver slowed down to honk.

Classy!

Today, I worked out my legs, arms and abs for 60 minutes with the fabulously toned Denise Austin. I read my daily meditations for "Women Who Do Too Much" and I enjoyed a lovely bowl of non-sweetened granola from the trendy co-op just down the street, topped with fresh raspberries. Now, I'm on my way to a meeting at the club with my brothers and sisters in Alcoholics Anonymous.

I have found a new life and I am renewed. I have introduced my body to whole foods and nothing died, fell off, or imploded. I have, like, three different kinds of lettuce in my refrigerator right now!

Gone are the days of eating my breakfast from a cake pan. Gone are the days of standing in front of my cupboards, desperately spooning peanut butter, chocolate chips (and sometimes coconut to make it taste more like cookie dough) into my mouth. Gone are those futile attempts at feeding my loneliness with drive-through malteds. The bakery section at Cub Foods is dead to me!

Today, when I look in the mirror, I'm backlit by the glow of my new sugar-free lifestyle. Today, I latched my belt on the tightest notch without having to suck anything in, pull anything out, or run to the toolbox. Today, I don't care if James ever calls me again. I mean, I'll talk to him if he calls, but I don't care if he does, is basically my point. Today, I am in charge of my food, my body, my life!

Today, I can see my future. And it looks tan, healthy, and about a size 9/10 tall.

Chapter 10

Day 9, *How sweet it isn't.*

James called. And I was doing *so well.*

Before I could even remind myself to demand one, he
started in with this big fat apology for New Year's Eve, and
another tired old "amend" for lying about hanging out with old
friends. He was with Cassie, he says . . . or was it Carrie? I don't
remember because I was too busy thinking about how I could
justify this all to Gloria when she inevitably got mad at me for
what I was about to do, which was unquestionably to let him
back into my life because I'm a world-class schmuck.

Cassie/Carrie is totally out of control with her binging
and purging and starving, he said. But they are *finished*, he also
said without even a trace of conviction, and he wanted to get
back to focusing on his *program* which, in addict-speak just
means that he'll be going to AA meetings all over town, talking
about how much he misses her.

He said he just wanted to hang with his old friend Estelle,
which made me feel like an IHOP or something where you just
pop in every so often when you crave strawberry pancakes, then
bad-mouth the food every other day of the year because it's just
too greasy for your otherwise metropolitan tastes.

He wanted to know if he could come over with a movie
and some of this new near-beer he's drinking which is from
Europe and it certainly isn't a relapse, even though I could totally
hear Bea dragging out her barber shop analogy on *that* one.
Irritated as I was by this half-assed proposal, I was more thrilled
than anything to be getting the attention, and I invited him over
with his six-pack of 3-2 heartbreak (which I now know tastes like
sweat socks), and his coy blues-musician excuses, and when he

was 55 minutes late, I panicked and wanted to cry.

I chalked it up to sugar withdrawals. By the time his cab pulled up in front of my place, I'd consumed three peach-flavored sugar-free Frescas and was eyeing my bear-shaped honey jar and trying to remember if honey counts as sugar, which of course it does because it's *awesome*.

As soon as he darkened my door, I could tell he was having second thoughts about being there at all, like maybe there was a phone call he'd rather be waiting for at home, but we sat a while on the couch and he did that thing where he asks me how I'm doing like he's my slightly smarter older cousin and we're stuck in the back of the minivan on the way to the family reunion neither of us wishes to go to.

He seemed to have forgotten the movie.

Finally I let him off the hook by saying he looked preoccupied and was something wrong? He said, "Oh, Cassie's on a 72-hour suicide hold because she told her roommate she didn't want to live anymore. I just found out."

"That'll get you put away?" I guffawed. "When I was in high school, I said that five times a day before I'd even reached first hour!"

And then we're off to the races again about Cassie and how she lost her job last year at Victoria's Secret because of her eating disorder (SHIT! Really?), and how her father never told her he loves her . . . blah, blah, 90210 blah.

After James had announced the extent of Cassie's pain, he jumped up and said, "How 'bout we go out somewhere? I know this great coffee shop. We could walk."

We found a booth, and I told him about my new sugar-free plan, and he just grimaced and said, "Anyway what are you worried about, twenty extra pounds? That's no big deal."

Twenty pounds? Fifteen at best. Damn it!

We were blowing on our super-hot Chi Latte's and trying to talk over Mr. Bungle blasting on the stereo when James reached over and touched my knuckles across the table. It only lasted a moment, just to emphasize a point he was making, but he pulled it off like the entertainer that he is, with his audience just hanging on and dying for more.

Holy hell, I just wanted him to keep touching me.

He did and did.

Later, he fumbled a little pulling his naked butt out of my soft-sided waterbed. He pulled his pants on quickly, then kissed me dryly on the cheek like I was his mother, sick with some kind of classic old-movie-type disease like consumption or dysentery.

Wonder where I put that sugar packet. I think I'm going to need that.

***

Day 10

James withdrawal. Good thing I have work and obsessing about what I eat to keep me busy. Good thing. Fun. Good times.

Then Jack was all mad at me for showing up late. Mad, in his passive/aggressive little way. Bea taught me that term. It means you're the type of person who often says "okay" when what you really mean is *Bite my ass.*

He said, "Everything okay?"

"Okay, sure. Sure. I'm good."

"You were a little late. I mean, no biggie. But you had me a little worried."

"Sorry."

"Okay."

"Radio?"

"Yep. Sure."

"Okay."

I flipped the power switch on Jack's stereo, eager to let the goofballs of the local classic rock radio show carry the conversation from there. I had been fifteen minutes late after sleeping through my alarm. *It's not like we can't make up the time. It's not like we really need two full hours to get him ready every day,* I fumed silently. It's not like we didn't sit at the breakfast table sometimes with half an hour to spare, sipping coffee and talking about nothing until he finally goes to work. Also, ten days in a row of watching Jack eat waffles with syrup while I eat mine plain is beginning to give me a facial tick.

Anyway, I worked in silence, going through the motions of Jack's physical therapy. First his legs, then his arms.

I retreated to the shower room and returned with the chair, a plastic wheeled contraption with soft arms and a large hole on the seat for easy backside access. I locked both wheels, turned with bent knees toward the bed, and smiled. *C'mon Jack, let's smoke a peace pipe. I'll never be late again.*

"Ready?"

I leaned over Jack, locking my arms under his; he locked his arms around my neck. Suddenly, he recoiled, and I almost dropped him.

"Jack!"

We dangled for the longest moment in mid air, with only one of his arms around my neck, the rest of him sliding toward the floor. I tightened my grasp on his free arm, then managed to scoot his butt enough onto the chair for it to support him, and for me to regroup. *What the hell?* I thought. He didn't seem to care about almost being dropped, or that his antics were about to break my back.

I slid his butt to the center of the chair carefully, without crushing anything important, but he still seemed pissed. He wouldn't look at me.

He just said, "You stink like cologne."

Chapter 11

Day 11:

Let's see… today started with a lovely fruit and yogurt smoothie, lunch was a rather large baked potato with salsa and a side of boiled broccoli because I'm all about pairing foods that don't have jack shit to do with each other, peppermint tea with a sensible amount of honey and oh I almost forgot…

Gloria is pregnant.

Yeah. And that.

I got the news when Gloria got home from Gas N Splash, bolted through the door, and christened our tub with morning sickness. I asked her whose it was.

She said, "The pizza man. You know? Red's Savoy. Down the street."

I was aghast. "Don't those guys deliver multiple pizzas? Don't they have to hurry to the next house or they'll miss out on a good tip?"

"I gave him a good tip," Gloria sighed, then started heaving again.

"For crying in the rain!"

"It's going to be okay," Gloria said, lifting her head. "Maybe you should sit down. Have you eaten? Are you still on that sugar thing? You're working out too much."

"Sugar abstinence is what it's called. It's totally awesome. Deprivation rocks. Anyway, what're you going to do?"

"I'm not giving up another baby for someone else to raise," Gloria said, quieter, switching her position from the tub to the toilet.

"Okay. That's okay. I could help you raise it," I said. "I'm a nurse's aide. I know things about … nursing."

"You're a *Home Health Aid*. And you're not the father."

Retch.

"Then what? What? Ugh, Gloria. Do you need a towel or something?"

"I'm going to … I'm going to the clinic. I'm not having another baby. I can't."

Flush.

"When?"

"Day after tomorrow."

"I'll drive you," I said. "You need me to drive you?"

"Dierks is taking me."

"Who the hell is that?" What the hell is a Dierk?

"Mr. Large Pepperoni."

"Oh."

Gloria rose from kneeling. Her face said she didn't need me to be okay with anything, but her limp arms kind of said, "Please just hug me you psycho bitch, and then go have a Snickers bar or something." I did neither.

After a long icky moment, she grabbed a Mountain Dew from the fridge, then retired to her bedroom for the day.

***

Day 12, Sugar-Free Journal

Today, I ate shredded wheat with Sweet n Low for breakfast, a dry sesame bagel, and for lunch, a bowl of rice with Sweet n Low. Jack calls it "sip n glow" because of some show he saw on the Discovery Channel about artificial sweeteners. I call it methadone.

Fittingly, today was suppository day at the Jack Mack residence. That's right. It was poop day.

Jack apologized for telling me that I stunk, though he didn't get real specific about why he said it, exactly, or whether I actually did stink, and I couldn't see his face because I had him turned toward the wall so I could put the suppository into his back end.

He just stared out the window at the other subsidized condo next door. Then he said something about me deserving to be treated with respect. Gah! How could I stay mad? Then I did that thing I always do, which is to accept his apology so fervently that by the time I was done gushing he was probably wishing he could take it all back.

It's just that I hate conflict.

Also, I was just so relieved. I can't lose Jack. Plus I had to tell *someone* about Gloria. Someone who wouldn't judge her.

He didn't judge her, but he didn't seem surprised.

"She doesn't want me to help." I sniffled. "She doesn't want me to take her to the clinic or anything."

"She's not *going* anywhere, right?" the back of Jack's head asked me. "She's not going to move in with this guy or anything?"

I lubricated the mini-torpedo and slid it in.

"No. I don't know. It's like she's not there *now*. She didn't even tell me she was sleeping with somebody. I never even had pizza from Red's with her for Pete's sake. We're supposed to be best friends. When I . . . I mean, if I was with somebody, I'd totally tell her."

Jack paused. I thought I heard a chuckle.

"Maybe she didn't want you to feel bad, since you're all alone and single, right?"

"Thanks! Asshole."

"Yes, that is my asshole, missy. Stop undressing it with your eyes."

I laughed too loudly for the occasion.

"Is this thing helping? This suppository?" Suddenly, I was anxious to change the subject. Even if it meant talking about Jack's anus.

"You'll know in a minute, girly."

"Oh, goody."

I sized up his backside for another minute, not for kicks, but to make sure nothing got hurt from his little stunt the day before. It was then that I noticed a dime-sized red mark at the base of his spine. It was too perfect and circular to be from the shower-chair incident, an angry little pressure point.

"I think you've got a bed sore, Jack."

"I know."

"What? How do you know?"

"I can't feel it specifically, but I know it's there because it's making me sweat."

Then I noticed the dew on the back of Jack's neck.

"We have to have this looked at."

"Nah." Jack sighed, "Not today."

"No, really. I mean it."

"You know what they say, beautiful."

"What, Jack?"

"Rectum? Damn near killed 'em."

***

Day 13

Getting a little bit lonely at the top of the sugar mountain and feeling like bashing some heads with my super-sexy hiking boots.

While rummaging through the kitchen for whatever type of lettuce I could find that tastes like a hot fudge sundae, I noticed that all of Gloria's Cherry Coke is gone. Then I checked the cupboards and found that her Fry-Daddy and her Belgian waffle maker were also AWOL. What the hell?

A less secure person would think she was moving out without telling me. I checked her room, and it looks different. She took her socks and her bras and her favorite white fringe jacket. I'm sorry, but something is rotten in the state of Denmark, my dear sugar journal. Plus, I got our phone bill today. $323 in collect phone calls from the Stillwater Prison. Who does she know in the pokey?

As they say in AA, if it looks like a duck and quacks like a duck...Is that AA? Or "Cops"? Anyway. I smell duck.

Gotta go. Jack wants me to make a Better Than Sex Cake tonight for some work function or something. Nice timing.

Chapter 12

Day 14

Well, it was Better Than Sex for a little while, then Jack took the damn thing to work, and now it's Just Like James Cake, in that it would have been beautiful, but then it disappeared and never calls me. Jerk. Jerks. Both of them. All of them. And I don't want to be sugar free anymore.

But I do.

Sick and tired of being sick and tired. Right?

One day at a time.

Easy does it.

Shit.

I was right about Gloria. She's gone. I finally called her mother, who said she'd gone to California. California! It's too warm for leather fringe jackets out there. She's really gone. When was she going to tell me?

Her mom said that she left with some guy. Not the pizza guy. Some other guy she used to go out with when she was "using." Some guy who did two years for forgery and got out yesterday. Some guy who called her collect while I was elsewhere watching sitcoms and Jack's butt.

Her mom said, "You should sell her waterbed. She said you could sell anything she didn't take."

As if I didn't already have an ad in the paper. Cold comfort, though. Wouldn't even cover the phone bill.

She said, "Gloria's really sorry. She wanted you to know that."

I couldn't sit around the empty duplex with all her stuff everywhere, so I went to the grocery store, bought forty-bucks-worth of the best fruit you can find, the best French bread they had, and a 2-liter of diet Barq's. I wasn't eating sugar, but I could still stress-binge with the big dogs, boy howdy.

I got to Jack's place by three in the afternoon. I'd barely unpacked all my booty when Jack got home; he was early.

He rolled in with kind of a flushed face. His collar was opened and his tie loosened.

"What's wrong?" I asked.

"Nothing. Just a little stomach thing today."

"Oh, God. The cake?"

"The cake was fine, Spaz. I just need to lay down a bit. Are you having a party?"

Jack stared at the huge bowl of cherries, the butter, and the bread on the cutting board.

"Uh, just . . . uh."

"Something happen?"

"It's Gloria."

"Help me get this monkey suit off," Jack said urgently, "and tell me all about it."

I followed Jack into his bedroom while he maneuvered his chair by the head of the bed. I pulled at the knot on his tie.

"She's gone."

"Gone where?"

I started on the buttons of his shirt.

"Gone to California."

"*With an aching in her heart*? I'm sorry. That's not funny."

"You want different pants on too?"

"Yeah. Shorts. I'm burning up."

Hastily. I threw Jack's arms around my neck, hoisted under his arms, and tossed him onto his bed with one angry motion. His expression was bemused until he saw mine.

"*She's gone for good.*" I wailed like a big baby, "And she left with some guy. Some convict! And I don't even care. I just want to eat a bus. A sugar bus. I just want to throw myself under a sugar bus, yeah! A ten-ton mound of sugar. I try so hard! And what does it get me? A fucking bowl of cherries and no best friend. A fucking waterbed I don't need!"

I knelt down by Jack and buried my face in the blanket by his chest.

"You're a good friend," Jack said finally. "But you've got to give yourself a break. And stop snotting on my comforter."

"Huh? Oh."

"I'm kidding. Snot all you want. I have people." Jack rested a hand on my neck.

"Let me take you out for a real dinner, Estelle. And eat what you want. Get a good meal. Sugar . . . no sugar. Give it a rest. Give yourself a break for once, okay?"

I suddenly wanted to kiss him. Was it his beautiful Bruce Willis face? His kind words? Or was it the offer of unlimited free food? Awkwardly, I backed away. I grabbed his hand, though, and gave it a squeeze.

"Thank you. I'd love to."

***

Day 15 or Day 1 . . . however you want to look at it.
I relapsed a little. But that's not even the half of it.
Jack is in love with me.

We finally got his temperature back to normal with some cold packs and Tylenol yesterday. So, after he'd napped for an hour, Jack started talking about taking me out to dinner again.

I figured *what the hell*. Nobody's waiting at home for me except a cat, and I'm not pathetic enough to let my *cat* start running things. Yet.

He said, "Where to?"

I said, "Where else?" Red Lobster. Home of the garlic/cheese biscuit. I could binge on those babies till the cows come home and still not break the cardinal sugar sin.

So, I ordered a Diet Coke, Jack ordered a Margarita, and I told the garcon to keep the biscuit baskets rolling. Jack's margarita came, and it was like a fish bowl on a crystal pedestal.

"So, did you talk to her yet?" Jack took a long pull on the straw swimming in his drink.

"No. She can't be troubled. I don't know. I guess they're staying with his family out there."

Jack gestured toward his Cesar salad, and I slid a fork into his right hand, which he gripped, albeit a little awkwardly. Jack doesn't bring his "special" utensils when he goes out. Can't say that I blame him, as much as people stare. His curled fingers wrapped around the fork, and he stabbed a chunk of romaine.

I shoved half a biscuit into my gob and gave him a big smile.

"Thanks for dinner," I chewed. "You're a big old sweetie."

"Is it hard to sit there with this big-ass margarita in your face?" Jack asked, taking another long drink of it. Alcoholic beverages. Just another item on my tediously long list of Things Estelle Can't Handle Without Going Apeshit.

"A little," I shrugged. "I want to reach out and touch the sugar on the rim."

"That's salt."

"Oh!" I'm an idiot.

"Maybe you really are a sugar addict," Jack grinned.

"Ya think?"

"This is nice," Jack said. "You're fun. Do you remember that day when you came for your first interview? Did I ever tell you why I hired you?"

The waitress came with our meals. Thirty fried shrimp for me. Tilapia for Jack. I started on my shrimp while the waitress leaned in awkwardly and cleared Jack's salad plate. She made a quick, awkward grab for the fork in his hand, then thought better of it.

"I'm still gonna need this," Jack smiled forgivingly.

"Of course," she said loudly.

"He's not deaf," I said tartly. "He's crippled."

"Woman, when we get back to the trailer, I'm going to beat your implants loose," Jack said in his best redneck.

The waitress ran off in a perfumed puff. Never trust a skinny server.

"As I was saying . . ." Jack's margarita was half gone. "You came in, and you shook my hand first thing. There was something like fifty other applicants, some with experience. Nobody shook my hand, though. But you shook my hand like a man . . . I mean like a person. And that's why I hired you."

I squirmed in my chair a little at the compliment. I felt like we were headed somewhere I hadn't read about in my Big Book.

"I guess what I'm saying, if I'm saying anything," Jack slurred with exaggerated enthusiasm, "is that I just plain like you."

"Well, I like *you*, Jack." There. Hopefully I'd put a period on that topic of conversation.

We ate in silence for a while. When we were done, a different server with nice wide waitressing hips approached and cleared our plates. She said, all sugary, "Did you two save room for something sweet?"

Jack cocked an eyebrow.

"Es? How we feeling? Sugar? No sugar? How we playing this one?"

"Um. Can you come back in a bit?" I whimpered.

"I'll definitely have another one of *these*." Jack had finished the first fish bowl and left room for another. Waitress #2 turned and jaunted off.

He was looking at me all goofy again, and I couldn't help but look right back. It was kind of amusing that my boss turns into Dudley Moore on wheels when he's tipsy.

"So, what are you going to do now, my little dove? Find another roommate? Try living on your own?"

"God. I don't know." I hadn't even thought about that. Not only did I have the phone bill to worry about, but also another three months' worth of full rent payments before my lease ran out. I couldn't afford it, even with all the hours I worked.

"You could move in with me." Suddenly Jack seemed quite sober. "You could have the extra bedroom. It's not very big. But it's free."

I reeled. It would solve all my problems. Still.

"I don't know," I stuttered. "I wouldn't want to put you out. You'd have no privacy anymore."

Across the dining room, Waitress #2 emerged from the kitchen with another enormous drink for Jack in one hand, pushing a dessert tray with the other.

"Privacy," Jack chortled. Not something a quadriplegic ever really has, I suppose. "Anyway, you *can't* put me out. You couldn't," he announced. "I love you too much."

Huh? Waitress #2 crept closer. Something layered and chocolate quivered on the tray as she nudged it toward us. Something cheesecakey and covered in berries began singing my name in the key of D minor.

Jack glanced nervously at the big empty fish bowl with the lime lying limply at the bottom as though the words had come from that opening, and not the one on his face. He lowered his forehead to his open palm.

"I mean I like you. Gah! I mean . . . I love you. I love you."

"Jack . . ."

"So how are we feeling about dessert?"

I pointed vaguely at something on the tray. Perhaps I pointed at everything. Whatever it was, Waitress #2 chirped "Alrighty then!" and went off to retrieve it.

I waited.

Jack waited.

"Oh, and I almost forgot your drink!" Number 2 bellowed. She bussed the old fish bowl away, replaced it with a new one, then left us to our conundrum.

I didn't love Jack, but I couldn't say it. So I didn't say anything.

Then he didn't say anything.

Then the waitress brought my mound of sugar and I just started shoveling it into my mouth, but the tension stayed, of course. It just got worse with every quiet minute. With every minute that just kept hurting the only friend I had left. My dear, sweet Jack.

     ***

Of course, we barely spoke the next morning; only the basics. *One, two, three, lift. Which tie do you want to wear? More coffee? More syrup on your waffles?*

Back at my empty duplex afterward, I rummaged for something to eat. I could get back on the wagon. I had one slip while eating out. No biggie.

I checked the cupboards for the food Gloria left behind. Half a box of Honey Nut Cheerios. Barbeque potato chips. In the fridge, she'd left lunchmeat. And, what's this? Slim-Fast in a can? She was dieting?

I went back to her cupboard again. Half a box of L.A. Weight Loss snack bars. So, she *did* give a shit about her weight. I mean, even a novice dieter knows that stuff doesn't work, but still. She was trying. Just another thing she never told me.

What would I find next, a C.I.A. badge with her name on it?

The L.A. Weight Loss bars looked so pitiful. Nothing but sugar, that's the scam. No food value whatsoever. Empty calories.

I pulled one out of its wrapper.

Such bullshit. *It's just a mini-candy bar is all it is.* I nibbled its chocolate-covered edge. I took a bite. Chocolate covered bullshit is what it is.

Hell. It was delightful. It was like a Butterfinger. It was sex in a wrapper with only two small fat grams. I did the mental math. If I ate the whole box, that's still only about 700 calories. If I worked out to Denise Austin twice in a row . . .

Fuck!

Forget it. I'm done.

I'm done not doing. It's too hard to not do. It's easier to just do and do and do.

I'm going to bake a cake.

Chapter 13

D-Day: Sugar meltdown. Damn the torpedoes. Full speed ahead. Take no prisoners. Women and children first. Er. Okay that's all I got.

The directions on a box of Betty Crocker Yellow Cake Mix are pretty simple, even for me. In a nutshell: Combine the cake mix with eggs, water and oil. Blend. Grease the pan. Bake for blah blah minutes. Allow cake to cool on a rack.

Allow cake to cool? Binges don't have that kind of patience. No ma'am. They don't wait for boyfriends to call back, they don't wait for friends to start making sense, they don't wait for bosses to stop loving you, and they sure as a mother-effing heifer don't wait for cakes to cool on a God Blessed rack.

I ate the damn thing hot, with melted chocolate frosting and my bare hands, sitting on my ass in the middle of the kitchen floor.

In the middle of all this madness, the phone rang. I knew it was Bea, but I wasn't going to answer with my mouth full, besides, just one more little piece, and then I could start the Denise Austin Step Workout. All this sugar should somehow end with a workout, I figured. The prospect of redemption through aerobics perked me up for a moment.

"You've reached Gloria and Estelle. We're out being rad twenty-somethings and can't come to the phone. Leave your stuff at the thing."

I cut a generous third piece of cake. I took a long last swig of milk, gently scratched Sesame's orange ears, and poured another glass.

Tomorrow will be better. Tomorrow maybe I'll go sugar free again.

Oh, who am I kidding?

From my answering machine, Bea's voice bounced off the walls of my half-empty duplex.

"I'm just done with work now, so I'm going to get some things put together and I'll be over in an hour or so. I've got sheets and a pillow and whatnot, too, just in case you don't. I've got some brownies leftover from work too. Oh, but I guess you're not eating that stuff, sorry. Or are you? Uh. Are you there? (Pause.) Well, anyway."

Click.

Bea . . . coming over. I'd forgotten about that. I'd called her bawling. Something about being so lonely . . . next thing I know, we're having a sleepover.

Excellent.

I'll have a couple brownies after my workout.

Shit.

No.

Maybe just one.

***

"Estelle? Are you in there? I'm coming in."

I listened to Bea's knee boots clicking on the hardwoods, and I pictured Hitler marching. I didn't get up.

Can't. Get. Up.

Denise Austin remained paused at the point of maximum cardio, and even though I had made a sincere effort to pump my thighs, calves, glutes, abs, and all other muscles that sincerely needed pumping, my bloated stomach had cramped up mid-tape.

"Estelle? What the hell are you doing?"

I had figured if I was too cramped for Denise Austin, I might as well finish the cake. About halfway through, my stomach had really started protesting. I ended up cussing at the cake and dousing it like a wicked witch in the sink, rendering it powerless over me at last.

"I ate too much," I shrugged. Bea placed a hand on my forehead, like she didn't believe that's what was wrong. Like no one in their right mind would eat to the point of illness and instead I must have some sort of virus.

"I'm starting to think this is actually a problem," she said, staring at Denise Austin in mid-lunge. I stared at her too. That Denise is a freaking machine: fully extended from her fingers to her toes, yet smiling, always. I'd like to punch the organic spinach out of her.

"You hear anything from Gloria?"

"What's the point? She's not coming back." The words came out like they'd been uttered by a cancer patient right after a long session of chemo. I wasn't trying to be dramatic; I honestly thought I could die of cake.

Bea sighed, lowering her impossibly light and delicate frame slowly onto Gloria's floral slip-covered couch. "So what's next?"

"I don't know. I mean. I don't know. You didn't have to come, Bea. In my life, this is just another night at the Roxy."

"It's my job as your sponsor."

"Not as my friend?"

"You're not well. I want to be here for you."

"Do you get a special medallion for the major head-cases?"

Bea slapped both hands onto the tops of her knees as she stood up.

"You haven't used yet; that's something. It's everything, actually," she offered.

"Is that why you're here? To make sure I don't drink?"

As if I could even crawl to a bar.

"Should we shut this off?" she said, grabbing the remote from my cold dead hand.

"Sure."

"Well…"

You must think I'm such a freaking load. Look at you with your size eight thighs and your cashmere sweater. If you're not here as a friend, then leave me be. Hah! Leave me, Bea.

"Yeah?"

"I'll go change into my night clothes."

"You can take Gloria's bed if you wish," I said, blinking from the pain of moving air in and out of my body. "I'll be here on the couch for a while."

"Okay, dear," Bea softened a bit. "Get some sleep."

"Thanks, Bea," I muttered. Suddenly, an unexpected a flood of feeling rushed over me. Whatever strange AA sense of duty brought her there, I was glad for it. If she hadn't, I'd have been totally alone.

***

If the phone had been ringing long, I hadn't heard it. Bea's sober, take-charge gait pounded the hardwood floor, marching toward me with the cordless phone. She was groggy, but strangely serious.

"It's for you," she told me with certainty, as if it could be for somebody else. As if she actually had a purpose for being there outside of babysitting me, or as if I still had a roommate, and was not alone in my own phone number.

"Is it late or is it early?"

"Late. Too late for phone calls," she said.

I straightened on the sofa for a moment and took the phone so Bea could stand down. I held it for a long moment. I knew who it might be. Then again if it wasn't, I wasn't sure if I could stand the disappointment. My belly ached the ache of ten thousand cakes.

"Hello?"

"It's me."

I glanced at Bea and mouthed, "Gloria." Comfortable with this little bit of information, she shuffled back toward Gloria's bedroom and sloshed into her abandoned waterbed.

"Hi," we both said at the same moment.

"Um, you go first, Estelle."

"Okay, where are you?"

"Sacramento."

Duh. I picked at a hangnail on my thumb. *All the questions I have for her, and all I can ask is one I already know the answer to?*

"Um. Now you go."

"I suppose you're pretty mad."

"Yeah. I mean . . . yeah."

"I'm sorry to leave like that. But, I mean, I think I can be happy with Zeke."

"Zeke who? Never. Heard. Of. Him."

"I know. I'm sorry about that. Really. It seemed easier not to talk about it. About either of them."

"Well, you got your wish. You don't have to tell me jack shit anymore."

"Es . . . I want to start over. There's nothing to stay in Minnesota for."

"Nothing?"

"Come on, Estelle, grow up! Were we just going to live together forever like a couple of lesbos? Just watching 90210 and ordering pizza every night?"

"Hey, pizza was *your* deal. Clearly."

"That's over."

"Right. On to the next felon."

"Estelle, he's a good person who's made some mistakes."

"Aren't we all?"

"Are you going to be mad at me?"

"As if I haven't started yet?"

"You're not so perfect, either, you know."

"Thank you! That needed saying."

Gloria paused, and I didn't contribute, but I wanted to. I wanted to tell about so many things. About my night with James, my dinner with Jack. I wanted to tell her how much I ate, then I wanted her to tell me she's done worse. That's the *least* she could do, to be at least five to ten times more messed up than I am.

But more than anything I wanted to punish her, so I kept quiet.

"You should see the people out here, Es. Everybody's so tan and healthy. I feel like I could be a California girl. I could stay off the drugs out here with Zeke, maybe start jogging and stuff. It's a fresh start. His dad's a minister, and I could even go to church."

"Church? Well, goody for you."

"Do you think you'll ever forgive me?

"I don't know . . ."

"Really?"

"Fuck! Gloria. You of all people should know when I'm trying to be nice."

Gloria continued unfazed. "You should come out here some time, I mean, if you ever get any time off from Jack."

"I dumped your ice cream in the tub," I said triumphantly.

"*That's* why my feet got so sticky," Gloria moaned.

I laughed like a true sap. Have I mentioned my feelings on conflict?

"Gloria, I've gotta go work out or something." At 3 o'clock in the morning.

"Okay. Take care of yourself. I really mean it about you coming out here."

"Really?" *I can't believe I'm even . . .*

"Really. Think about it."

80

Chapter 14

Day blah. Blah Blah Blah.

*So, let's review. Gloria is in California, James is
Godknowswhere and never calls me anyway, Jack loves me but
hates me, and as soon as the rent comes due, I'm homeless. Oh,
and I'm off the sugar wagon for good and back on the high-
fructose warpath.*

*Today: two bowls of Golden Grahams for breakfast and a
third for elevensees. Fillet-o-Fish value meal for lunch, and
Meatloaf sandwiches with mashed and gravy for dinner with
Jack. How does he stay so skinny? He's crippled, for God's sake!
I think I had an apple in there somewhere, too, I don't know.
Like it matters.*

*It's liberating not to care. It's good. This is good.
Loosened my belt by one notch. Otherwise, wearing sweat pants
whenever possible. My boobs get bigger when I get fatter, which
I do like. Counting my blessings. One. Two.*

More later. Must go grocery shopping.

***

For a single girl who doesn't get out much socially, the
grocery store is a place of infinite possibility. At any given point,
I may meet the man I'm meant to torment for the rest of our
married lives. In any given aisle, I may look past the Crystal Lite
end cap and spot the man who will someday put a ring on my
finger and begin to learn, better than anyone else on earth, just
exactly how deep my various neuroses really extend.

Sigh.

If this happens, I'd generally like to be wearing
something a titch more tied together than plaid pajama pants,

Ugg boots, and a maroon UMD sweatshirt caked with cat fuzz. I usually like to have a little more makeup on than *none*.

So, I guess I should at least be grateful that I didn't run into that special guy. Instead, I ran into James.

The kicker is that given enough lead time, either one of us would have *gladly* pretended not to see the other for our own individual reasons: James because he was with *her*, me because I was basically dressed like I'd taken a wrong turn on my way to detox. But it was fated. Predetermined. I just rounded the corner from "condiments and spreads," and there they were, Ken and Barfie. I didn't even have time to hide, or to add some produce to my cart, or to put back two of the three boxes of cake mix I had grabbed.

I had often imagined how this would go in my head, if I ever saw them out somewhere. I even had a grocery store fantasy on file, where I gestured to her cart and ask her if she likes her sesame bagels and strawberry cream cheese better on the way down or on the way back up.

But you know how those things go. Instead, I smiled my super-wide I Hate Conflict smile and said, "Oh! It's! And. Um. Well, look at you. There you both are."

Cassie/Carrie laughed, not knowing at what.

James looked stoned. "Yeah. Yeah. Honey, this is Estelle."

"Hi!" she burbled. God Damn she was cute. Her hair bounced like blond mini-marshmallows. Her Lauren Bacall waistline made me want to find out where I could purchase some ipecac for personal use.

"I really like your sweatshirt," she said, when nobody was saying anything else. "It really, um, looks warm."

Hmm. She wasn't quite the soul-less bitch model tramp I pictured in my revenge fantasies. She was thin, but not Vogue Magazine thin. She had a big, eager laugh. She was sweet.

Maybe she needs a sponsor in OA.

Oh, honestly.

I was struck mute, which gave James just the out he was seeking. He nodded, smiled, and steered their big plastic cart the hell away from me. "We'll see you, then," he tossed over his shoulder.

Back home, I hadn't even gotten my new box of Golden Grahams open when the phone rang. "Yost, James" on my caller ID. Amends so soon? I let it ring.

***

Sold Gloria's waterbed today, to some pervert who tried to tell me about a threesome he had on a waterbed once. Ickiest $110 I ever made. Bea went back home after two nights at my Duplex of Dysfunction. She wants to know what I'm going to do.

I'd like to know too.

Gloria said everyone was so skinny in California. She said I could come to stay with her some time. I think that's what she said. Could it be she's my only real friend? I've missed two women's meetings in a row and do you think those twelve-step-thumping cows bother to call me to see if I'm okay? Probably at Byerly's right now talking about my shitty program and eating tuna melts and kettle chips, which sounds delicious.

Wonder if Gloria meant what she said about being happy with Zeke and about me coming to live with her out there. Did she say stay or live? Maybe I could stay for a little while; maybe get a job as a home health aide out there. Or work at a nursing home. I was so skinny when I worked at the nursing home in high school. Running everywhere back and forth down the halls, changing diapers, answering call lights. Except I wouldn't work the Alzheimer's wing again. Those people are nuts. But I bet I could be skinny and happy in California, living with Gloria and working in a nice, ocean-side nursing home. I could find a man out there to love me. It's a big state, right?

I could meet Denise Austin. I have some questions for her. I have a lot of questions for Denise Austin.

Okay.

Okay, then. I'm going to California.

Shit.

What do I tell Jack?

Chapter 15

I'm not running away from anything this time. I am moving on. I'm not quitting; I'm changing direction.

I've read all the books and kept all the journals. I've taken all the pills that started with "metabo" and ended with chest pain. I've played all the fitness tapes, the Tae Bo tapes, The Firm, Richard Simmons, Yoga, Yogalates, Hip Hop Abs. I've rewound them and played them again. I have made the celery soup and I have peeled and quartered the grapefruit. I've taken a deep breath in and exhaled out. I've squeezed and I've released. I've gone to all the meetings and read all the readings. I've chanted all the affirmations, written them on post-it notes, and strewn then on my mirrors. I've measured every portion and read every label. I've gained and I've lost. I've sucked it in and zipped it up.

And I'm done.

I had hoped to tell Jack the very night I made my decision, then didn't because it was "ER" night, and Noah Wiley's character just found out his girlfriend's baby would be stillborn, and it was good TV, for sure, and we were both so into it. I didn't want to ruin it. I vowed to tell him the next morning during our morning coffee. But he had the cold sweats for some reason, and then I couldn't get his tie straight, and it just seemed wrong. I meant to tell him tonight when he got home, but just as I was about to go back to Jack's, I got a phone call from Linda at "Absolute Home Health Care."

"Estelle, is that you? This is Linda from Absolute."

"Oh, hi. Did I forget my time sheet for last week?"

"No. No, that's all fine. I'm calling you because Jack went to the hospital from work today. Did you know about that?"

"What? No. What?"

"He's okay, don't worry. He's got a fever, though. They say he's got an infected sore on his rear end."

"I know exactly which one you're talking about."

"Really? Because I didn't see it on your charts or anything."

"But I told him he had it. That it was there."

"I didn't see it on your charts. You're supposed to chart that sort of thing."

It had never occurred to me to "chart" something that Jack already knew about. *He's a grown man.*

"Um, I have to talk to you about something, long as I've got you on the phone," I said, eager to change direction.

"Oh?"

"I'm leaving. I'm going to California, to live. Which would make it hard for me to work for . . . Jack."

It was the first time I had said the words out loud. Sitting alone in my room, packing all my size-10s (still holding out hope for the 12s) for Goodwill was a silent commitment to leaving. But saying it out loud, that was another thing. I liked how it sounded. *I'm going to California.* I had made it public. Linda wasn't supposed to be the first person I told, but I figured it was good practice for more difficult conversations to come.

"Are you giving us two weeks of notice?"

"Yes. Almost. Very close. One week."

"So, one week?"

"Yes. I guess that's one week less than two weeks."

"Yes, it is. Well, *Jack* will be sorry to lose you."

"Do you think?"

"Yep."

***

I headed to Jack's house to wait for the ambulance to deliver him home. I'd tell him then. I'd have to.

I searched his kitchen for something to start a good meal with, maybe make some homemade pizza and malts for Jack to wash the bad news down with. I could make a cake for later. Cake always cheers things up, right?

I glanced across the butcher-block countertop in Jack's kitchen. I'd spent a lot of time there, cooking, wiping, cleaning, gorging. I'd prepared countless dinners, with Jack acting as the foreman, leaned back in his electric wheelchair, dictating his mother's old recipes for me to replicate. Jack always liked advising me on things like what it means to "whisk" something instead of "beat" it . . . or telling me the difference between a "pinch" and a "dash."

Once, when we were in the kitchen together, he swung his arm around while I mashed the potatoes, smacking me in the ass.

I basically ignored it; I figured perhaps an "oops" or a "'scuse me" was forthcoming.

Instead, Jack, irritated, said, "Aren't you going to hit me or anything?"

I said, "Oh. Um, no. I didn't think you meant it."

"Well, I did. I meant it. I smacked your ass and it wasn't an accident. Now what are you going to do?"

"Well, I don't know."

"Why don't you know? A man smacks you on the ass, you should do something about it. One way or another."

I had laughed and turned away. Standing in the same spot I had been standing then, I wished I'd have acted differently, but still didn't know in what way. Which way would have spared his feelings?

I opened Jack's cupboard to get flour for the pizza dough. A paper bag of C&H Pure Cane Sugar sat front and center on the middle shelf. It stared back at me at eye level. I tried to imagine what Jack would say; or would he say anything at all? I decided to make the cake first.

Then I heard Jack's ambulance.

***

~~Dear Sugar,~~
~~Dear Diary,~~
~~Dear,~~
To whom it may concern,

I am leaving. It's official. I've said it out loud to three people now. The agency doesn't care, my mom thinks I'm joining an AA commune on the coast like she saw on 20/20 the other night, and Jack won't speak to me.

I don't really care about the agency, I'm not joining a commune, AA or otherwise, and as for Jack . . .

The last thing Jack said to me before he stopped speaking entirely was that he hopes I'll be happy, which of course means that he hopes I get pecked to death by chickens or perhaps run over by a Krispy Kreme delivery truck.

And since I told him right after pizza and right before making a cake, well, I never got to make the damn cake, which was just on the menu to make me feel better, I mean, who are we kidding? Anyway, twelve hours later and I'm still without cake.

Instead of dessert, I dialed the numbers for Jack while he called the agency. Jack has an earpiece that allows him to have private phone conversations, but he kept it on speaker. He told Linda I was leaving and they should start looking for a replacement. She told him that she already knew. He paused for a minute when she said that. Then, he said, "I want someone to start tomorrow."

Tomorrow? I'm so not feeling the love.

Linda balked a little at the whole "tomorrow" thing, but in the end, she made a few phone calls and got it done. God only knows what kind of a low-life they got on that kind of notice. One-night notice. I'm gone.

No turning back. No changing my mind. Homeless, jobless. Gone.

Normally, it takes me about 45 minutes to get Jack washed up and into his bed. Last night it took three years. When you touch without talking, the sound of the touching is more like smacking and smooshing. Just breathing and touching. Breathing and touching. No eye contact. Smack. Smoosh, smack.

The hospital bandaged his bum really well and gave him a bunch of instructions to follow for continuing to treat it. Glad I won't have to deal with all that. Sterile procedure and bandages and antibiotic ointment. I'd probably do it wrong. I'd probably make it worse. It's for the best, I think, me leaving. Maybe now he'll have someone who really knows how to take care of him. Maybe a real nurse. Not some sugar-junky scatter-brained bonehead.

I hope he'll be OK. I kissed his cheek right before I left. It seemed like if he could have, he would have ducked me.

Chapter 16

Dear friend,

I'm calling you that now instead of "journal" because frankly I can use all the friends I can get, and of course the sugar thing is out the window . . .

When I dropped Sesame off to stay with my parents, my mom took one last shot at getting me to "look at my life." I saw the rosary beads on the table and knew that if I didn't act with swiftness, I might never get out of there.

"Here's his soft food," I said, handing her a large plastic bag full of Fancy Feast cans. "He likes it in the afternoon after his twenty-two-hour nap."

"I'm serious, Estelle," she said.

"He's really into the Harry Potter series lately, but don't bother renting the movies. He's a purist."

"Estelle!"

"I love you, mom," I said, kissing her on her wildly furrowed brow. "Tell dad to tell you I'm going to be fine."

***

The best thing about traveling alone, I think, is being in charge of when you can pull over for a meal. Growing up, my dad's idea of a successful trip was one where we got from point A to point B in well under Triple A's estimates. This was achieved by launching at the earliest possible hour and, once all adults and children were within the confines of a moving automobile, moving at the highest speeds allowable for the longest time without stopping to eat, pee, or anything else.

We'd stop maybe once or twice in a five-hour stretch, and even though I wanted to get to where we were going (*are we there yet?)* another, much larger part of me wanted to make sure I didn't miss all the killer noshing opportunities we passed. Billboards and highway signs invited me to stop and try this pancake house or that small town pizza parlor; it seemed rude to just blow by like we always, always did.

"Don't you want to get where we're going?" my dad would ask with a big relaxed smile on his face; he was happy to be anywhere but at his job as a house painter.

"Yes, but I want to be at Sam's Smokehouse too, eating burgers and fries."

Since I had a lisp, statements with multiple "s" sounds would send my parents into a giggling frenzy over my insane cuteness. Hungry and humiliated, I would crawl into the window of our 81 Grand Prix and sleep (remember cars with backseats where you could seat seven?). Two hours later, I would wake up when the car turned onto my grandparents' gravel driveway. Then I'd start wondering what was waiting in my Grandma's candy tin, or what was for dessert.

Grandma's candy tin was a cheap old dime store tobacco tin with sea-shells sloppily glued to its round top by a grandchild who had long since gone off to college and who would never have blamed her for throwing it away.

It wasn't conspicuous, but it made a really loud sucking noise and then a loud metallic "pop" whenever it was opened. The sucking/popping combination was usually enough to get my mom's attention from anywhere in Grandma's house. (Mom also had special radar for the whooshing sound of the hallway linen closet where Grandma kept the Tupperware tub full of oatmeal or molasses cookies.)

Once the sugar patrol had been alerted, there was nothing I could do but wait patiently for my brother to do something to distract her, like petting the cat with a G.I. Joe tank. Greg never seemed that interested in making an entire day out of obsessing about pilfering butterscotch nips. Therefore, we were never close.

***

The first time I ever tasted booze was at Gramma's house, in the pursuit of sugar. I stole the cherry out of my dad's Brandy Manhattan. That night, I graduated from cookie-thief to cherry-picker.

Booze-soaked cherries made everything just a little bit better. The Benny Hill Show (Grampa's favorite) got funnier, (though I still didn't understand it because I wasn't a repressed married white man), and Greg got less annoying (though I still felt he breathed too loudly). In my mind, I got wittier, prettier, and more like those perfect little girls in the Sears Catalogue, with their skinny ankles and their teensy little patent leather belts.

Pretty soon, cherry-picking took precedence over all other once-cherished pastimes of cookie-sneaking, cat-pestering, and day-dreaming. I became a devoted distributor of the cherries to the drinks, and then the seeker of the almost-finished drinks I had helped garnish.

I had finally found a fun activity, and wasn't that mom was always encouraging me to do? *Estelle, get out from under my feet and find some kind of fun activity*. After dinner, I would follow Grampa down to the basement bar where he prepared the drinks, snatch the clear glass bottle from the refrigerator door, and immediately offer my cherry placement services.

"Wait just a pea-picking minute," he'd say. "You don't put cherries in everything."

"Pea-picking" is an expression Grampa used as a modifier to a wide variety of nouns, but mostly in reference to time. A pea-picking minute is a minute that could have just as easily been spent in sweet solitude, without the world's most

93

annoying ten-year-old breathing down his neck and futzing with his drink condiments. "Pea-picking" was likely dusted off and recycled from Grampa's childhood vocabulary, specifically meant to replace "God Damn" in an effort to spare my unbelievably tender feelings.

I would drop the cherries in despite Grampa's protests, never suffering any actual consequence for disobeying. Maybe he thought it was cute. Maybe he thought it was annoying as hell, but allowed it anyway, since he needed me to carry the tray with the drinks or they'd never make it all the way up the stairs. Years of hard drinking had not only eaten his liver, but also given Grampa a permanent tremble, which no one ever talked about. I learned early to grab the tray before Grandpa ever had a shot at it, just like Mom had learned to take the keys from him on our way out the door to church or out to dinner, saying, "But I haven't driven your new Cutlass yet!" When everyone knew she already had half a dozen times.

Once the drinks were distributed, with my assistance of course, came the monitoring faze of the cherry pick. The trick was to solicit the cherry in time enough before it was consumed by the drinker, but not so soon that the drinker could protest.

Too many objections can register on a mother's radar, and then I'd find myself banished to the basement TV room, forced to drink Seven-Up from a metal tumbler and watch "ABC presents Rudolph the Red-Nosed Reindeer" for the seventeenth time on the floor with all the great-grandchildren I was too old to hang out with, and who thought liquor-soaked cherries tasted "ocky."

Careful observation and patience were key. *Aunt Lee is almost half done with her vodka sour. Dropped two in her drink. She usually gives one and keeps one. Mom's drink has barely been touched, but she's the one to watch. Managed to drop four into hers before Grampa got mad. She's good for at least three, if not all four, depending upon how much she's drunk so far tonight, and how much she knows about how much Dad has drunk.*

On a good night, depending on the number of aunts, uncles, neighbors and drinks, I could nail down fifteen to twenty cherries. Fifteen to twenty cherries were almost enough to make my brother's breathing tolerable.

One New Year's night, after harvesting the two cherries I had planted in my dad's brandy mix only half an hour earlier, I had a realization. If the booze made the cherries better, wouldn't it make sense that the cherries made the booze better too? Then wouldn't the last swig of my dad's glass -- which he wasn't paying attention to because Benny Hill was on -- wouldn't that last swig taste heavenly too?

And then another? And another?

Sixteen years later, sitting in a "family group" session at the treatment center, my mom asked me where she and Dad had gone wrong. Why did I do the things I do? But I had nothing to offer. No story and nobody to blame. Knowing that made the urges to drink again, or do drugs, come back like a madman.

I had a good childhood. I had summer vacations and school uniforms and Tupperware tubs filled with homemade cookies. All I could do was shrug and think about bright red cherries in the jar.

***

The last time I took a road trip, it was with a man named Jude. That time, I didn't call my mom until we were halfway to Florida. I was eighteen and Jude was 25; she was thrilled. I told her Jude had a job lined up or some such dribble we both knew wasn't true because Jude wasn't really *job material* with his long hair, scorpion tattoo, and Crippling Drug Addiction.

This time is different. I'm sober, I'm making my own decisions, and I even called AAA for a trip ticket to San Diego. I forgot to bring it, but the point is that aimless people don't even bother calling AAA when they take trips. They don't give notice at their jobs and they don't secure safe lodging for their cats.

Because my trip ticket is sitting in my now abandoned duplex, I'm not real clear on how to get where I'm going, but I'm pointed west on Highway 94.

Anyway, I don't need AAA to tell me where all the waffle houses are.

***

Maybe if I'd never been skinny, I wouldn't hold it up like it was the end-all, be-all of female existence. Maybe if I'd never slipped on a size 8 mini-dress and watched it shimmy over my tiny little hips like it did . . . maybe if I'd never worn a bikini in Myrtle Beach and felt like I was in a David Lee Roth video. Maybe I wouldn't want it back so badly if I'd never had it. But once upon a time, for one precious year, I'd lived it.

I lost the weight the summer before my senior year of high school. I'd been dieting since I was twelve, but my heart was never really in it because I never had a goal. Then one sunny May day, some asshole dumped me.

Bradley worked at a cart factory by day and played drums in a band on the weekend. As far as the average high school junior knew, he was extremely cool. Actually, the guy was a major goober and I was going to break up with him anyway, but he did it first. He out-dumped me! I couldn't cope.

The pain is torture, I wrote in my journal, humiliated. Then I memorized and hand-wrote all the lyrics to Bob Dylan's "Knockin' on Heaven's Door" and taped the page to the inside of my locker. It wasn't that I wanted to kill myself . . . it was just that I wanted to make people wonder about it so that they would fall in love with my mysteriousness out of a sense of urgency. *What if she really is knockin' on heaven's door? We should probably invite her to the party on Saturday while we still have the chance!*

Eager to make Bradley want me, I was inspired to really, truly starve myself. I burned for the chance to show up at Plaza Billiards thirty pounds lighter, in a half-shirt and suede boots and make Bradley eat his cart-factory heart out. I was becoming a real woman!

My diet went like this: Diet Mountain Dew for breakfast, school salad bar for lunch (or a pretzel, depending on mood), and a bowl of cereal (preferably raisin bran due to regularity issues related to nearly starving myself) for dinner.

Exercise plan: walk to the gas station at every opportunity to buy cigarettes. Four nights a week: five hours of running up and down the hall of the old folks home where I worked as a nursing assistant. Occasionally: jazzercise on the VHS.

I lost 40 pounds in 4 months.

Being skinny was a beautiful high. Everything fit. Everything looked right. One day my Spanish teacher told me I looked *too thin*. I blushed, sucked my cheeks in like Linda Evangelista, then floated on air for the rest of the day.

Sometimes I craved chocolate, but the high of lightness always kept me from acting on it. The sugar buzz paled in comparison to the delirious, dizzy feeling of a flat, empty stomach, the way my abdomen sometimes seemed to be sucking itself inward, the tight, achy feeling in my thighs. I became so slight, I could take two aspirin for a headache and it would be gone in seconds. Rings I wore as a child slid off my knuckles.

Prospects for boyfriends improved greatly. There was the clerk at the Amoco who could barely look me in the eye when I sauntered in with my cut-off jeans and my Harley-Davidson tank top (I was a trucker's dream!). There was Tim Budrow in eleventh grade, who wrote a metal song called "Estelle, my belle" and played me the tape in the study hall. His cousin played guitar. It wasn't bad; a little too much on the cow bell. But I wasn't about to date a boy one year younger than me.

I preferred older guys like Jude; they added to my "knockin' on heaven's door" mystique. Plus, since he could never actually enter the school, I could talk about him like he was some kind of guitar hero super-stud, and not some mooch who couldn't get a girl his own age to date him.

When Jude first noticed me at the mall, I was busy not eating a slice of cheese pizza from Sbarro's, and gulping down my third free refill of Diet Coke. He seemed to know (and like) my best friend, DeAnn from somewhere, but DeAnn had a boyfriend. I was wearing my favorite jeans: stonewashed and tight, with suede laces strung up the back of my calves. He shook my hand, looked me up and down, and told me to come to a movie with him. I went, only knowing his first name and that he came from New Jersey.

We smoked a joint and went to the Rocky Horror Picture Show. I didn't smoke a lot of pot, usually because I didn't like getting the munchies. But with Jude, I felt like a different person. DeAnn said I *acted* like a different person, and not in a good way. He made me laugh; he made her nervous. He smoked Camels without the filter.

Two weeks after we met at the mall, Jude and I stayed at a party on the East Side until almost all the other guests were gone. Then Jude put a glass pipe in front of me and told me not to let the smoke out right away.

"This won't give you the munchies," he told me.

Two months later, Jude and I were on the road with all our clothes in garbage bags, running from his warrants and some drug dealer we'd stolen from. We lived like kings when he had money, like bums when we didn't. Sometimes I'd call my parents and beg for money, but they wouldn't send it because someone gave them a copy of *Codependent No More,* which should carry the subtitle: *How to fuck up your alcoholic while wearing a big sadistic smile on your face.*

Something tells me my mom is re-reading that book right about now. But that's not the kind of road trip I'm on. I can be civilized. I can behave, and I'm not out of control.

Anyway, the civilized traveler takes time to stop for pancakes and directions. Wouldn't want to get lost on my way to paradise, eh?

Chapter 17

Jack

Estelle is gone, and now some nursing student named Rock is wiping my ass.

He's perfect; the guy's a machine. He was a starting halfback in high school. I had no idea what to expect, letting Absolute hire me someone new on such short notice, but they really hit it out of the park with this guy.

He picks me up like a ten-pound sack of potatoes, but he's careful about it. He knows his way around a wound site, which is important. He's good with the charting, he knows about proper skin care, and when we have down time, he wanders off with his laptop and leaves me be. No drama. No hassles. Just a run-of-the-mill English Lit major who makes a kick-ass Denver omelet.

I never told Estelle, but I'm really not that big on waffles. I just said I liked them because I thought that would make her happy, eating those things every damn day.

She's such a sugar-hound, she doesn't even realize that there are some people out there who just (gasp) eat to live. Some people just eat their breakfast and forget about it. They don't need to write three pages about the fucking thing in a "food journal" or go to a meeting or starve themselves for two weeks just because they had a lousy damn meal.

I'm fine without her. Better than fine. I don't miss her. I mean it.

***

Dear . . . oh, dear.

This morning I woke with a headache, crashed out on a bare cold ply-wood kitchen floor, in the trailer home of two twin sisters whose names I could only remember both started with the letter *R*.

Roberta? Renee? I pondered the possibilities.

There was a truck stop cafe, and the *R* with the name tag that said "Town Tramp" had struck up a conversation after watching me wolf down two enormous pancakes in one minute flat. *R* had offered me one more free of charge, which I accepted happily.

Then there was a bar and a lot of attentive truckers who wore button-down plaid cotton shirts. The other sister, the good one, the one who seems to want to take care of everybody, she had been the designated driver.

I rolled onto my back and stared at some water-damaged 12 by 12 ceiling tiles. Someone, probably the codependent *R*, had given me a musty sleeping bag to crash in, and a throw-pillow. I was still wearing my traveling clothes from the day before, the clothes I had on when I ran into James and Cassie at the grocery store, the pajama pants and sweatshirt of a woman who has lost all interest.

Town tramp *R* must have left a six-pack of Budweiser on the poker table in the dining room, so I crawled on my knees to grab one. It's been a while since I've needed the comfort of a beer at 9:20 a.m. Yet another bad choice in what I assume will be a long series of more.

"Good mornin' sleepy head!" came a high-pitched chirp from the adjacent living room.

Quick. Ricki? Rolanda? Rutabaga?

"You remember me? I'm Roxanne."

Oh, thank God.

"Oh, hi!" I said, though in my head it registered more like a high-pitched squeal. "Hi Roxanne. Yes. Thank you. Thank you for the sleeping bag."

"You were pretty wiped out from all the pancakes and the slow gin probably, too," Roxanne said cheerily. "Did you sleep good?"

"Oh, you bet."

I joined Roxanne on the couch in front of the *Ellen DeGeneres Show.*

"So!" Roxanne bounced the cushions a little with her enthusiasm, and it sent tremors through my nausea. "Are ya ready for your first cruise, ever?"

Robert Pattinson, star of the movie *Twilight* was telling Ellen about how he still drives a crappy car, despite being the tween heartthrob of the new millennium. He was tall, disheveled and most calculatedly British. I could totally see myself falling for a guy like Robert Pattinson. He pulled at his hair anxiously, unconsciously. He talked about all the screaming girls. He seemed a total mess. A project. Completely and utterly hot.

Wait. Cruise?

"Cruise," I said slowly.

Robert Pattinson laughed nervously.

"Oh my goodness." I reached for my own hair and started tugging. Various scenes came back to me. Rhonda. The slutty twin was Rhonda. "A cruise! Yeah," I breathed. "Um. Remind me. Just real quick. What was the plan with that?"

"Oh, we're going to have so much fun!" Roxanne beamed. "We're going to have one last fling before Rhonda gets married, remember? We got you all booked and everything. Houston to the Caribbean! Don't forget to put your credit card back in your purse, by the way."

"Right." I scanned the trailer for my purse. "How are we getting to Houston, again?"

"We're taking your car. I totally hope that's still okay."

"When?"

"We leave tomorrow! Do you want to drive the first shift?"

"Um…"

The sound of a toilet flushing announced Rhonda's entry into the kitchen, and the sight of her reminded me to stop remembering anything more from the previous night.

Rhonda is one popular girl in Fergus Falls, especially with men who drive eighteen-wheelers and wear Carhartt apparel. Not pretty by any stretch, but bold. Not dangerous, but just brash enough to make most other women fear crossing her. She's the kind of woman who would happily belt you in the mouth over the last X-Box on sale at Fleet Farm on the day after Thanksgiving. She's the kind of woman who buys her Lee jeans with the expandable waistband, and her Wal-Mart v-neck T-shirts in size full-to-bursting.

"You sure as fuck *better* be taking the first shift," Rhonda said to the inside of their refrigerator. "You barfed gin all over my new Keds last night."

I retreated to the bathroom to see if I could unload a little more of that gin, and that pretty much brings us up to date on Estelle's Ill-fated California Vacation That Ain't Going To Happen Quite Like That.

As the Ellen show faded to commercial, Robert Pattinson gave America a long, deer-in-the-headlights kind of gaze. He said quite clearly, for all his crazed fans to hear, "Estelle. What the bloody hell were you thinking?"

I couldn't even eat the Fruit Loops Roxanne gave me, which I absolutely wanted more than anything until they were placed in front of me and I could smell them. I wished instead that it could be a bowl of Tylenol floating in 2-percent. I don't *know* what I was thinking, Robert Pattinson! I wasn't thinking. I wasn't. But, you know? It felt good. It felt like something, and not nothing.

So, now, I'm going on a cruise with Rhonda and Roxanne, two friends I made last night when I stopped to gorge in Fergus Falls because I realized at some point that I was going *northwest* on Highway 94, not just west, and that I don't know what I'm going to do with California anyway, or what it's going to do with me, or why I'm chasing Gloria's friendship like a little paper receipt in the wind. A receipt for something I'll never need to return, like toilet paper, or Twinkies.

Rhonda and Roxanne are not identical twins in any sense, least of all by appearance. Roxanne is a pink cable-knit sweater. Rhonda is a bright-red push-up bra with the front hook busted.

I don't know why they took to me the way they did. Boredom is my best guess, or that they needed a cheap mode of transport to Texas. Roxanne laughs at every stupid thing I say. And when they got off work, we all headed over to the VFW for drinks.

I wasn't going to really drink, of course.

But then I just started doubting everything I thought I knew.

Then I thought about all the reasons I don't drink.

Then I crossed them all out, one by one, as irrelevant.

Then I thought about Bea.

I thought about treatment.

Then I realized that I was sitting on a bar stool and that I really like gin and that Rhonda had bought the first round.

When I stopped thinking, I just started *feeling.* With every drink, the feeling grew stronger. The change. The old familiar change.

Right off the bat, Roxanne started saying how guilty she felt about me drinking when I'm an "AA person." That's when I realized something wonderful; someone's worried about me. I have a co-dependent. I'm not all co-depending on some jack-off and his bulimic girlfriend, and I'm not all co-depending on Gloria and all her crap. Somebody's co-depending on *me.* And I'm not going to let her down. I'm going to be the biggest lush/addict/sugarfiend anyone ever met.

I'm going to be that girl.

I *am* that girl.

I called Gloria to tell her I'm not coming. I really was quite drunk when I did that, but I swear I heard her say something about Jesus right before I let her go. Now, if I was still her co-dependent, I'd be on the phone right now asking her what the hell that was all about.

But I don't care.

She wants to take up with Jesus, she could do worse. At least she won't get pregnant.

Hah! I'm still a little drunk.

Anyway, Rhonda is marrying Roxanne's therapist next week, and this trip is their last hurrah as single twin sisters. Probably for the best. They don't actually seem to like each other, or have anything in common. And Roxanne's still pretty sore about having to find a new therapist in a town this small.

I've never been on a cruise, so this should be interesting. I don't remember all the details, but I know exact the phrase I heard right before I dove into my purse and whipped out my MasterCard:

ALL-YOU-CAN-EAT.

Chapter 18

Gloria

I never meant to hurt her, just like I never meant to hurt a lot of people. That's my problem, I just do the next thing that comes along, I guess, and it's nothing personal. Zeke loves me. He's not perfect, I know. If the perfect guy fell for me, I'd never trust it anyway.

I know I owe her one, and I know I really talked it up, but when Es said she was coming to California, it kind of threw me. Zeke was not *happy about it. He says we need some time to ourselves, some time to be newlyweds, and I agree.*

And just when I'd spent half the night trying to smooth all his feathers down about it, I get another call from her, and I remember just exactly who we're talking about. Instead of going straight west, she accidentally went northwest from Minneapolis, and is now halfway to Fargo. She's in a bar somewhere getting drunk and talking about going on a cruise with some twin sister waitresses she just met. She's not coming to see me; she's getting on a boat with two perfect strangers. Somewhere in the last week or two, all her biscuits fell out of her basket.

Honestly, am I to blame for all of that? Zeke says no. I don't know. I never asked her to care as much as she did. I don't know why anybody cares about me, but I'm working my way out of that, and someday I'll really deserve all of the concern.

I'm just glad I wasn't there when she relapsed. Judging by the way Es and I binged on food together, I can't even imagine the kind of damage we'd do after a couple bottles of Absolut and a gallon of grapefruit juice.

Anyway, I don't want that life anymore. I'm tired of being tired. Zeke says prison taught him some good lessons in self-

control, and that's why he doesn't drink or do drugs now. Sheer will power. I don't know what self control feels like, and I don't do will power. But I know that when they took that baby out of me, what was left on the table was an empty husk. Empty, but ready to be filled up with something entirely different.

The first thing Zeke and I did when we got out here was we got married in a real church by a real minister, Zeke's dad, Richard. Can you imagine? I'm a married woman. It gets better: Then I got baptized. As it turns out, Jesus loves me. Jesus loves me! After all of my shenanigans. After everything.

I'd heard it before, of course, when my mom went through her phases in and out of churches here and there, but never at the right time. Never with my new husband at my side, with water running all down my face and hair, hunched over at the belly. My belly still hurt that day from the "procedure" as they'd called it at the clinic. Until that day, I'd hated my belly anymore for what it meant to me. My big, saggy, empty belly where I stuff the food to hide the pain. My big stretched-out belly, where life just comes and goes, comes and goes, into me and out of me. One baby, two babies, then a third torn away.

Richard put his hand on my belly and asked Jesus to heal it. And asked Jesus to heal my heart, which I didn't know needed healing until just that moment. Like a cancer I didn't know I was dying of. Richard asked that it be healed. And then. Jesus. Did.

And I was full, finally. I was filled.

Hallelujah!

I'm worried about Estelle. Just before she let me go so she could go off and plan her big cruise with her new twin friends, I told her I'd pray for her.

She said, "I'm sorry . . . What?"

And I said, "Jesus loves you, Estelle."

And she said, "What did you say?"

It really threw her, I'm sure.

I still can't believe it myself. But it's true.

***

Road Trip: Day One.

See? Life can be pretty darned exciting. Two days ago, I was a pathetic little jobless, homeless, boyfriendless goof running around trying so hard to keep all my eggs in a basket and not crack any shells. Today, I'm still all of those things, but I've dropped my basket and there are eggs everywhere . . . yolks and whites and shells everywhere, and I'm going to leave them for somebody else to pick up, thank you *so very much.*

R. and R. and I got halfway to Houston when Roxanne asked me if I had a passport. Apparently, you have to have proper international ID to eat at the Big Floating Buffet. I checked my trunk, which contains all my worldly possessions now, and found it. No good drug addict/alcoholic gets to age twenty-five without at least a trip or two to Cozumel to vomit on a foreign beach, you know. But that was a long time ago, and my passport expired in 2008. What to do?

Rhonda came up with the idea of altering it just a wee bit. The old me would have never considered it. Fraud! I would be committing, like, international espionage or something, just for the opportunity to board a boat and deplete half of its food supplies.

But the new me said, "Hell yeah!" Thanks to a safety pin and a fine-tipped magic marker, my passport now claims to expire in 2018. Hello, naughty! I'm like a pirate. *Sugarbeard.*

We stopped in Wichita, stayed at a Motel 6, and ate at the IHOP. We bought two six-packs of wine-coolers and drank them in the hot tub. I got a little drunk and told R. and R. about Jack. Nothing big, just that he was my friend, and that I wonder how he's doing. Roxanne said, "Why don't you call him?"

I said, "Cuz that's what the old Estelle would have done."

"Well, La, De fucking Da" Rhonda said in that tone that makes me remember how much I sometimes fear her. "The new Estelle eats too much, drinks too much and doesn't talk to cripples."

"He's mad at me!" I protested.

"I would be too."

"Don't go growing a soul, Rhonda, you're the wind beneath my relapse."

"Have another cooler," Rhonda belched. "And call the gimper."

I found a phone in the hotel lobby and started dialing. One ring, two, three. I checked my watch. Eleven-thirty? Shit. This might wake him up. Four rings. He should at least be home on a school night like this. Five, six. Maybe he knows it's me and won't answer. Ten. I gave up and headed back to my party of three.

Chapter 19

Jack

When you're somebody's patient twenty-four hours a day,
eventually, that's how everybody sees you. Patients are referred
to more in numbers than in names. It starts in the hospital the
day you wake up. You're a C6-7 fracture. You're the patient in
1801. Your pulse rate jumped to 90. Your O2 saturations are
down to 70. Your pain is a seven on a scale from one to ten.

You leave the hospital eventually, of course, but you learn
to be a patient everywhere. Who's going to help me in the
bathroom? Who's going to come to hoist me into the bed?
Physical therapy. Doctor's appointments. Specially adapted
forks and spoons. Post traumatic stress. Nursing assistants.
Urinary care.

Then you get out into the world, sort of. But you're
always that one guy . . . that one guy in the wheelchair. And
there's always someone in the background on the ready to dab
your chin with a napkin, hold a door, empty your leg bag.

I've been a quad for nineteen years. Soon it will be
twenty. Twenty years on my feet. Twenty years in a chair.

Quad; another number, meaning four, of course. I'm
defined by the number of limbs that don't work anymore.

But five precious days a week, I get the chance to pretend
I'm not a patient. I drive my own van downtown to Fortis, Inc.,
equipped with hand controls and a hydraulic lift. I wear a tie,
pressed shirt, trousers, and leather loafers. I wear expensive
cologne, (not that the women ever seem to notice.) Mark from
HR sends me the occasional dirty joke on the company email.
Lionel, one cube over, complains to me when his teenage son

dents the family car or when his wife spends too much on decorative candles. Delilah from auto claims actually seems a bit smitten; unfortunately, she's married to an auto mechanic who I think has done some time for assault.

Anyway, after four years on the seventeenth floor, nobody really sees the chair anymore. And I do my very best never to remind them. If I'm in my cube and I drop my stapler, I wait for housekeeping to pick it up when they vacuum on the weekend, even if I drop it on a Monday. If I drop my fork in the cafeteria, I stop eating and head back in. Sometimes my leg bag gets so full you can see the protrusion alongside my calf, but I let it ride. I don't want anyone picking up after me, and I sure as hell don't want Ron from Accounts Receivable handling my piss.

I work my ass off all day, toiling over whatever project they give me. My intellect is all I have, and I never want to give anybody a reason to doubt my abilities. My income makes me less of a chair and more of a man. It's going to get me out of section-eight housing forever. One less number in my life. One less quad in the projects. Instead, a homeowner who happens to use a wheelchair. A man and his house.

So, today, when I got a fever at work, I ignored it. I'd already left work early just about a week ago for the same thing; I didn't want anybody grumbling. That guy in the wheelchair is always sick. *Michelle came in with the file from the Kenmore account, said a few things, and left. I didn't catch a word of it. My ears were ringing; my skin was gray. When she came back for her copies, I was slumped over, with long strands of drool reaching down to the matted Berber floor.*

When I woke up, I was the patient in room 1801. Bed 2.

***

Dear Estelle,

~~I guess you're still mad, but I'm writing this letter because~~

~~I know I don't deserve an explanation, but~~

You probably don't care, but I'm writing because I'm worried about you. I tried to call you, but everything's disconnected so you really must be out on the road like a gypsy.

I think about you every day. What the hell are you doing?

Speaking of hell, after our last conversation, it sounds like that's where you're headed. You've probably fallen off your bar stool by now, but it's true. Because I'm bound for heaven, and I want to help you find your way. I owe it to you. That's right. It's still me. It's Gloria. Only better.

Call me again. Please. Soon. I have found peace and love in Our Lord Jesus Christ, and I really want to tell you about it. And it would also interest you to know that I've lost four pounds. I prayed about my weight issues, and one night I had this dream. I was stuffing myself full of biscuits from Kentucky Fried, and feeling like I was about to barf, and here comes this handsome Latino guy in a red uniform (my Savior looks a lot like Benicio Del Toro, by the way) and a KFC hat, and he said, "Daughter, I gave you this body, and all I want you to do is stay sober and eat three good meals a day. And walk with me."

So that's what I've been doing. I don't binge anymore, and I take long walks by the beach every day. Can you believe it? Jesus is not just my personal savior, he's my personal trainer!

Call me soon. Your friend in Jesus Christ,

Gloria

***

Road Trip, Day 2: Trip to H . . . E . . . double hockey-sticks.

Dating the Son of God? I did *not* see that coming.

I called my mom, who read me Gloria's letter with a joyous lilt in her voice. My mom's not *born again,* but let's just say the biggest sin she's committed in the last 45 years was to forget to bring the Krumkake to the annual St. Pius Catholic Church Bake Sale and Ski Raffle six years ago. She'd love nothing more than for me to give Jesus all my woes and follow down the path of cheesiness.

But I'm not interested, and I told her as much.

Then she said, "Well, where are you going, Estelle Marie? What are you doing with your life?"

I said, "I'm letting the wind take me." (I have no idea what the hell I'm saying. I'm not boarding a sailboat, after all.)

"What does that mean?"

I could just picture my mother standing in her kitchen, talking to me on the last corded phone remaining on the planet Earth, holding her crystal Rosary, which thanks to me will eventually be rubbed down to nothing but pebbles. The old Estelle would have felt guilt at this point.

"It means what it means. I'll call you in a week, okay, Ma? Don't worry."

Telling my mom not to worry is a bit like telling Denise Austin to stop looking impossibly perfect and borderline psychotic. It's just what she does. But I say it anyway, just before I say "goodbye," because for some reason, "I love you" just seems so, I don't know, *ominous.*

Truth is I don't know what I'm doing; I don't know what happens to Gilligan at the end of the seven-day cruise. But isn't that the way I'm supposed to live it, according to AA, OA, NA, FAA, CIA, etcetera, etcetera? One day at a time? Keep it simple, stupid? Maybe not quite what Bea had in mind.

Anyway, tonight, another southern town, another Motel 6, another whirlpool full of empty Seagram's bottles and Zingers wrappers. Tomorrow, R. and R. and I board the S.S. Decadence, destination: the Western Caribbean.

I hear the smoothies are like heaven.

Chapter 20

Day 1: Cruise me to the moon.

I have found Sur-Vana. Get it? It's sugar meets nirvana with a big old booze-soaked cherry on top. That's what a cruise ship is. We haven't even started moving and I've had two huge meals and four strawberry daiquiris. See, Gloria? Kathy Lee Gifford is *my* personal trainer.

We had a bit of a kerfuffle at the customs gate, exacerbated by the fact that I was all jazzed up on IHOP stuffed crepes and a large caramel latte. (Too much sugar combined with caffeine makes me overly humorous and cutesy; picture Drew Barrymore with about thirty pounds of extra water weight and a bit of a lisp). In the end, they decided that while my passport may seem a little *weathered*, I looked more like a harmless chubby white chick than an Al Qaeda operative, so they let me by. Whew. If they hadn't let me aboard, I'm not sure exactly where I would have taken this traveling relapse show I'm starring in. Broadway? Nashville?

After customs, we got our room keys, which are actually cards, which are actually our credit cards for the week. Roxanne and Rhonda didn't have credit cards, so the tab for our room is going to get charged to mine. Roxanne swore up and down she'd pay me back for anything they bought, and I'm sure she will because she's a good girl, and responsible, like I used to be. Besides, how much can you spend on a cruise? The food's already paid for.

We *embarked* (who's fancy?) about noon, and took our carry-ons to our "state room" which must be a Maritime term for "a suite too small to sneeze in." If I don't know R. & R. too well yet, I certainly will after living in this windowless shoe box with them for a week.

The bathroom is so small you can pee, shower and brush your teeth all at the same moment, depending on what the tide is doing. The sleeping area consists of two bunk beds protruding from the wall on one side and one single bed on the other. Mercifully, R. & R. claimed the bunks.

In the middle of the room is about a foot-wide console with a nine-inch TV, which is always on and streaming live footage of all my dear shipmates as they pass through the main lobby snapping photos and grabbing handfuls of free Dramamine packets at the information kiosk.

We stuffed our clothes and our various soaps and shampoos into the small crevices the room offered, then set out to explore the ship.

***

Day 2: Ship happens.

And I've barely seen my *state room* since, or Rhonda, for that matter. Now I know how they get away with designing them so small. How can I go to bed when the sailing circus of fat white middle America never sleeps?

Rhonda disappeared right off the bat with a couple of German brothers we met at the Karaoke bar, who sang Sir-Mix-A-Lot and claimed to make "more money than David Hasselhoff." If I wasn't so worried about *their* wellbeing, I might take time to worry about hers.

One of them, I think his name was Carsten, kept trying to make eye contact with me, but I basically ignored him. Thing is, I think they were lying about the money thing, and it kills me that anyone would bother even embellishing on this kind of a trip. There are something like 2,000 of us here, brought together by various travel web sites or booking agents, all here to get blitzed and stuffed and possibly laid (if we aren't too blitzed or stuffed), and destined never to see each other ever again. There's no point in pretending we're something we're not, especially while sipping thousand-calorie smoothies out of plastic neon tumblers.

Carsten said, "So what is it that brings you to traveling?"

I said, "I'm an undercover Vogue reporter writing a story about cruise ships and the bulimics that love them."

He said, "I completely understand that you are saying that."

So I said, "Let's get down to brass tacks. How much for the ape?"

He nodded, smiled, and looked at my cleavage for a long minute. Then Rhonda grabbed him by his Hawaiian-print polo shirt, and dragged him to the dance floor, where she showed him a little dirty dancing Fergus Style. (This is like any other dirty dancing, really, only your partner is wearing a Wal-Mart sundress and plastic thongs.) I haven't seen him since. Poor bastard. He's going to need Roxanne's therapist when Roxanne's therapist's fiancé gets through with him.

Anyway, here's a fun fact I wouldn't have guessed: There's a fitness center on this binge barge.

Roxanne and I stumbled upon it on our way from the Beach Blanket Barbeque Buffet to the Make Your Own Sundae Bar on the pool deck. Enclosed by large panes of glass, the fitness center was a sea of hardwood flooring speckled with treadmills, various machines and weight benches, towels and Culligan water jugs. The walls were painted a relaxing tea green, and it would all have looked kind of pretty, if it didn't remind me so much of the treadmill I jumped off of when I left Minnesota and surrendered to my inner slob.

Taped to the glass were various announcements of fitness-related activities for the duration of the week. *Kickboxing* on Monday and Tuesday, *Spinning* Tuesday and Wednesday. *Yogalates* on the pool deck Thursday morning. *Get off the diet rollercoaster! Join us for a Two-hour Detox Seminar* boasted a hot-pink eight by ten. Detox? What the hell? *Don't miss Walking Club every day at 7 a.m. Meet new fitness friends and win a free water bottle!*

Adjacent to the workout room, some brunette cutie with crooked teeth and spandex hips was barking out orders to a kickboxing class, a group of about half a dozen women and one man trying to keep their balance while performing Tae Bo moves against the ebb and flow of the ship's movements.

Roxanne laughed out loud while the group shifted left in unison and started punching the air. "Who exercises on vacation?" she scoffed.

"I know, right?" I breathed.

Motherfuckers.

I stared at myself for a long moment in the glass. I felt the old shame creeping back. I stared at my baggy red t-shirt, my gray cotton shorts with the elastic waistband. I realized my fat clothes have become my regular clothes again. I put my hand to my belly, trying as always to smooth down my lumpy mid-section. To suck myself in.

And once again, always and forever, I hated what I saw. Suddenly, I felt guilty for not being one of the kicking masses.

No! This is ridiculous. I'm here because I'm done with all that. I'm done with guilt. I'm done with the weight war. Feel the ship's prevailing energy, Estelle. It's about food. It's about over-feeding. These are just seven people working out in some pathetic little studio . . . but outside of here and all around, are about one thousand, nine-hundred, and ninety-three people who are gorging themselves silly with booze, bratwursts, cream pies, all manner of filth! God bless America! Freedom Fries! Apple Pie! If you're not for us, you're against us!

This silly little group of stumbling kick boxers is the minority. They're just here to show you the misery you left behind. Who wants to be a number on a scale? Who wants to be a poster on Jack's wall? Who even understands a word Richard Simmons ever says? Who is a friend of fitness? Not me.

I re-focused on the class.

Why did I ever even try? Is this what I looked like? Fumbling around, trying to jiggle my way to happiness? I bet I'll see every single one of these sweating maniacs at the Midnight Chocolate Buffet, chowing down and undoing all their precious hard work. Or worse, sitting there with their families on vacation, just picking at their low-fat brownies and sticking to their stupid little weight-loss programs . . . on a cruise ship! The thought of it started a burning rage in my belly. How dare they spit in the face of decadence? How dare they exercise restraint? How dare they exercise . . . anything?

I hated them all, and they would feel my wrath.

"Let's go get our sundaes," I muttered to Roxanne, who seemed to be getting impatient to do just that.

We got in line at the Sundae Bar, my gut on fire with revenge. We loaded up our bowls with everything there was to offer from cookie dough chunks to pineapple, then piled whip cream on top of all of it. We took several red cherries apiece. Then we headed back to the fitness center.

"Why don't we just enjoy these on the lounge chairs by the pool?" Roxanne whined when I started back up the half-flight of stairs we had just come from.

"Because I want *everyone* to enjoy our sundaes," I laughed ruthlessly.

"What are you talking about?" Roxanne lumbered behind me, stealing bites as we walked. "Have you tried the hot fudge yet?" she gurgled, "It's like heaven. Hey, what are we doing back up here?"

"Have a seat!" I chirped. We were smack dab in front of the windows of the fitness center again. To my delight, the kick boxers still labored away, this time moving to some sort of Samba beat and looking continuously more and more exhausted. I plopped down cross-legged, facing them, and began digging in with even more fervor than I would normally exhibit while stuffing my face full of ice cream.

Roxanne guffawed. "Just exactly what are we doing?"

"Nothing! What? I'm just like Marlin Perkins," I slurped. "Observing the animals."

"You're so bad," Roxanne whispered, joining me on the floor.

The group didn't notice us at first because they had their backs to us . . . but the instructor did, and at first seemed puzzled. Then as they all pivoted to kick, three of them glanced our way. Then the other four. Two of them lost their places and forgot to kick with the rest. Another simply stopped and huffed angrily.

I giggled and shoveled another large spoonful into my mouth. The instructor flashed a crooked-toothed sneer at me and started barking her orders even more loudly.

"Ooh, she's maaahd," Roxanne said somewhat anxiously. "I'm going back by the pool."

"I'll meet you in a few," I said happily. "I don't want to miss the cool-down."

Chapter 21

Day 3: Left to my own devices.

Early this morning, we docked at Cozumel, and the grazing masses slowly filed off the boat for a day in the sun. Most people, including R. & R., signed up in advance for "fun excursions," but not me. I figured with everyone off snorkeling, slogging through Mayan ruins, and buying five-dollar shell bracelets, there will be almost no line whatsoever back at the Waffle Bar. Dibs on the blueberry syrup!

I filled my plate and found a poolside table.

"This seat taken?" I looked up to see a thirty-something blond guy wearing an orange T-shirt exclaiming, "You Better Belize It!" and a shark-tooth necklace. His hair was light, short and spiky, his face smiling, his build tall and lanky, and his slight belly pushing his cargo shorts a little beyond their intended limit. Not in a heavy-person sort of way, but in a *kitten that just had too much kibble* sort of way. Skinny people get that sometimes. Thanksgiving belly. Generally gone within two hours of the meal. He cocked his head to the side, and his shades fell from his forehead onto his sun burnt nose.

"Not technically, no."

"May I?" He pushed his shades up onto the bright red bridge of his nose.

"Sure," I smiled, wondering why I'm always so popular when I have a bucket-load of food in front of me. Or is it that I just always have a bucket-load of food in front of me?

"Your friend leave you again?"

"She's off touring lovely Cozumel," I said, uneasy. My friend? "Have you been watching me or something?"

"It's more like you've been watching me." Still smiling. Smirking.

"Huh?" His accent was southern. Had I been an asshole to him at some IHOP on the way to Houston? Had I insulted his best Kid Rock in the karaoke bar? That's the trouble with me drinking again. Things get fuzzy. *Perhaps today should just be a straight sugar day,* I noted. No booze. Maybe just one fancy drink after dinner. One? Hmmm. Okay, four. I'll only have four.

"Well, I thought it was funny," Spike shoveled half a sausage link into his mouth. "A touch cruel, but still funny."

What? Then it hit me. I heard a distant Samba beat . . . the faint smell of treadmill oil . . .

"Oh," I muttered. "You're one of . . . them."

He howled with laughter. His shades fell off.

"In my defense, aerobics classes are a great way to meet chicks," he said after a moment.

Chicks. Skinny boy was there to meet chicks. I put my fork down. Something churned in my belly, and it wasn't the Jell-O-marshmallow salad.

"What's your name?" I asked calmly.

"Bill," he held his hand out. "Bill Baker."

"Well, Bill Baker," I stood, ignoring his hand, "I'm Estelle. And I think you should know that the old Estelle would have already apologized for what I did yesterday."

"Oh, I'm not asking . . ."

"But the old Estelle also would have sat here trying not to eat in too much front of you. The old Estelle would have sat here holding her gut in and waiting for your approval. Trying to look . . . tiny. Trying to be your little anorexic Cassie or Carrie or whatever the fuck her name is."

"I'm sorry?" Bill had the look of a man who'd walked into a movie theater, thinking he was going to a Jean Claude Van Dam movie and finding a Kate Hudson movie instead. *How to Lose a Guy in Ten Days*, if I had to pick one.

"You should be sorry!" I was outside myself. "To you, a fitness center is just some place to ogle women while they run in place all day, sweating their asses off, just praying that someday, some bean pole with a beer gut like you will find them pretty, so they can feel like they're worth something!"

"I don't . . ." Bill Baker was at a loss. He sucked in his gut a little; oddly, he was still smiling.

"I bet you think exercise is just *fun*. Don't you? Good times. Well it's not. Exercise is a device . . . a torture device. Just one more thing we *chicks* use to flog ourselves to death with, like diet pills and deal-a-meals and Ab Rollers . . . and *fucking Denise Austin!*"

I was yelling; people were looking.

"Well, *my*," Bill Baker guffawed. "I thought you were cute . . . had a wild sense of humor maybe. But hell. You're just about a baker's dozen different kinds of fucked up." He piled his coffee cup and utensils onto his plate and picked them up nervously. "It was interesting talking to you, *New Estelle*."

"Likewise," I said, imitating Bill Baker's drawl.

I plopped down angrily, picked up my fork and carved a huge chunk of waffle for myself. Oh, I thought pensively, it's going to be *that* kind of a day.

***

After the Bill Baker Incident, I tried to find someplace where I could avoid personally insulting anymore of my fellow shipmates. I fled to the Starlight Lounge, where I hoped a sea of easy chairs and ash trays would keep me at a safer distance from, well, anyone. Not only can you smoke and drink in the Starlight, but there is almost always some kind of live music you can lose yourself in. Almost never good, but always live. And while you nurse your various regrets, you can fantasize about the supersexy keyboard player whose name is probably Diablo or Enrique or something equally Latino.

Bill Baker. What a fucking name *that* is. Probably Bill Baker from Baton Rouge or something else equally ludicrous. Still, an innocent. A casualty of my unraveling. Poor guy had no warning about the dump truck full of crazy I drag around, waiting to unload. How could R. & R. leave me alone for a whole day? Alone in my head? Alone and relapsing all over everybody. I'm clearly not suited for human company. Who will be my next victim?

A young waitress with a Swedish accent approached me, and I recalled the rather unfortunate promise I made myself earlier about drinking. Immediately, I found a loophole. I had vowed to have only four drinks *after* dinner. I'd made no such promises about *before.* And the day was oh, so deliciously young.

"I'll have one of those sugary coffee drinks with Bailey's in 'em," I said, handing her my key/credit/magic card. "How many calories do you s'pose are in one of those bad boys?"

"Uh?" the waitress smiled uncomfortably. Her black knee-length pencil skirt and white blouse looked to be about a size five or maybe a seven. She knew what the hell I was talking about. Unless she didn't. Unless she was one of those freaks like Bea, all self-controlled and smug, with no food obsessions to speak of, one of those "eat to live" people. Skinny. Bitch.

No. Calm yourself. She's just a waitress with a favorable metabolism. She's just your garden variety Pretty Girl With Not Unattractive Thighs. She's done nothing *intentionally* wrong.

"Well, I don't care, is my point!" I threw my legs onto the lounge chair across from me. "Keep 'em coming."

And so she did. As fast as her perfect little calves would carry her, my little Swedish Dolly kept me supplied with coffee drinks all afternoon. By the time R. & R. found me hours later, it was time for dinner, and I was the most alert drunk in all of the western Caribbean.

"You guys are totally awesome," I told Roxanne while Rhonda stood idly, letting her twin lift me out of the lounge chair. She swung my arm around her shoulder and began limping me toward the door.

"And by you guys, I mean Roxanne," I slurred.

Rhonda grunted. She was sun-burnt and wearing a new T-shirt she'd bought that day: a white baggy number depicting a skinny, bikini-clad body that I guessed none of the three of us would ever have unless we wore it on a T-shirt.

"You need to learn how to handle your alcohol."

"You need to learn how to handle your *alcoholic*," I retorted. "Take a lesson from your sister. She's the awesome-est codependent, ever."

"Maybe you should eat something," Roxanne codepended as we limped along.

"Oh, hell no," Rhonda snorted. "She'll never keep it down. We're taking her to the room to sleep it off." And by "we" she meant Roxanne.

Food sounded good, as always, even if it didn't get to stay long. I started forming my opinion on the matter in my head. Just then, I caught a glimpse of Bill Baker. He was walking toward the "Freestyle" dining room, the ship's 24-hour buffet, talking to some *chick* with Paris Hilton sunglasses and Nicole Ricci thighs.

"Take me to my room," I whispered.

"What?" Roxanne yelled.

"I said take me to my room!" in a very loud whisper.

Bill Baker looked away from Paris long enough to see that it was me. A look of concern flashed across his face.

Swell.

"You ladies need any help?" he stopped mid-flirt.

"No. We. Do. Not."

"Yeah," Roxanne panted. I wasn't exactly making it easy for her.

"Looks like you've got a couple of cocktails on board," Bill Baker grinned. Paris Hilton walked off, disgusted. Can't blame her. Who talks like that?

"You better go after her," I said urgently. "*Chicks* like that come along only once every cruise ship."

Bill swung my arm under his shoulder and took a load off Roxanne, who pulled away briefly to stand up straight.

"What room is she in? I can take her for you," Mr. Big Helper announced.

Roxanne seemed ready to protest, but Rhonda took over.

"Room 3145. Here's her key card. You're a fucking prince, whoever you are."

"He's the fucking Boston Strangler as far as *you* know," I sneered at Rhonda.

"He looks more like Officer Friendly to me," Roxanne chimed in.

Bill just smiled this big stupid Aren't Chicks Funny smile and punched the elevator button.

"You're fired, Roxanne," I yelled over Bill's shoulder as he led me away.

Alone in the elevator, I pulled away from Bill's steadying grip.

"I don't need the help."

"Maybe not. Maybe I just think you're cute."

"You're full of shit."

"You're full of *something.*"

"I'm full of mad," I stuttered. "I mean I'm . . . I *am* mad."

I could feel something derailing. What is it about this guy that does that?

"Mad at what?"

"Mad at men. Mad at women. Mad at Size Seven Swedish waitresses. Denise Austin. Mad that I'm so . . . addicted."

"So you're taking it out on yourself?"

"I'm mad yet strangely passive!"

"You're cute."

"You're condescending, Bill Baker from Baton Rouge."

"I'm not from Baton Rouge."

"And I'm not cute."

At last, we were in the hallway, searching for my state room. I was grateful for the distraction. God knows what else I might feel compelled to tell Bill Baker about myself. Maybe my weight? Bust size? That I like to eat raw cookie dough until I see spots? He just had this look about him. This neon sign on his forehead, blinking, *Tell me all your troubles.*

In my room, Bill Baker carefully picked the fancy origami towel dog housekeeping had left on my bed and placed it on the TV. Cruise ship housekeepers are all about origami towel art, if you weren't aware. He turned the bed covers back.

"I'll grab you a bucket just in case; you want the TV on?"

"Sure." I flopped onto the cot, praying that he would go and not linger. It was one thing being pampered by my very own co-dependent, but entirely another being babied by some strange man named Bill Baker who was suddenly starting to look like halfway-decent boyfriend material. This is not the kind of situation that gives one the upper hand even in the best possible doomed relationship.

Bill Baker turned the TV to the worst station – one that broadcasts the ship's various goings on after-the-fact. We both stared lamely at it for a moment. It was something cleverly called the "Oldy-wed Game" that took place over the lunch hour, emceed by the ship's "entertainment coordinator." An elderly male contestant struggled to remember his wife's favorite sexual position. At stake was a 25-dollar on-board gift shop certificate, which he would certainly need to make up for the fact that he couldn't answer the question. Typical. Probably a blues musician. Married five-hundred years and still doesn't know how mamma likes her sausage.

"Missionary," Bill quipped. "She looks like a traditionalist."

I tried not to laugh. Upper hand.

Mercifully, he turned for the door. As he flipped the light switch, he said, "Would the New Estelle like to have dinner with me tomorrow?"

The Old Estelle would have said yes. Yes. Yes. Yes. Which is why . . .

"Um," I paused. I thought about James. Gloria. Jack. Waterbeds. Slim-Fast bars. Strawberry waffles. And how everything, no matter how hard you try to steer it, no matter how good you are, how bad you are, how fat you are, how skinny, everything always ends up the same. The scale never lies, but it also doesn't tell the whole truth. The more you strive for perfection, the faster it slips away. The more you want someone, the faster they go. The best thing to do is cut him off at the pass.

"No, thanks," I said pitifully.

"Okay." Still smiling? Asshole! "Goodnight, New Estelle."

"Goodnight, Old Bill."

Chapter 22

Day 4: Acting Normal.

I slept through Roatan. Just as well. Somebody told me there's a sand flea issue on the beaches. That's all I need to add to my resume: Alcoholic, sugar addict, sand flea carrier. Maybe there's a meeting for that out here on the swinging seas.

I got up around 2 p.m., took a long shower in our tiny stall, and rummaged around for something to wear.

The TV was still on of course, and some little spa-tart with purple fingernails was giving a demonstration on how to perform your own, at-home Caviar Facial. She smeared a blob of black mess onto an eager old woman's face while others looked on, nodding feverishly about the healing benefits of fish eggs.

Fish eggs. Fingernails. Paris Hilton sunglasses. Who was that girl with Bill? Who cares? I sure as hell don't.

Still. What to wear?

After some looking, I found a rather comely sundress I'd forgotten I had: kind of a tie-dyed number with pleats and gatherings all in just the right places to promote maximum sin concealment. I slipped on a pair of strappy leather sandals and checked myself in the mirror. Today, I figured, would be a good day to act human for once. I'd had my little melt-down. I'd said some really *fascinating* things to some basically innocent people, and I'd more than made up for lost drinking time. I'd spent so much time at the sundae bar that the lady behind the counter already knew my name, my cat's name, and my preferred ratio of hot fudge to scoops of ice cream.

Purple fingernails rinsed all the sludge off the old lady's face, who suddenly beamed like a new bride. "Don't forget ladies," spa-tart hissed. "Join Lauren tomorrow at 9:30 for a

Detox Seminar in the fitness center! Learn the secret to lasting weight loss once and for all!"

I found my brush and turned on Roxanne's curling iron. I rummaged in her makeup kit for some foundation, some lip gloss. Just for today, I vowed, vaguely remembering the old post-it note affirmations that used to frame my mirror, just for today I will be different. Just for today . . . I'll act normal.

***

I headed to Mama Mia's, the ship's Italian buffet. I wish I could put the pasta bar in my pocket and never have to be without it again. The spicy meat loaf is also a little slice of dehydrated soup mix heaven. Whatever would I do when it came time to go back out into the world of foods with limits? I was sitting by my cute little lonesome when the next best thing to All You Can Eat came walking up in semi-snug button-flies and a t-shirt that said, "Chicks Dig Me."

"You got a hankering for some pizza?" Bill Baker said in his typical twang. He was loaded for buffet bear, but he didn't sit down. This represented his third attempt to fraternize with me, and he'd learned to expect disappointment, I suppose.

"Did you really just say 'hankering?'"

"Yes, ma'am."

"Well, sit on down, ya big hayseed."

"Really?" He checked the chair next to me for alligators, fart cushions, and live grenades. "I'd be delighted."

"But what?"

"Huh?"

"You'd be delighted, but what?"

"Damn it, woman, I *am* delighted. I'm fucking elated. I've been talking to you for sixty seconds now and I still have both heads and both balls attached."

"Am I that big a shrew?"

"Yes, ma'am."

Bill sat down, then took a long sip on his iced tea.

"Well here we are having dinner anyway," he proceeded on down the icy highway like a truck driver hauling a load of eggs. "And you said it couldn't be done."

"Nice t-shirt," I said, and imagined myself taking it off of him.

***

I'd like to say that the next part of this gets blurry, but it doesn't because I wasn't drunk . . . or even the slightest bit buzzed. I hadn't even had dessert. I mean, I wanted dessert, but Bill asked me to take a walk with him, so I did that instead. That should have been my first clue. The shitty ones: they try to separate you from the things you love.

"So what do you do out in the real world?" he asked me as we strolled past a gaggle of shuffleboard players. It was a normal enough question.

"I lose friends, disappoint employers, and eat at IHOP as much as possible," I said, wondering instantly if I ever said anything that didn't make me sound like the half-wit love child of John Cusack and Minnie Pearl.

"Where are your friends tonight?"

"Roxanne and Rhonda? Dunno. I don't even know if they're really my *friends*. I actually just met them less than a week ago. I feel pretty certain that Rhonda's done time in Attica."

I hate how I keep telling this guy shit I don't even like to admit to myself.

"And you're on a cruise with them?"

"They gave me pancakes and got me drunk. I really, really like pancakes."

"Do you like getting drunk?"

"No, that's just something that tends to happen lately since I stopped caring about anything. I know, right? Insanity."

Babbling. Find your words. Use your filter.

"So, what do *you* do out in the real world?" I attempted a swift re-direct. Normal. Normal. Normal people ask other normal people what they do for a living. Normal people don't spill all their cookies every time somebody asks them a polite question.

"I spend fifty weeks a year working and fantasizing about the two weeks I spend on vacation," Bill sighed, staring wistfully at the ocean.

"You're going to make me cry," I giggled. Oh, gag. First dinner, next flirting. I thought, *This goes against everything New Estelle stands for.* Then I tossed my hair with my hand like a freaking high school sophomore.

"Don't cry for me, beautiful. It's just life." He flashed a big toothy smile.

Beautiful?

I tried to look away from the mouth that had just spoken the word . . . the word that had shot straight to my bikini area. But I couldn't. I couldn't not want for somebody to think it. Some. Body. To think I'm beautiful.

Bill Baker cocked his head and looked into my eyes. I could totally see at that moment why Chicks Dig Him.

Then he kissed me.

Then the New Estelle jumped out of my body, over the railing and into the water, probably creating a size 14 crater in the ocean floor. Poor old New Estelle.

I haven't been kissed like that in forever, like Bill was starving and I was the last ice cream cone on the planet. We stayed like that for several minutes, until one of the shuffle boarders said, "Cheese and Rice! Get a room."

So we did; we went to Bill's.

My state room wasn't safe, of course. Roxanne and Rhonda had to be roaming around somewhere with matching

Roatan flea bites, and could show up any time. Bill's roommate, he said, was off watching one of the stage shows with all the ex-ballerinas in pleather and sequins.

Thank Blessed Merciful God, he turned off the lights first thing. *I* don't even know what I look like naked lately. I sure as hell didn't want *him* looking. We squeezed onto his tiny cot, kissing, touching, breathing hot buffet breath into each other's ears.

At first it was all so familiar. Same old sex: fumbling around in the dark with some guy, wishing like hell that I had some prettier, skinnier, better version of myself to offer. *Maybe someday I'll have sex like a normal girl,* I thought, traipsing down that dark and dangerous alleyway also known as my psyche. *Better yet, I wish I could have sex like one of those girls on Jack's wall. Perfect, skinny, big boobed, flat-bellied sex.*

Suddenly, Bill rolled me out from under him, positioning me astride. And because God hates me, the ship shifted just at that moment, and the bathroom door fell open, causing light to stream in and shine across *my* belly, *my* breasts, my horrified expression.

Bill took it all in. All me. Back lit, front lit . . . mortified.

"Oh my God," Bill breathed; he grabbed my hips and pulled. "You are incredible."

The poor man. The poor, half-blind, half-witted moron. All I could think was that desperation had brought him to this point. But he just kept on with that stupid grin, like he'd just won $500 in scratch-offs or found his lost schnauzer.

"Look at me," he said. "I want you to do whatever feels good. You're in charge."

"What?" I squirmed. What kind of kinky-ass, trailer court, battery-operated sex with a virtual stranger had I gotten myself into?

"Just do whatever you want," Bill rose onto his elbows and kissed my chin. "*Beautiful.*"

How the hell would I know what that is? God. I could have died. I stayed motionless for the longest time, wondering why anyone, ever, *ever* talks during sex.

Then the ship rocked again, slamming the door shut, extinguishing the light, and returning me to my comfort zone. I was free again. Free, and apparently *in charge.* Instead of dying, I braced my two hands on his chest like a marathon runner on the starting line. Then, I did exactly what Bill Baker had asked me to.

I just did, and did, and *did.*

***

Bill Baker's state room was neat as a pin, by the way. A little place for everything and every little thing in its place.

"I'm ex-military," he explained when I opened his closet to find all items hung perfectly or folded neatly at the bottom. "Plus, Stevie took all the other storage." He laid back and rested his hands behind his head.

"Lay with me, woman. I'm not *even* done with you yet."

"Well, sir, yes, sir," I saluted. I scooped my sundress off the floor and pulled it over my head. Bill sighed.

"Okay, okay," I said, and slid my hips down next to his tiny little ass, suddenly feeling all the weight I had managed to forget about just half an hour before. I jabbed his ribs with my elbow.

"Sorry," I moaned.

"S'okay," he said, making room for my girth and turning toward me, staring intently. Staring at me long enough, I surmised, to begin to see every little thing that is wrong with me.

We stayed like that for possibly five minutes to three days. It's too bad for Bill. You can take the psycho sugarfiend out of her clothes, but you can't get her out of her own head. You can call her beautiful half a dozen times, and even get her to have

136

an honest to goodness orgasm for once in her pathetic life, but you can't fix that what's hopelessly broken. Somewhere between my head and my skin lies the problem. My head and my skin and every single addicted, insecure, cell in between. Ay, dear Bill. There's the rub.

"Are you uncomfortable?" Bill finally asked.

"Yeah," I exhaled loudly. I was *so thoroughly uncomfortable.*

"You don't have to stay," he volunteered. "I just want you to."

"Um, I should go take a shower and change clothes," I said, squirming.

"Okay, then," Bill sat up a little. "Meet you later at the Starlight?"

"Yes!" I said overly emphatically.

"Okay, gorgeous."

I had to run. Just had to run.

But cruise ships are confusing if you're not paying attention. I started off in what I thought was the direction of the elevators, and next thing I knew I was at the butt of a dead end. I doubled back, then took a left down another hallway, thinking I had it right, then spotted the same discarded room service tray I had passed on my way to getting lost. Fuck!

I circled around again and checked the room number I stood next to. I was back where I started. But where was I even trying to go?

Gorgeous. Beautiful. Do what you want. Why was I running, and from what? Kindness? Love or something resembling love? A man who seemed to . . . gasp . . . want me?

I tried hard to think what the new Estelle would do about this situation, then realized I had trashed her earlier. So which was I, the New or the Old Estelle? I couldn't remember. I didn't care. I wondered if he was still there, waiting for me to lie back into his arms. Suddenly, his arms sounded softer, more pliable.

Given permission to take him or leave him, I wanted him. Wanted him bad.

I started back down the hall toward his room, increasingly sure where I was headed. I smoothed my hair down a little and sucked in my stomach. For a moment, I pondered that detox thing I'd seen advertised. What if I could get back on track? What if I could find my way back to normal? Surely at some point in my life I've been marginally normal. Maybe I can lose a few pounds . . . since I had someone to lose them for. Maybe try out one of those elliptical things . . .

Just then, walking toward me down the hall I noticed a girl with Paris Hilton sunglasses. Seeing her made me sweat instantly, and I couldn't remember just why. Not Denise Austin sweat, but "I'm about to sing a song two octaves above my vocal range in karaoke" sweat. She strolled casually, failing to notice me the way most skinny girls fail to notice anybody who isn't attractive.

She stopped at Bill's door. I froze.

She knocked.

I turned myself away and rushed toward the nearest door I saw. I knocked casually, praying nobody would answer. I snuck another peek at Paris Hilton. Jesus. My *cat* has thicker ankles than that woman. She was knocking impatiently. Pink tank top and matching sling-back sandals. Insanely adorable.

Because God still hates me, a tan, leathery woman who could have either been 45 years old or 75, with orange hair and wearing a yellow terry-cloth robe answered the door I'd been knocking on.

She sized me up. "Yeh?" Her accent was either Russian or . . . something else.

I said, "Uh . . . yes. Is Jemima home?"

"Who? Jemima?"

"Yes," I stuttered, "Er . . . Aunt . . . Jemima."

Two rooms down, Bill's door opened for Paris Hilton. Without a moment's hesitation, she stepped inside and closed it behind her.

Chapter 23

Day 5: What a long, strange ship it's been.

It's funny how a meltdown happens. Before my little tango with Bill, I pretty much thought I was already having one. But melting is a gradual thing. It takes time for a candle to drip down to nothing. And then when it's all down to nothing, if there's nothing to catch it, no sensible fire-proofed candle holder, then the wick just keeps burning and burning and pretty soon the table's on fire and then the whole kitchen, and then of all things the damn gas stove is on, and next thing you know you're on the Channel 6 Shipboard, half-naked, covered in chocolate syrup and yelling "I'm ready for my colon cleanse now, Denise!"

Point of clarification: Denise Austin is not directly responsible for my behavior of last night, which thanks to half a dozen more coffee drinks, stretched into this morning and ended with a half-crazed bang right around nine forty-five. But she is not *un*responsible.

Admittedly, Denise Austin did *not* make me do the following:

1.   Head straight to the Starlight lounge after watching the Bill and Paris show and immediately belt back three to twelve shots of Peppermint Schnapps. (I figured if I was going to get all up in that bastard's face, I was at least going to do so with minty, come-hither breath.)

2.   Leave the Starlight after waiting for a full hour for Bill, then head to the Chocoholic's Midnight Buffet with a belly full of booze and a lobster bib. My memory fails me a bit on this one. Suffice it to say that I came, I saw, I bathed in chocolate. Eye-witness accounts intimate that I was "asked" to retire to my state room for the night some time around 2 a.m.

3.   Fail to retire to my state room. If Ms. Austin had been consulted on this, I'm fairly certain she would have told me to pack it in, hit the shower, and wash the chocolate cheesecake out of my hair.

4.   Continue to drink all through the night and into the morning, stopping only to treat my shipmates to my own special karaoke interpretation of *Crazy*, during which I dragged Patsy Cline from her grave, beat her poor bones to submission, then threw her down in a mangled heap begging for mercy.

5.   And this one's a biggie: Show up for the detox seminar, fagged, lagged, and 100-percent in the bag. I'm pretty sure the words, "Give me high fructose corn syrup or give me death" were uttered, and not by Denise Austin. Anyone needing to know the details of this incident need only tune in to Shipboard Channel 6, where the now-infamous detox-debacle has been replayed twice so far, due to popular demand I assume.

I'll tell you what I do blame Denise Austin for. For making me think I could ever be normal. For looking at me with those Smurfy-blue eyes and telling me that firm thighs, toned arms and a flat belly were my ticket to happiness -- and that they were just one good workout, one salad, one protein shake away. For looking a little bit like me, only skinny; for smiling at me with those awesome sugar-free teeth of hers. For leading the fitness revolution, inspiring millions of women just like me to eat grapefruits, drink teas with special antioxidants, to get up off our fat butts and imagine that we could live the fitness dream. For spreading her ilk so far and wide that a girl can't even get on an all-you-can-eat cruise ship without having to be reminded of how far she falls short. How very fucking far.

When I woke up, Roxanne was resting in the cot across the room from me.

"Where are we?" I asked, having a bit of déjà vu over that first day, which seemed eons ago, not a mere eleven days, when I woke up, hung over, unsure of my surroundings, on the floor of Roxanne's little trailer.

"We're stopped at Belize City for a little while longer," she whispered, anticipating my headache. It was nice to see her, my little caretaker, obviously perched and ready to give me just exactly the Advil and sympathy that my situation clearly warranted.

"Is it over yet?" I sighed.

"Is what over?"

"Am I done being me? Can I be done yet?"

"You're one crazy bitch," Roxanne giggled.

And she hadn't even turned on the TV yet.

***

We ordered room service pizza. In a startling show of human emotion, Rhonda took pity on me and ventured up to the sundae bar, bringing my dessert back to the room. I'm on something of a "house arrest," in the care of my codependent and her twin, confined to my state room by security, as a result of *the incident.*

We'd watched it all on Shipboard Channel 6. I'd entered the detox seminar quietly enough, though I was five minutes late and my once-lady-like sundress was torn up one side (when performing the karaoke classic "Her Name Was Lola," one's dress must be slit, I'd surmised) and splattered with chocolate and raspberry goo. I'd taken a seat in the back row. Lauren, of kickboxing instructor fame, was talking while a twenty-something guy with a Jamaican-looking head and a Lance Armstrong body dutifully manipulated a PowerPoint presentation projected overhead.

The word "CRAP" was spelled vertically, with a word for each letter spelled horizontally:

Caffeine
Roaming toxins *(huh?)*
Allergens
Processed sugars

"You see," Lauren explained in a clippie little British accent, "You try and try to eat the right things, to manage your calories, to be good little boys and girls. You exercise your little bums off. And what? Nuffing. So you get disgusted, don't you? And you revert to your old ways."

Energetic head-bobbing all around. I recognized most of the faces, like they were the woodland creatures in my own little tripped out Disney movie. There was Linda, the soccer-mom from Indianapolis, who can't stop eating the cheese bread and who I'd heard sing "I Will Survive" three times in five days. There was Judy, who works in the lingerie department at Macy's in Cleveland and says that this cruise is her last hurrah before signing on for that diet that Perky Marie Osmond hawks on TV. There was Sandy, a twice-divorced state trooper who'd apprehended at least three willing suspects on this cruise with her big, tan Wisconsin thighs.

It was an all-female crowd, with few exceptions, and they were eating it with a spoon. Lauren had hit on something we could all relate to: hope and hopelessness. We were all there because we were tired of trying, yet not done trying. We thought we could eat without shame, but we couldn't. We thought we might take a vacation from the Big Fat Lie, but it stowed away in our make-up bags and followed us here to paradise. We thought we could be skinny. We hoped we could be lovable, finally. We thought British Lauren had the answer to the Big Question. We counted on her for that. She had damn well better. We were missing "Crepe-palooza" on the main deck for this fucking thing.

"With this program, you'll see results right away because it's like not a diet. The answer to your new life is not in your *head*, your *heart* or even your *stomach*." Lauren beamed shamelessly. She was building up to something big. Her audience perched on their folded chairs with baited breath. Bring it home, British Lauren!

"The answer is in your colon!"

My . . . colon?

I looked around at us all, and waited for the other shoe to drop. Lauren had taken it too far. The insult was too deep. The scam too shameless. The claim too ridiculous. I waited for the crowd to descend upon her, to tear her gorgeous flesh to pieces. But it didn't happen. Quite the opposite, in fact. All around me, approving nods and positive words uttered.

For God's sake, I thought. *I'm the only one who can save us.*

I stood up; It took a moment for me to find my equilibrium, and it wasn't because of the ship's movement. I focused on my target: my big, British, gap-toothed target.

If Jack Lalanne and Denise Austin had ever stopped flexing their various muscles and had a love child, it would have been Lauren. One could just imagine the first infant ever to come out completely dressed in spandex and Asics running sneakers. She was blond, toned, and her white-hot smile just begged to be punched.

Which is, I imagine, what I was thinking when I stumbled into the aisle between the folding chairs, squared off like a size-fourteen Technicolor bull, and lunged at the poor girl suddenly from the back of the room, yelling at the top of my voice, *"It sure as fuck is in my colon, you Nazi Fitness Bitch!"*

Of course, British Lauren was way too agile for the likes of me, and jumped nimbly out of the path of danger, clearing the way for me to tackle the overhead machine like I was Mickey Rourke in *The Wrestler*. There was quite a ruckus after that. Sandy the State Trooper had me hog tied with her sarong in about ten seconds flat. From there, the angry mob kept me down with nothing more than their basic feelings of fear and loathing until shipboard security and medics could arrive.

I figured resistance was futile. Plus, I vaguely remember one of the EMTs looking a lot like Benjamin Bratt, which had a certain mellowing affect. As they rolled me away on the stretcher, I was muttering something about "Don't drink the Sugar-free Kool-Aid!" Then I ordered Mr. Bratt to stay the hell away from my colon . . . at least until our second date.

Chapter 24

Day 6: At sea.

Our last day was spent at sea, ironically. At sea is pretty much where I've been for the last two weeks. Drifting. Eating. Drinking.

Bill knocked on the door a time or two during my confinement, but that cowboy is *dead to me* (insert loud spitting noise.) If he wants to knock his boney little hips with some cheerleader camp refugee, then he's welcome to it, by God. Makes no difference to me. God. I could really use a bucket of Daiquiri to swim in.

But no. I'm off that stuff 'til we hit terra firma. I've had my fun. I'm starting to miss things, people, places. I miss Minnesota. I miss my cat. My mom. Gloria. Shit. Jack. Double shit.

Oh, evil hangover. Why must you vex me with crystal clear hindsight? I realize I've lost or abandoned everything I once had. When I disembark this ship, I'm homeless. I could travel back up north, but what have I to return to? Gloria is gone. My job. My sweet crippled confidant. My cat awaits, but how will I feed him with no job? And me? Where will I live?

I lay in my cot, sweating, fighting overwhelming anxiety, deep regret, pre-menstrual confusion, and the desperate urge to break house arrest and crash the waffle bar for one last time.

On Channel 6, an events calendar streamed lazily to a backdrop of a Muzak version of "Some Kind of Wonderful." But since the Advil I had taken had begun wearing off, it felt more like all three members of Grand Funk Railroad were trying to bust out of my head with guitar-shaped chain saws.

I popped twelve Dramamine and washed them down with a Diet Coke.

The last thing I remembered before I fell asleep again was watching R. and R. packing their suitcases. Though I should have, I don't remember caring all that deeply about it. Somebody had switched the tube to the movie channel, and *Titanic* was in full swing. Oh, Kate and Leo, you smarmy, doomed, skinny bastards. I reached a hand out to the screen and muttered "Put your hands on me, Jack!" And out I went.

***

Day 7

I woke to the sound of a Philippine man singing, "Dees-embarking time; time to go. Come on, detox lady. You wear out your welcome now."

I checked my surroundings. Ernesto from Housekeeping had busted in, turned on every possible light, and was far enough into my dance space for me to tell that he smelled of urinal cakes and thin mints. The room was empty, but for me, Ernesto, two towels on the floor, half a can of Diet Coke, and everything I'd brought onboard stuffed into two gift shop bags.

"Roxanne?" I muttered, helplessly. This did not look good. On first assessment, one would think that those shyster bottle-blond hash-slingers had stolen my luggage and left me high and dry.

I rolled gracelessly off the bed and stumbled to the bathroom.

"Detox lady, you go now," Ernesto said as though he were wishing me a Happy Birthday and not kicking me off the ship like a cockroach.

I slammed the door and locked it. "That's exactly what the fuck I'm trying to do," I told him.

Think. Think. Think. Why would they bail on me like this? Hadn't we had just loads of fun with a few notable exceptions? Why didn't they wake me up? I'd expect this much from Rhonda perhaps, but Roxanne?

I peed. And peed. And peed. How long had I been unconscious? Had they tried to wake me and failed? Had I . . .

"Come on now, Miss Estelle. No more cruising and bruising for Miss Estelle."

I pulled up my jogging shorts and opened the bathroom door to find Ernesto holding my bags impatiently. No more origami towels for Miss Estelle. Ernesto was not even playing.

"Check out is on the main deck. You go now. You had too much fun, detox lady."

Thanks to Ernesto, I arrived at the checkout turnstiles in two different-colored flip-flops, wearing lime green jogging shorts, and no bra under my T-shirt, which was one of about seventeen that I'd purchased at the gift shop during one of my *episodes.* They really should warn you about those key cards. It's like Monopoly money, only you can clean puke off them.

The line was short, since almost all the other passengers had left. A dapper young brunette with thick, pasty eyelashes and Bettie Page bangs slowly straightened her navy blue uniform blazer as she waited for me to lug my bags up to her station. It was a gesture not unlike when somebody scratches his or her nose as a hint that you've got something on yours. Her eyes said, "Good God, woman, straighten yourself."

Her mouth said, "Key card?"

Key card. Of course. Eek. I fished around in the bags for my small purse, and, thankfully, found it without too much delay; this seemed to relieve Bettie Page. She had figured it would take longer; she had seen my kind before. I handed her my key card triumphantly, as if to say, "See? I'm a wreck . . . *with a key card."*

She swiped the thing along the side of her computer and paused for it to process something. I was going to miss that little key card. So much freedom. So much convenience. So many sweet, chocolaty coffee drinks.

The computer emitted low, ominous tone, causing Bettie Page's sculpted black eyebrows to shift. She gave me a long look, blew her bangs out of her eyes (which was unnecessary because they weren't really in her eyes), sighed, and said, "Your account is *flagged*."

This *flagged* thing seemed important. At least to her.

"Flagged?"

"Flagged. Didn't you get the note we left under your door?"

"Uh." As if my friend Ernesto and I had had time to read notes! "No."

"Well, you spent more on your key card than you actually have *credit* on your credit card. You're going to have to give us another card to put the rest of the charges on. Or you can give us cash, of course."

"Wait. I went over my limit? I went over my card's limit?" *My card had a limit?*

"By quite a lot, yes."

"How much?"

"Let's see . . ." Ee, gad. She needed a calculator. "Looks like one thousand, six hundred, and fifty-four dollars."

"Wha . . .?"

"One thousand, six hundred, fifty-four. *Dollars.* That you owe."

"But I didn't get the note," I muttered as if that mattered. I didn't get the note that said, *Dear Estelle, You're a fat, drunken dumb-ass who trusted two perfect strangers with your key card, and thereby your credit card, and now they're God-knows-where and you're here with little miss prissy bangs, and this ain't no joke, and you ain't got no other credit cards, and you're good and truly fucked. Love, Destiny*

"I'll print you a new list," said Bangy Bangerton. Oh, goody.

I watched the pages slowly stream out of the printer. One. Two. Three. Ten. Twelve. Shit. Shit. Shit.

I read and read. Bar. Gift shop. Bar. Bar. Bar. Excursion. Excursion? I hadn't gone on any. But, of course, my good friends Barbie and Skipper had. Bar. Casino. Bar. Bar. Tobacco. In-room porn? *Fucking Rhonda.* Bar. Bar. More excursions.

How could this happen? I could expect this from Rhonda, but Roxanne? After two weeks, *you think you'd know a person.*

Immaterial, I realized. Beside the point. I was in big debt, had no more money, and was completely on my own. Bangs was staring daggers at me. I'd stalled so long at this point that she'd picked up the phone to call Somebody Important. I realized quickly, that somebody was Three Large Security Guards with Mace On Their Belts.

There was only one thing left to do. Surrender, you say? Nothing doing. I would run. I would run as fast as my substantial-sized legs would carry me, I would jump in my car, and I would flee this boat, this life, this binge . . . forever. I would return to Minnesota, beg my mom for mercy, and start anew. Maybe Absolute would take me back and give me a new client or two. Maybe Jack? Oh, Jack.

Suddenly, I ached for my old life. I ached for my old aches. If I could get it back, even half of it, I'd do it all differently. I'd take one day at a time like Bea always said. I'd eat in moderation. Drink in moderation. Go to meetings. Work out to Denise Austin . . . in moderation. I'd moderate in moderation.

I reached down for my bags slowly, like I was about to pull out two machine guns and start calling everyone a "cock-a-roach." I clutched the handles tightly, I squinted briefly at the sunlight beyond the ship's exit signs, and I curled my toes tightly into my sandals.

Then I bolted.

Really, not a bad plan, as plans go. Nobody was expecting it; it was completely un-cruise-ship-like behavior. Uncivilized. Most of the gate people were busy cleaning up their areas, probably talking amongst each other about what they were going to do with their time off. The security guards were still off in the distance when I started my dead run.

As I sped down the long carpeted planks that connected the ship to land, I envisioned my blue Dodge Neon where we had parked it a week earlier. It would likely be easy to find; the huge lot was close to empty. I continued to the open gates of the lot. It was just as I'd thought: sparse. Almost no cars. *Should be no problem finding my blue Dodge Neon. No problemo. Should be here somewhere. There it is! No. That's a blue Celica.* I looked to the east, no Neon. I looked to the west. I saw only Ernesto unlocking a champagne Lexus. *Ernesto you rich towel-folding bastard! No! Focus, Estelle.*

Where is the damn thing? Exactly what won't those two Fergus Farm Whores stoop to? My mind reeled.

I looked behind me to see three pissed off Asian security guards taking the safeties off their mace cans and approaching me on short, efficient legs. I reached into my purse for my keys, though I had no car to unlock.

And by that point, I pretty much knew they weren't in there.

Chapter 25

Jack

They say I'm going to need surgery.

To clarify: I mean, the constant parade of medical professionals who come in here day in and day out to stare at my ass, x-ray my ass, poke my ass, rub q-tips on my ass . . . say I'm going to need surgery. And I guess they probably know what they're talking about. Certainly not for lack of studying. Seems like everyone within ten miles of this hospital has had a good long gander at my crack. Ironically, I haven't seen it in twenty years.

The dime-sized sore that Estelle found just a couple of weeks ago is now the size of a half-dollar and goes almost completely to the bone. In an effort to be thorough, Rock had taken all the padding off my wheelchair to clean it, then put it back wrong. I've been sitting my semi-sore butt on a rumpled crease for hours and hours at a time. I don't blame him. I blame myself for how much I depended on him. Just thinking of that makes me prickle with angry heat up and down my spine. I was too dependent, once again. Maybe that's why Estelle left. How could she fall in love with a 170- pound pet rock?

Now I'm just being pathetic. It's hard not to go there. It's hard not to go all sorts of dangerous places in your head when you spend all your waking hours counting the color specs on a floor tile.

To his credit, Rock came to visit me on the second day and babbled a little about "sorry this" and "sorry that." He said he'd make it up to me, then turned toward the door and appeared to be trying to stifle a sniffle. I couldn't take that. I said, "Dude. Come ON." I mean, what the hell? Guys aren't supposed to cry around other guys. Especially guys named "Rock."

Other than blubber-puss, I've had no visitors. Not that I would have wanted any, given the compromising position I'm in, but I'm lonely as hell. Maybe that's why I miss Estelle so badly. I admit it. I miss her. Maybe it's love; maybe it's desperation. Also, I'd kill a basket full of kittens if I could just smoke a joint. One fat joint.

My mom has called a few times. Both my parents and my sister live in Myrtle Beach, where I'm from, but they can't come running every time I get a booboo. My boss is letting me float for a while on a "medical leave," but I haven't told my work friends where I'm at. It would hurt too much to have them know, then never come. It would also bother me if they came. It's complicated. But, Estelle . . . she would have been here, and it would have been comfortable. She would have eaten all my Lorna Doones, but she'd have been here.

I wonder how she's doing in California. She's probably found some out-of-work actor/waiter/alcoholic/commitmentphobe to fall in love with . . . and into bed with. Fuck. That's the thing about sitting alone with your thoughts for days and days. You have all the time you need to mentally flog yourself up one side and down the other. Time and television. That's what I have right now.

Sometimes when I'm awakening from a deep sleep, I think I see her at the door for a moment out of the corner of my eye. Then I start a little fantasy about it. We're awkward at first because of how we left things, but then she trips on something, or I say something stupid, and next thing you know, she's laughing and I'm laughing and it's like old times. Like we're listening to talk radio in my rotten old welfare condo (which I now miss like hell), and we're talking about what a smug fuck that Rush Limbaugh is, or about the ethical dilemmas of legalizing pot. Her hair is long and braided into two braids. She's wearing a Vikings football jersey and nothing else. Hey. It's my fantasy, after all. Go Vikes.

On the darkest days, when the nurses act like they don't care, when the toast is burnt and the coffee is stale, when the morphine stops working and the pain shoots BBs into my temples, I think about Holly.

Holly was my first girlfriend, after, and we were engaged, for a time. Holly was the first girl who made me realize I could still be a man. The first time I saw Holly, I thought for a second that I was standing upright; she made me forget that I can't.

Holly had beautiful transition areas, like the space where the ass becomes the lower back, the pale skin where the breast meets the ribs, or the spot just under the jaw that becomes the neck. She let me study them all, at length, with the appreciation of a newly-freed man who'd spent the last five years as a prisoner of war, thinking he'd never see his homeland again.

Holly was a paramedic student trying to work her way through a two-year degree without her parents' money or help. They were quite wealthy, she told me, and couldn't understand why she would settle for anything less than a doctorate. But it was impossible to imagine my Holly, with her potty mouth and skin-tight U of M tank tops, wearing a lab coat and writing prescriptions. Back when she was my Holly.

Holly used to complain about how hot it got in the mornings, lugging me from the bed to the shower to the bed to the chair in the welfare condo with the 1982 Sears Kenmore window air conditioner chugging uselessly away, making more noise than cold air. So, one day I said, "Take your shirt off if you're so hot."

"Really?" she said, like I was doing her the favor.

"Uh, yeah," I muttered, nervous. I should have known she'd do it; I could tell she had a certain air of freedom about her. She was the kind of girl who would tell another girl she had a nice ass, or tell a stranger that she was on the rag. She was

155

uninhibited, and aware of her attributes. Suddenly, her shirt was off and I was in another world. Her black, lace designer bra hinted that she was still getting some money from her parents, and otherwise hid very little from me.

I told her she was beautiful, then waited for the backlash, or at least, the subtle rejection.

Instead, she just blushed and grinned. She was not the type to blush. Suddenly, I remembered the significance of that from my able-bodied days. I vaguely recalled what it was like to realize you'd made a girl tingle somewhere without actually touching her; I was too stunned to act.

Nothing happened that day. But the day after, and then every day for three months, everything happened, sometimes clumsily, but most times magically. And it always ended with her head in the crook of my armpit and my hand stroking the roots of her long red hair.

Jesus. I'm deep in it, alright. It's a one-man jack-fest.

It ended when we tried to take that next big step that most normal people like to call "commitment." It ended the moment her folks saw me . . . saw the chair underneath me. In that moment, Holly she saw me through their eyes.

We met them at a middle-of-the-road Italian restaurant they'd probably never been to judging by the slow way they took it all in, the plastic hanging plants, the tomato-red walls. Holly's mom looked like a Chihuahua with her smart wool suit and her Jackie-O haircut. Her dad smelled like cigars and custom leather car seats. They asked me whether I was ever going to finish school; they asked me if I was always going to live in a subsidized apartment. Valid questions about their daughter's future that I had no idea how to answer. I was twenty-five years old. My fracture was five.

I'll never know what her parents said to her, but I can imagine. How are you going to raise kids with him? How is he going to take care of you? How will he carry you across the

156

threshold? How will he afford your manicures and pedicures? How can you do this to us?

When she showed up for work two days later in a conservative turtleneck (in the middle of October) I cocked an eyebrow. When she kept the ugly blue thing on all morning, I knew it was over. She didn't have to say anything. She was also carrying a new leather case I hadn't seen before, big enough for all her school books. "Coach" was the brand name. She said they lasted forever; it was the first time she looked me in the eye all morning. I said that was ironic, about how long they last.

She called the agency the next day and quit without notice; I suppose she didn't need the money, anyway.

Christ. What am I doing thinking about all that? Much better just to think about Estelle. Much better to pick at the fresh wounds than go re-opening the old ones. Trust me, I know. When it comes to wounds, I'm pretty much an expert.

Chapter 26

Day 1: Totally incarcerated.

Oh, you might think being tackled to the ground by three really enthusiastic security guards would be something of a cheap thrill, but you would be dead wrong.

Okay, I wasn't tackled so much as I was tussled. Molested? No. Rough-housed. Anyway, it was no picnic. I've never been maced before, so that was new. The nice thing about mace is that is that it knows not who's guilty and who's innocent. When one person gets maced, pretty much everybody gets maced. Or at least when you're maced by the three stooges, that's what happens.

The last time I was arrested, I was in Fort Lauderdale, Florida trying to buy cocaine from some kids in a neighborhood where white folks are only seen after dark if they are there to buy drugs or a ten-dollar blow job. I got a little bit tackled on that night as well, for trying to run. How was I to know that cops on bicycles even existed? How could I respect the authority of a man with a bread bowl strapped to his head?

My boyfriend at the time had something like four or five out-of-state warrants, so we got treated like Bonnie and Clyde for a little while at the police station, until they realized none of his warrants were serious enough to extradite. Still, we spent three nights in jail for loitering. Anyway, it wasn't bad, what I can remember. My roommate shared her hand-rolled cigarettes with me, and all our meals included Little Debbie snack cakes for dessert. The rest of my *time* was spent sleeping, which was just what the doctor ordered after the six-month cocaine binge that I had been on.

I wondered if I kept drinking like I'd been drinking on the ship, how long before I got back into cocaine? And if I did start up again, would I at least lose some weight? Could I go back to treatment and get coddled, fed and sheltered for another 28 days? What kind of moron wants to go back into treatment?

These are the things you think about when you find yourself back in some familiar state of hopelessness you promised never to revisit. At least, these are the things I think about when I'm not thinking about Little Debbie Snack Cakes.

I wondered if they'd book me into a real jail at some point, which I suppose would be the Houston PD. They couldn't keep me in their little conference room/security office, handcuffed to a chair forever. What was I being charged with? Some kind of theft? I wondered if I'd get a phone call. Who would I call? I wondered if they'd let me take a shower so I could wash all the pepper spray out of my cleavage. Speaking of cleavage, phone calls, and showers, I wondered what Jack was doing. If I called collect, would he accept?

So deep in thought was I that I didn't see who'd sauntered her way into the security office.

Not five yards away, British Lauren was chatting with the three guards, but looking at me. She wore her blond hair in a tight pony tail, the end swishing back and forth across the straps of her hot pink sports tank as she spoke. Was she flirting? She held a loose stack of paperwork, which she occasionally used to point in my direction. After a long pause, one guard gestured to another, who quickly picked up a phone and started dialing. The third guard just looked at me, shrugged, and wiped a blood-shot, pepper-sprayed eye with his thumb. This did not bode well.

Next thing I know, Tea And Crumpets is charging straight at me in her turquoise take-charge canvas sneakers, and looking more triumphant by the stride. She took a seat at the conference table across from me, beaming.

"Blimey," I leaned toward her slightly, hoping my breath was every bit as ripe as I suspected it was. "You're even more perk-tacular up close."

"You go ahead and take a tone," she smiled, laying her papers on the space between us. "But I'm your bloody savior. You'll thank me."

Actually, it was more like she said, "You'll *f*ank me" so I did my best to make her say it again. It made me giggle.

"I'll what?"

"You'll *f*ank me," she sputtered. "You will. You wait and see."

***

Gloria

Jesus, my Lord and Savior,

Thank you for this day, and for food and shelter. Thank you for Richard and Lana, without whom, I'd be homeless and lost. Thank you for Zeke.

Please be with all of those who still suffer from their addictions. Please deliver Estelle from her demons: sugar, alcohol, cocaine, and most of all, herself. When she looks in the mirror, Lord, let her see someone she could love. Or if she can't, then please, Lord, keep her away from too many mirrors.

Please comfort Zeke and give him guidance. Please help him keep our marriage vows. Please help me keep him. He's all I have. No, that's wrong. I have you, Lord Jesus, and You are all I need. I'm just scared.

161

He keeps disappearing. An hour here, two hours there. What little money we have, he never lets me at it. His eyes were all screwed up yesterday, like his pupils were practically vibrating, not even trying to see me, or anything. Richard says that to worry is to lack faith, so I'm sorry, Lord. But let's just say, if Zeke is using again, as I suspect he is . . . I'm screwed.

Amen.

Chapter 27

I am walking through turn-stiles, getting back on the cruise ship; Jack is with me. It's a hot, shiny morning, and I'm feeling that anything goes *feeling up and down my spine. There's a strawberry-sweet taste in the back of my throat, and my pockets are bloated with cash. As my hips move the metal bar, it hits me that Jack won't be able to follow me in his wheelchair, not if this is the only entrance. When I turn to find him, I look down, but he is up. He is walking; he is looking me in the eye, more than six feet tall.*

Seeing him like this makes me so happy that a tinge of guilt registers in my gut. But he is walking, strutting actually, like he's never been paralyzed. He's one of the handsomest men I've ever seen, and I take him in the way I might normally take in a billboard featuring a man in only Calvin Klein underwear. He's so incredible, he's barely real. And I'm not the only woman staring.

At the sight of him, the whispers start. Old women, young women, ship clerks, gate agents, men, women, everybody wants him. They hiss and sputter among themselves about his eyes, his ass, his broad shoulders.

The whispers persist and the questions start. Who the hell is she? *What's he doing with* her? *Her face, her butt, her girth. Look at her. It must be true what they say. Love is blind.*

I reach down to straighten my sundress, sucking in my stomach. But there is no sundress. It's just me. Just naked. Though I'm not cold, I shiver and pull my arms around me and over my bare breasts. Self-consciously, I run my hands down my shoulders, my arms, my stomach, my hips, my thighs. Under this harsh scrutiny, my body starts to react. My skin is hot and sticky. The flesh on my legs feels heavy and gelatinous.

The whispers slowly turn to shouts, and the shouts echo in my head. Not good enough. Not good enough. Never. Never worthy. Fat. Fat. Fat.

Jack and I finally make it to our state room, and I am frantic to cover myself, even though we're finally alone. I rifle through my suitcase for something to wear, but I only find clothing big enough for a small child. It's not my suitcase. When I turn to tell Jack, I find him gone. No surprise; the rejection is expected.

The strawberry taste from before has turned sour. Now the back of my throat wants everything I can give it. It wants all of the worst things, the best things. It wants and wants and never feels satisfied. At last, I find a t-shirt and a pair of pajama bottoms to drown myself in. Now I can go out onto the ship and feed all of it, to quiet the voices. At my feet is a pair of brand new running shoes. I tie them on without questioning where they came from. I feel the bounce under my feet, the promise of movement.

With my hand on the door knob, I look down to see that a note has been slid under the door. The handwriting is barely legible, as if the author held the pen in his mouth to write it. It's from Jack.

It says, "Lucky you."

***

Day 2 of total incarceration, I think. Or could be a continuation of day 1. Like it matters.

I woke up in jail. They say the innocent pace like rabbits in here, while the guilty sleep like stones. I was one of the stones, I guess.

On waking, it took me a while to sort the fantasy from the reality. Jack was the fantasy. He's not walking and he's not with me.

I recalled my visit with Lauren. Lauren was my odd, cockney, gap-toothed reality now. Back at the ship, before the police hauled me off for booking, she had made me an offer someone like her thought I couldn't refuse. It was an offer that would make me a better person. It was an offer that made perfect sense. She had given me a get-out-of-jail-free card. And I had told her to go flog herself.

Then I went for a ride downtown. When they booked me in, they had allowed me to make a call. I called Jack and got no answer. Worse than no answer, actually. I got a message from his voice mail system that said his "inbox" was full. Now I'm in panic mode over Jack, and completely powerless to do anything about it.

Powerless. That's the first step, isn't it? In the twelve-step watch-a-ma-callit? We admit that we are powerless over *insert addiction here.*

So powerless, in fact, that when Bill came to see me in my cell, I could do absolutely nothing to stop it. Sure, you can turn visitors away when you're in jail. But not ones like Bill. Why? Because he's a cop. He's a Houston freaking police officer.

I should have seen it. The buzz cut, the squared, military stance, the vague aura of a man who enjoys eating pastry *while* engaging in high-speed foot chases.

He sauntered in like he owned the place, said "hello" to the female guard, then stood in front of me like he thought I would be happy to see him.

"Really?" I sputtered, taking in the badge, the gun, the uniform, the handcuffs . . . handcuffs, eh? Not bad, actually. No. *Focus!*

He just nodded and smiled sheepishly, and then I remembered Paris Hilton.

"I don't want to see anybody," I snorted.

He moved in on my bars and rested a hand on one.

"But, why? Why *don't* you want to see me?"

"Because you're not what I thought you were. Clearly."

"I'm sorry I didn't tell you I was a cop. But who did you *think* I was?"

"Someone who could . . . appreciate me." I chuckled at the thought of it.

"Why do you think I'm standin' here?"

"I don't know. Maybe you have a fetish for chubby girls. Or maybe you're just afraid you'd break your skinny little wife in half with all your fancy positions, so you go looking for sturdier stock on the side. Or maybe . . ."

"My what?" Bill glanced at the guard nervously to see if she was paying attention to my tirade.

"Your wife! Your girlfriend! I don't know. Shades the size of her head. Knobby knees. Smells like Diet Red Bull."

A look of clarity registered on Bill's brow. "My *sister*, you maniac. Stevie's my sister." Bill stood back a pace then. He muttered, "Classic."

"I was just thinking that same thing," I hissed. As if I could believe him, anyway. As if . . . I slumped back onto my bunk, suddenly conscious of my matted, wet hair and my orange jumper.

His sister "Stevie." It was starting to make a little sense. It made a lot of sense. What the hell kind of a name is "Stevie"? Shit. I'm a moron.

Bill broke the silence with a chuckle.

"Sturdier stock?"

"Fuck. I don't know."

"Shee-it," Bill drawled. "Is that what you think of me?" I saw something on Bill's face I hadn't seen. The boy looked just plain *blue*. Jesus. Hurricane Estelle wastes another innocent with her big freaking tidal wave of crazy. Imagine the fun Bill and I could have had on that ship if I'd just . . . Oh, what the hell, anyway. Suddenly, being a big fat load didn't seem as fun as I'd once thought. How do people do it? I pondered. How do people go on dumping and dumping on others for years and years? Practice, I suppose.

"It's what I think of all men," I said.

Officer Bill straightened up, and with the rising of his shoulders came an invisible barrier. An Estelle barrier, I assume. "Well, you're wrong about that. And you're wrong about me."

I just shrugged. Even if he was right, we both knew all of the things that it didn't change. Cop. Inmate. Normal person. Freaking lunatic.

"I'm going to take off," he said finally, and that familiar relief flooded my dank little cell. It's that relief I feel when I get a chance to be alone so nobody will hear me say anymore stupid things. "Is there anything I can do for you before I go?"

I pondered Bill for a moment. Officer Bill.

"Yes," I paused. "Yes. If you would."

"Anything. Well. Any *legal* thing."

"I have this friend that I used to work for. He's a quad. A quadriplegic. I left on bad terms with him, and every time I try to call I get no answer. It didn't seem too surprising at first, but now his voicemail is full, and I'm worried."

"He lives in Minnesota?"

"Yeah. Minneapolis."

"So, kind of a welfare check sort of thing? You just want to know if he's okay? 'Cause I can't make him talk to you or anything. God knows what you could've done to a poor paralyzed guy who can't defend himself . . ."

"Yeah! A welfare check. I just want to know that he's alive. Quads . . . they can get sick easily, and things can happen kind of fast."

With that, Bill looked me in the eyes like a Boy Scout ready to earn his next merit badge.

"I'll look into it, OK? I'll find the guy."

"Thank you, Bill."

"And where can I find you?

I considered that.

"Bill, what are they going to charge me with? If someone doesn't step in and help me?"

"Depends on the investigator. Some would say this is felony theft because of the amount. It could also be argued that it's a civil issue between you and the cruise line."

All I really heard was "felony theft." Apparently, I was going to make some biker chick a very good wife.

"Is the food good in prison?"

"Estelle. Seriously. Do you have parents? Call them. Get a good lawyer. Get yourself back to Minnesota and dry out. You're not a criminal. You're just a garden-variety, unstable alcoholic female, at best."

Holy labels, Batman.

"You big charmer! Trying to get in my pants again?"

Bill didn't laugh, or even smile.

Why'd he have to make me think about my parents? I envisioned my mom with her rosary and her worried eyes. Then I thought about my dad, who'd just plain *hate* this, and with good reason. Collect phone calls. Bus fare sent by Western Union. Hand-wringing. Treatment centers. Twenty-five years old, sleeping in my parents' basement by the winter coats and the frozen meats. Is she sober? Is she using? Is she ever going to give us our ping-pong room back?

"Will they give me another phone call?"

"Yeah. I'll get the guard."

"Bill? If you find Jack, just get a number or an address, OK? I'll call you tomorrow morning from the dock before the next cruise."

"What? I don't get it."

"I'm going to make a phone call, then I'm getting back on that boat. You're looking at the newest employee at Gilligan Cruises, Inc."

Chapter 28

Dear Jack,

Holy shit, man!

First of all, I just want to tell you how glad I am that you're okay. My cop friend, Bill, (someday I'll tell you more about how I came to have a "cop friend") told me you were in the hospital and that you'd had surgery for a decubitus ulcer, which thanks to Google, I now know is a "bed sore." I should've figured. I tried to call your room, but the phone just rings and rings. Duh. You can't reach the phone without help. That's why I'm writing. I just want you to know that I've been thinking about you, and that I miss you, and that I'm sorry for how I left things.

You wouldn't believe everything that's happened, Jack. Or maybe you're the only person who actually would. First of all, I never made it to California.

If the mere mention of my name doesn't cause you to spit on the floor and curse in Arabic, then I'd love to see you when I get back to Minnesota some day, whenever that is. Right now, all I know is that I'll be on a cruise ship for the next two months. Long story.

Oh, what the hell, you've probably got time. See, I hooked up with these two chicks on my way to California, who I thought were kindred spirits, but who turned out to be just another set of chubby twin truck-stop waitresses who will likely someday be found pulling each other's blond roots out on *Maury Povich,* willing to eviscerate each other over both their Baby's Daddy, who is also their therapist, that is if both their lives aren't first claimed in a tragic trailer-fire ignited by the often-fatal decision to start the oven for a frozen pizza just after closing down the VFW, then passing out in a drunken heap in on the couch in front of Craig Ferguson.

I digress.

Blinded by the lure of warm weather, cheap lodging, and the 24-hour-feed-fest that is the modern day cruise experience, I signed up to go with the Banger Sisters on a week-long "excursion."

When I woke up a week later, they had taken off and left me with the tab! Which of course, I can't pay. I'm not saying I didn't also charge a cocktail or seven, but I swear, Jack, if you're ever in Mills Fleet Farm and you see a couple of puffy-cheeked twenty-something twins wearing matching Gilligan Cruise Line ponchos and bright orange Crocs, please just run them over with your 600-pound electric buggy, will ya? Even if you get the wrong twins, you'll at least have done the fashion world a favor.

So, I'm picking pepper spray out of my ears and waiting for the Houston Fuzz to pick me up when in walks the fitness director for the cruise line, Lauren. I'll skip the details and just say that Lauren and I had already *met* a couple of times during my stay.

She told me she had been "monitoring" me on the cruise, and thinks I'm "bloody fascinating." Which from someone like her, means I'm a freaking disaster. You should see her, Jack. Nothing but British grizzle from fore to aft. A pure disciple of Denise. Along with trying to convince people they should be jazzercising in between buffet-binges, her job is to hawk this bullshit "colon detox" diet right there on the ship, plus the gobzillion-dollar seaweed supplements that go along with it.

"What does this have to do with Estelle?" you ask.

Well, Lauren wants me to be her detox guinea pig. She wants to take me under her super-toned little wing, make me eat only the things she lets me eat, make me exercise half the day, take supplements, and basically transform my "fascinating" body into her very own live on-board "Before and After" poster. In exchange for successful completion of my sentence, the cruise line will excuse my debt and give me a $5,000 bonus.

At first I refused out of pride.

Then they trucked me down to the clink, threatened me with "felony theft" charges, made me shampoo with government soap, put me into an orange jumper, refused to give me any sugar for my cold Malt-O-Meal, and that's when it hit me. I have no pride. I have nothing. And if I'm going to live without sugar, I should at least be doing it in the lap of luxury.

When you think about it, Jack, this is the opportunity of a lifetime. At last, I can be the type of person I've always absolutely hated, yet fully aspired to be: a certified health nut. I'm finally getting treatment for my sugar addiction, more or less. Right?

I know what you're thinking, but, Jack, I can't fuck this up. It's too important. I mean, five thousand dollars! And think of the weight I'll lose! It will almost be worth it to smell like a bucket of seaweed when I get to my goal weight of 65 pounds.

OK, OK. At the very least, let's hope I don't *get caught* when I inevitably fuck this up.

Well, I've gone on and on, and who knows if you even made it past "Dear Jack" before trashing this? But if you did, in fact, get this far, please know that I intend to pray for your backside every night when my British Best Friend tucks me in. I'm also praying that right now, a really hot nurse in tight, low-cut scrubs is reading this aloud to you just before she takes you for your whirlpool bath.

Your friend,
Estelle

***

Jack

Well, my nurse goes about three bills, his name is Judd, and my doctor hasn't approved anything but sponge-baths yet, but, thanks anyway, sweetheart, for giving me one more fantasy to keep me occupied.

I cried a couple of big sissy-boy tears onto the speckled linoleum when Judd read me Estelle's letter. How can I stay mad at that girl? She had me at "holy shit."

I wish I could talk to her right now; I'm shitting a brick over all this stress. Surgery is tomorrow, I'm in constant pain, and I haven't pissed in two days. The doctor tells me if I don't pee soon, they're going to stick a tube in there to drain my bladder. This is my nightmare. Never mind the bedsore. My ass is just another dead limb on the tree. I can't have a catheter. This is what I've been trying to avoid for twenty years. Somebody wants to stick a tube in my dink. Oh, they say they can take it out later when I'm better. But it's like anything else you don't use. It doesn't get better. It just gets lazy.

When Judd was done reading to me, before he could get away, we got on the phone. Time to call Rock and cash in a favor. After all this, that boy owes me one.

Chapter 29

Day One. Cruise Ship Cleanse. Or, the first day of the rest of my colon.

I woke up early to the sound of my Drill Sergeant brushing her teeth. We're bunk mates, we are. And work mates, and play mates, and breakfast, lunch and dinner mates. The better for her to see me, guide me, *control* me, my dear.

The crews on this ship have it far more primitive than the passengers. These little sardine cans haven't been re-decorated, re-upholstered, or re-carpeted since before Pop Tarts were invented. The "H" on my hot water faucet actually stands for "hesitant."

Anyway, the accommodations hardly matter. Every day will be just another opportunity to wake up and realize anew that there will be no joy. Under my new diet plan, I am allowed to eat exactly Jack Shit. Actually, shit would likely be a violation of this diet, since it may contain additives, may have some sort of flavor, and might actually make me feel full for more than thirty seconds.

Yes, indeed. I'm surly.

The booze has completely worn off, and reality completely soaked in. I'm trapped in the Garden of Eden for the next two months, and an apple is about the only thing I *can* eat.

OK. Focus. Think of this as an opportunity. It's an opportunity to pay off my debt. It's an opportunity to spend the next two months of my life cruising the Caribbean. It's an opportunity not to go to jail.

If I had some post-it notes, I could affix these messages properly on my teensy little bathroom mirror, reminding me to keep a positive attitude about my situation. Shelter-wise, the situation is good. I have some. Job-wise, again, good. I work for a cruise line as a "guest spokesperson." Friend-wise, the situation is a bit bleak. I could hardly call Lauren my "friend." Man-wise, I'm good. No boyfriend, no cry.

Food-wise, the situation is dire.

Given that I have been dieting on and off for ten years, I thought I knew deprivation. I've done low-carb, no-carb, abstinence, South Beach, North Beach, Atkins, Grapefruit, Acai Berries, Nutra-shitty, Jennie Craig, Dr. Phil, Dr. Joyce Brothers, Dr. Oz, Richard Simmons, Gene Simmons, Carmen Electra, and that skinny chic from *Clueless*.

I ain't seen nothin'.

First off, Hitler won't let me call it a "diet." It's a "cleanse," she says. Which brings us to the heart of the matter, which is not my heart at all, of course, but my *colon.* The focus of my life, and Lauren's, will be to turn my colon from a dirty, polluted, unhappy, argumentative organ that processes shit into a clean, happy-go-lucky, grime-free, cooperative organ that processes shit.

This can be accomplished very simply by consuming only raw vegetables, very lean meat, raw vegetable juices, flax, bulgur wheat, oats, and other high-fiber items I've heard of but didn't realize anyone but horses actually ate, and only occasionally . . . fruit. Three times a day, I will take a Neptune's Trident Seaweed Supplement. No sugar. No bread. No booze. No red meat. No whole wheat crackers, for God's sake. No raisins! Seriously. Raisins! The list of "no's" is as big as a cruise ship.

Incidentally, Neptune's Trident is the reason Lauren even exists. Three years ago, Neptune's Trident and Gilligan started working together to hawk 90-dollar-a-bottle wonder pills to gals just like me, who have enough money to get on a cruise ship, and who can't even wait until the end of the week to start planning their next failed attempt to lose all the weight they just gained. It's genius, really. Fatten them up, shame them to tears, then offer the cure on their way out the door. The objective is not to clean the world's colons, of course. Nor is it to get everybody to discover the beauty of carrot-beet juice. The purpose is to sell a 10-dollar bottle of sea sludge for nine times its worth.

If I stick to the program, Lauren assures me, incredible changes will take place inside of me and out, which will be carefully documented by the cruise line and showcased in print ads, posters, and of course, on The Gilligan Channel. Footage of me busting up my first detox seminar like a raving lunatic will be shown alongside footage of glowing, skinny, jump-suited me professing my detox devotion after at last realizing that it has changed not just the color and consistency of my excretions, but my Whole Entire Life!

Conversely, if I don't stick to the program, if I'm caught sneaking non-approved food items, beverages, booze or drugs, I'll be kicked off in Houston and back where I started: carless, jobless, homeless, and in debt. Not to mention the peril my colon will be in.

It was when Lauren started talking to me in low, serious tones about the changes about to take place in my lower digestive tract that I began to really, truly understand how fucked my life is. Here's how fucked my life is:

My life is so fucked that I have to have long conversations with British schoolmarms about crap. Literal. Crap. My life is so fucked that the only thing that makes me feel good anymore, I mean really good, is drinking felony amounts of over-priced cruise ship smoothies. My life is so fucked that I have contracted out my colon for two months just to stay out of jail.

As if that wasn't enough, Lauren then pulled out the testimonial pictures of strange and awful items that other "cleansers" claim to have successfully flushed from their systems while detoxing. Some objects were long and twisted. Some thick and knobby. All were greenish brown. I had to take a knee.

"Are you alright?" Lauren knelt next to me, mercifully, turning the photos face down on our little state-room dinette. Still, some things you just can't un-see.

"Oh, you bet," I sputtered. "I'm just a little squeamish, is all."

"These are worst-case scenarios, of course," Lauren said apologetically. "I'll not present them anymore. But you will let me know if something really obnoxious comes out of you, won't you? The big-wigs at Neptune just can't get enough of that shit, er stuff."

"Oh, sure," I muttered, waiting in vain for Rod Serling to appear and introduce the next episode of *Twilight Zone.* "If I shit anything wild . . . a Smurf, a foosball table, an I-pod . . . Jimmy Hoffa . . . you'll be the first person I call."

Lauren patted me on the back triumphantly. "That's a good girl, then."

Chapter 30

Here's a little snapshot of the cleanse that is my hell:

0700: Arise, pee, rinse the bile out of my gob, pray for death or monsoon.

0705: Weigh-in. Today, I weighed in at one hundred and holy-shit-those-smoothies-pack-a-lot-of-hidden-calories pounds. In my defense, the ship's movement makes it hard to get an accurate reading. That's all I have to say on the weight issue.

0715: Walk two miles (20 laps around the ship) with Hitler.

0815: Breakfast: One cup of rolled oats with apples and herbal tea.

0900: Yogalates with Lauren and about twenty other chicks who apparently don't know the proper meaning of "vacation."

1000: Mid-morning snack of twenty unsalted raw almonds (yes Hitler counts them) and one pear.

1005: Consider eating the crumbs from meager mid-morning snack, then realize twigs and berries don't really make crumbs. Imagine, then try to erase from my head, the image of fifteen hundred happy cruisers just one floor above me, tipping their heads back and pouring strawberry syrup directly down their happy throats and chasing it with Reddi-Wip.

1006: Break time. Here's where any self-respecting sugar addict would find a way to cheat. However, there's a lot at stake here, so today's break, I decided, would simply be a reconnaissance mission. I skulked around the upper levels of the ship for almost an hour, surveying the layout (hadn't seen it much sober) and observing all the various possibilities for procurement of sweets, cakes, candies, etcetera. They were endless. Buffets. Snack bars. Sit-down restaurants. Unfortunately, it's not just a matter of where these things could be found, but where they could be *consumed*.

I was overwhelmed. Hungry. Scared. What if I couldn't get my fix when I needed it? What if I could? Would I do it? Would I risk losing everything? Would I have a choice? I found myself in front of "Shaky Grounds" coffee bar and computer lounge. I found an empty stool and sat down slowly. The boat rocked ever so lightly. I felt I could faint.

"You look like you could use a bump, hey?"

I don't know why I didn't notice her before. She was completely Geek-tacular. Her name tag told me her name was "Tweezer." She looked to be about thirty, but dark-haired and pierced all about the lips and eyebrows. Her eyes were heavily-lined, and her moon-shaped mouth was porn-star perfect. Her short plaid kilt showed off nice round hips that could be trusted to easily hoist large bags of coffee. Her combat boots were there, I supposed, to kick the ass of anyone attempting to watch too closely while she did that. Stunning.

"A bump?"

"A shot. A jolt. A kick in the ass!" She smiled brightly, which alarmed me.

"Uh," I stuttered. "I don't know if I should." I truly didn't. I knew sugar and carbs were off limits, but I didn't know about coffee. Could I have caffeine? Decaf? Would a shot of espresso be worth the risk? No. I'd be damned if I was going to wreck my big payday on anything less than seventeen waffles and two gallons of syrup.

"I'm not sure I can have coffee," I shrugged.

Tweezer stared for a long moment, then smacked the counter triumphantly with the palm of one henna-covered hand. "Oh, you're that chick! You're the one in the picture everyone's been talking about."

Picture? Everyone? "What picture?" I asked.

She reached under the counter and pulled out an eight by ten black and white photocopy. On it was my mug shot from the day I was booked, and under that were these words:

This is our newest employee, Estelle Brown. She is joining our health and fitness department as an independent contractor. During her time with Gilligan, she will be representing Neptune's Trident as a detox success story. Because of this, Estelle is going to be following a strict cleanse (diet). Please help Estelle to reach her detox goals by refusing to serve her any of the following:

Sugar in any form, alcoholic beverages, fruit smoothies or juices, breads, baked goods, cheeses, meats, sauces, coffee drinks or snack items.

Anyone caught supplying these items to Ms. Brown will be reprimanded immediately with the possibility of termination.

Thanks, crewmates! Let's make it a great cruise!

The whole ship was under Hitler's thumb.

"See right there? Coffee drinks," Tweezer pointed with a pearl-blue fingernail. "No coffee for you! This isn't the best job in the world, but you'd have to look a lot more like Benicio Del Toro for me to lose it over *your* ass."

I folded my arms onto the bar and lowered my head down. Deep sadness enveloped me. So much sadness over this loss, I'm ashamed to even admit it.

"What the hell is it with Benicio del Toro?" I muttered.

"Are you kidding me?" Tweezer enthused. "I'd crawl fifty miles over broken glass just to listen to him fart on the phone."

I opened my eyes to the glass case below me. Blueberry muffins. White chocolate scones. Some sort of chocolate blob with chocolate frosting. They were my dear friends, my family, my crutches, my peace, my every happiness, and an entire ship full of people was conspiring to keep them from me.

I felt a hand on my head, tapping lightly.

"Hey," Tweezer whispered. "I know it's hard to give up something you love, trust me. You can have tea though, hey? Try some of this tea we have. It's chamomile, peppermint and just a touch of jasmine. It's relaxing, really. It's even kind of sweet."

I lifted my head slowly. "Can we put a cup of honey in it?"

Tweezer ignored that, grabbed a big green mug, and started pouring the hot water. "Hey!" she snorted, her full volume returning as she plopped two tea bags in. "Have you ever been to a twelve-step meeting?"

1200: Lunch with Lauren: Chickpea spinach salad with vinaigrette and Green Tea. Though we ate the same lunch, Lauren allowed herself a bread stick, since she is not currently detoxing.

1207: Entertain a gorgeous fantasy involving beating Lauren to death with a ski-sized breadstick, then slathering the enormous thing with honey butter and washing it down with a caramel latte.

1300: More bloody exercise – this time disguised at "fun." But who ever heard of playing ping pong on a moving vessel? It's like scrapbooking in a wind tunnel.

1430: Snack. Tofu dill dip with carrot sticks. Seriously. As if I could have made that up.

1500: Merciful heavens, a nap. I've never felt so tired in all my life. No. Tired doesn't tell it. I feel as though a hole has been cut in my big toe through which an industrial strength vacuum has just Hoovered out my very will to live.

1700: Dinner. One grilled chicken breast, one unbuttered, unsalted pile of steamed broccoli, and one barely-seasoned clump of brown rice. Half a grapefruit for dessert. Apparently one entire grapefruit would have been Just Too Decadent.

1712: One. Pissed off. Sugar Addict.

1800: Twenty minutes on the elliptical machine. While working out, I catch twenty minutes of *The Biggest Loser*, realize I could be going through all of this bullshit on national TV, and for about 17 seconds, feel somewhat fortunate.

1830: Twenty minutes in the sauna. This is supposed to steam all those nasty, dirty toxins out of my system. Lauren blabs the whole time about her fiancé back in Paris.

1900: Another shower.

2000: Lauren offers another walk, then admits that it's optional. I can't say "NO" emphatically enough. Instead, I bug out for an hour and go to an onboard AA meeting, starring Tweezer and the Gang.

Hello. I'm Estelle and I'm an alcoholic and a sugar addict, and I don't know what step I'm on, but I do know that without a doubt that I'm in the sun-soaked, fruit-punched, barbequed belly of hell.

***

Dear Estelle,

Now here's me writing and hoping it finds *you*. Right now, I'm cashing in a favor from the PCA who screwed up my rear end. For his penance, and for a good job reference, he gets to come in here a couple hours a day with his laptop to transpose and send emails for me.

The cruise ship development is interesting, to say the least. And I'm not hoping at all that you fuck it up, yet I fear you might. Your cop friend is nice, if a little hard to comprehend. And I'm not mad at you. Anymore. Brat.

My operation was a success, if by success you mean that three days ago, there were two holes in my ass, and today there's only one. But if by success, you mean that I didn't wake up with a tube sticking out my wiener, then, no. It was not a success at all.

181

The bastards did it while I was under. They cathed me. I don't know who I'm more pissed at, the pock-faced she-male bitch nurse who inserted the fucking thing, or my dead-ass penis for just sitting there, not peeing, not fighting! Allowing it.

You're the only one I can tell all this to, Es. I really hope you get this note, that you check your email, and that you write me back.

Anyway, I owe you an apology too, Estelle. I'm sorry for saying that I loved you that night at the Red Lobster. That was a bastard thing to do. There you were, trying to make a living, trying to stay sober, your roommate's AWOL, and I go and put the moves on you. I was lonely. Am lonely. Still, I should have been paying less attention to your ass and more to my own.

Anyway, I do miss you. Hope your detox (?) is going well. Someday, you're going to have to explain this all to me in greater detail, I think.

-Jack

Uhg. Why do I hate apologies so much? Conflict. Hate it. Apologies are an acknowledgement of conflict. I must have read that somewhere in one of my super-smart self-help books.

After the meeting, Tweezer went back to the coffee shop with me, showed me how to log on, and there it was. Mostly, I was relieved. Jack's not mad at me. I still have one friend in this world. Two if you count Bill.

Anyway, Jack seemed different somehow, in his note. He didn't say whether he still loves me. And how sick am I for even wondering?

They cathed him, those em-effers. I wish I could be there for him. Wash his hair. Hold his straw. Something. Anything. I wish I could go back to that night at Red Lobster and be more clever, less of a ditz. I wish we were back in Jack's apartment eating waffles and listening to KQRS. I wish I was anywhere eating waffles. I wish I was on Planet Waffle, swimming in a sea of syrup.

After the meeting, Tweezer hugged me and said, "You're exactly where you need to be. I said, "Did Bea send you?"

But I hugged her back, hard.

Chapter 31

Day 2, Detox.

Hope rises, hope flounders, hope flushed down my teensy state room toilet.

Good Morning, Gilligan Cruisers. It looks like the second day of our trip is going to be every bit as lovely as the first, with mild winds out of the east and not a cloud in site. Join us on the main pool deck for the International Breakfast Bar, featuring French Toast and German potatoes! Husbands, be sure to check out our duty free gift shop, where you can receive a free box of chocolates with your hundred-dollar purchase of Swarovski Crystal jewelry. Ladies, once you're wearing your new tear-drop earrings and eating sweets from your sweetie, you won't mind at all if he spends some time at the blackjack tables at Professor's Casino, will you? We didn't think so. Have a wonderful day, one and all. And if you haven't signed up yet for a shore excursion, remember, we disembark on the beautiful island of Cozumel at 8 a.m. tomorrow. You wouldn't want to miss out on any of the fun, would you?

The stops. I'd forgotten all about them. This cruise makes three stops at three different exciting Caribbean destinations during the week, and I'd forgotten all about them because I didn't even bother with them last week when I was attempting to eat my weight in hot fudge sundaes. Suddenly, those stops were my last hope for a little taste of freedom. And any freedom would be so, so sweet.

As Lauren and I started our morning walk (picking up the pace just slightly as we reached the *French Toast* side of the ship) I thought of how I might broach the subject of "disembarking" without giving my bad intentions away.

I could tell her how I was looking forward to getting my cardio on the beach in the form of an hour-long run.

I could play it cool and act like I didn't even want to go to stupid old Cozumel, but would check it out anyway out of sheer boredom.

There was also the option of not broaching it at all. The old "better to get in a little trouble later than be denied permission in advance" tactic.

But as we passed the International Estelle Can't Fucking Have Anything In Here Bar for the second time, my stomach pulled ranks, as always, took control of my mouth, and said, "So, uh, Cozumel tomorrow, then, huh? How 'bout that? Sounds pretty awesome, for sure."

Lauren stopped, then, and looked at me with alarm.

"Oh, dear," she smirked, then wiped a wisp of hair away from her forehead. The color of her lip gloss and her nail polish matched the "swoosh" on her Nike jogging shoes. I couldn't have hated her more at that moment than if she *was* Denise Austin.

"Oh goodness, no, pet. You can't be trusted. God only *knows* what kind of trouble you'd get yourself into."

And that was pretty much that. For a moment, I felt like that little girl at my grandma's house long ago, trying to open the candy tin without alerting my mom, only to look up to see her peeking around the corner at me. Only, I don't think I ever fantasized about beating my mom to death with a shuffleboard cue.

"Anyway, look over here, then, Estelle. There's someone I want you to meet."

Lauren gestured toward one of my fellow Gilligan employees, standing behind one of the coffee stations, reloading the creamers. Heni was a stout, sweet-faced woman in her forties. She wore a chef's hat and frock and neon pink plastic boat shoes with white socks, which made her feet look like

Christmas candy. She shook my hand vigorously, but glanced back at Lauren warily.

"Estelle, this is the lady who's going to be cooking all your meals for your detox," Lauren beamed as if she'd given birth to the poor woman."This is Heni. She's from Belize."

Several other pained niceties were exchanged, I imagine. It's a bit blurry now. I wasn't really paying attention.

Can't be trusted.

Can't be trusted.

Can't. Be. Trusted.

All I could think was: *She's so very right. She's so incredibly, unbelievably right.*

***

So, then . . . Day 3.

Same as Day 1, and bloody Day 2, plus homicidal thoughts and fresh blueberries for my mid-morning snack.

Lauren and I took our morning walk and her lips never stopped flapping, but I was somewhere else entirely. I was in a deprivation spiral. Without sugar, there's no joy. Without my crutch there's no walking. I sense a poem coming on.

I imagined how simple it might be to hurl myself over the railing and into the deep blue waters. I imagined floating in the freezing abyss until sharks began biting at my toes. I imagined that they would spit my toes right back out, since they likely taste like hummus and carrots.

Talka talka talka kept on spewing from Lauren about her lover, her travels, her enviable body-fat content and her sparkling clean lower bowel. But the only words echoing in my brain were: sixty days, sixty days, sixty days.

Minus two.

So, fifty-eight days.

"One day at a time!" yelled a teensy little cartoon Bea on my shoulder.

Then a cartoon Rhonda punched cartoon Bea in her size-8 stomach and said, "Fifty-eight days, you big spaz. Hah! You'll never make it."

Fifty-eight more days without any sweet taste. Fifty-eight days without a satisfied belly. Fifty-eight days of empty. Fifty-eight days of nothing but twigs and nuts banging around in the hollow, feeding nothing.

All around us, passengers scurried hither and yon, preparing for Cozumel. Cozumel, which, after being denied a visit there, I was convinced was actually made up of entirely sugar. Brown sugar beaches. Graham cracker buildings held together with cream cheese icing.

Cozumel: yet another sweet thing I would never get to taste.

All passengers disembarking to Cozumel shall report to the fourth level atrium. Don't forget to grab a coupon for Senor Frog's Bar and Grill for your Buy One Get One Smoothie drinks, valid all day! And thanks again for choosing Gilligan.

Suddenly, walking was just too enormous a task; my legs felt like Lauren had strapped 20-pound ankle weights on them (which I'm sure she will do at some point on this insipid journey.) But she hadn't. She was a half a ship ahead of me when she finally noticed I wasn't next to her anymore. By then, I was leaning over the safety railing, giving the waters off Cozumel a taste of my super-colon-friendly berries and muesli.

I stepped backwards, then wobbled forward, then fainted head long into a shocked young couple who wore matching Green Bay Packers sun visors.

When I woke up, I was on the bed in my state room and I smelled like shuffleboard.

"Good mahning, sleepy hayd," spoke a female voice in a Creole accent. I turned away from the wall to face the origin of the voice. Heni.

My head pounded. My stomach reminded me that I'd thrown up what little I'd eaten earlier. I sighed a long, heavy sigh. Heni let out what can only be described as a scoff . . . in a Creole accent.

She said, "Yah, Dey tole me you was a drama queen."

"They? Who? I don't even know you!"

I call bullshit!

"Everybahdey. Dey tole me you like Scarlett O'Hara on de crack."

Really.

I stomped into the bathroom, searching for my toothbrush. "Heni, is it?"

"Yah, lady."

"Heni, does everyone from Belize talk like Bob Marley, or is that just *your* deal?"

"Don' have a deal," Heni said.

"Everybody has a deal.*"* I finished brushing and turned to face my tormentor, whose ruddy, tanned smile just grew annoyingly wide.

"Come on den, Scarlett. Wipe dat frown off yah face and let's go make you some-ting good."

"Where's Lauren?" I said, as if there was some chance that she'd be leaving me alone for any period of time.

"You wit me for now; Jane Fonda come back layta."

Heni marched me up to the 24-hour buffet, through two sets of double doors and into an enormous kitchen, which was a sea of steaming stainless steel dotted with white porcelain cups, saucers and plates. She then hustled me past the grills and the ovens and the smells of real food to a makeshift employee leisure area behind a large cluster of industrial dishwashers. Except for the occasional white-coated bus-boy, we were alone. She gestured for me to sit, hastily moving magazines and aprons off a small table.

"Okay, now, lady," Heni said loudly, clasping her hands together. "Now we goin' ta make ya some soul food. An' ya goin' ta tank me for it."

While I waited, I paged through a dog-eared copy of Spanish *People Magazine.* Valerie Bertinelli had lost 40 pounds as a spokes-celeb for Jennie Craig and was wearing a bikini on the cover and she was so freaking happy, her teeth were almost bigger than her teensy little buns.

Though all the words were in a language I don't know, I knew. I knew all the words; I'd read it all before. She dropped the weight by keeping a positive attitude, by working out six times a week, by eating fewer donuts and more spinach, by taking the stairs instead of the elevator, blah blah inspirational blah.

I stared at Valerie's toned, happy, inspired thighs. Smile all you want Val, you know it's not going to last. You know this is just another diet in a lifetime of diets. You know in three years, you'll be sitting on Kirstie Alley's couch eating Nilla Wafers, crying into her puffy shoulder and wondering why the hell any sane woman would embark on a weight loss program in front of the whole damn world.

"What ya laughin' at?" Heni popped her head around a pot rack with a big smile.

"Just a woman who's one bad TV-movie away from a three-day Krispy Kreme blowout."

"Oh, she so pretty. Look at dem eyes."

"Those eyes. You know what those eyes say to me? I'll take a number three with a Coke. And supersize it."

"Why you do dat?"

"What dat?"

"Why can't food just be food? Why can't Valerie be happy?"

"Hey . . . I'm not the one selling seaweed pills to the mentally handicapped."

"I don' know 'bout dat," Heni snorted. "But she's not da one who come on a ship an' try keel herself with food. Dat was you."

"I'm sorry, Oprah Winfrey, will you please explain what the fuck I'm doing back in this kitchen with you? 'Cause if it's to get my palm read or something, I'll take a pass."

Heni disappeared for a moment again behind the pots. When she reappeared, she held a steaming pile of stir-fry.

"Food just food," Heni muttered, placing the plate in front of me. "Some good, some bad. But food is food. I make all mine with love, anyway. Maybe you taste it in there."

The aroma turned my head. Despite the fact that it was clearly vegetarian in nature, my meal was grilled heaven on a bed of brown rice. I couldn't place the spices -- or even some of the veggies -- but didn't really care. I ate it like it was trying to run from me. Heni shook her head and stepped back like she'd just dumped a loaf of bread in front of a gaggle of geese. Five minutes later, I looked up to see Lauren holding a glass of ice water and my daily supplements. I wanted to thank Heni, but she was gone.

Chapter 32

Dear Jack,

I miss you, too. It's been a tough day, but I'm still sugar-free, still "detoxing" properly, and I still have a roof over my head. I'm so sorry the bastards stuck a tube in your junk. I know that's the last thing you ever wanted.

But all is not lost! I had a little time after the meeting, and I did some internet research on all things urinary. Here are some things you can do to get the little man back in business: For one, you need to drink *a lot* of clear liquids. For another, (and you're not going to like this) you're going to have to give up the coffee for a while because it'll dehydrate you and make you more vulnerable to infection. I attached a list of foods that are good for the urinary tract, according to the great and powerful Dr. Oz.

Also, and this is very important, make sure when all those cute nurses are handling your business that they're using sterile gloves at all times.

Basically, if you keep your stuff healthy, and infection-free, pretty soon they'll *have* to let him off-leash again! This has been a public service announcement brought to you by the Penis Advisory Council.

Anyway, you read right. I'm going to meetings again, such as they are. Generally, there are only four of us, plus whatever odd passenger may wander in. There's me, of course, Tweezer, Blender, and Paulo.

Tweezer is a coffee barista with two years clean from Heroin and booze. Blender is a straight-up dry-drunk who does stand-up comedy six nights a week in front of a crowd that's generally been drinking all day. He's been known to smash a bottle or two over the odd heckler's head. Paulo is on the housekeeping staff. As far as I can tell, the only English he knows are the following phrases: "Housekeeping, please put your clothes on," "My name is Paulo and I'm alcoholic," and "This today I wanted to drink something but deed not."

So much for anonymity, eh?

It wasn't hard, getting back into AA. The only requirement for membership is a desire to stop drinking, they say. Whatever. It beats after-dinner ping pong with the Food Nazi.

Well, I'm off to bed. Starvation combined with ludicrous amounts of exercise can be quite exhausting.

-Estelle

***

Day four. Berries. Yoga. Veggies. Walking. Grains. Meeting. Bed.

Day Five. Repeat.

Day Six. And again.

Day Seven. One week survived onboard the U.S.S. Deprivation.

Today I watched the faceless masses file one by one off of my ship. It's my ship now, you know. One week, and already I'm institutionalized. I realized, as they shuffled their bulky bags and their sunburned noses toward land, that I hadn't really met any of them. I hadn't really seen a single face.

I walked the landing dock a bit, examining them more. Nothing. Didn't recognize a one of them. It was like I'd spent the week on an empty ship.

Then I saw one face I didn't expect at all.

Bill.

He was dressed in khaki trousers and a pullover sweatshirt, thank goodness. I'd had a bit too much of "Officer Bill" the last time we'd met.

"What are you doing here?" For the first time in a week, I thought for a moment about how I looked. Jogging shorts. "Gilligan" t-shirt. Baseball cap. Pony tail. The best things I had going for me were my lip gloss and my farmer's tan.

"Been thinkin' about you," Bill took a step into my personal bubble. Danger. Danger.

"I've been thinking about cheesecake," I admitted. AA is a program of honesty, you know.

"I'll bet," Bill laughed. "They working ya pretty hard?"

"Yeah," I stuttered. "Yeah," I sighed. Then I remembered something about Bill. Something about Bill brings things out of me. I thought, *Oh, Jesus here it comes.* I braced one hand on Bill's shoulder, then, and felt like a cartoon coyote waiting for the anvil to drop on my head. I began to bawl. It was a real, guttural, hearty bawl.

Bill sat me down on a wooden bench, holding me calmly by my arms.

"Why do I feel like this?" I whimpered when I could finally talk.

"Like what?" Bill asked. "What happened? Did somebody hurt you?"

"No! No. Well, I mean, they won't give me any real food. I just feel lost. I feel lonely. Everybody knows what a freak I am. The whole ship! I'm the Valerie Bertinelli of the Western Caribbean."

Bill scooted his Dockers closer to me, then held me. I could tell he had not even one clue what I was talking about. That comforted me.

"It'll get better," he said finally.

"What will?"

"I don't know," Bill shrugged. "But, something. Something *will*, without a doubt, get better. Always does."

From behind me, I heard someone clearing her throat in a British accent.

"There you are," Lauren chirped.

I pulled myself slowly away from the arms that comforted me.

"What's so wrong, Love?"

Bill seemed to puff up a bit at the sight of her.

"Y'all are feeding her *something* right?" he shot Lauren a look. "She looks a little pale."

I held my breath and tried to look sunken.

"Oh, *honestly*," Lauren spat. "She's eating better food now than she probably has her whole bloody life."

"I'm fine," I interjected in a tone that instead suggested I may actually be dying of consumption. "I'm just . . . fine." I swooned a little getting up.

Bill stood also, and pulled me into a quick embrace. "I'll meet you same time next week, kid," he said, winking like a true jackass. His hair smelled of coffee and Head n Shoulders. I suppressed the urge to lick his shoulder. It was going to be a very long week.

***

Dear Estelle,

Sorry it took me so long to write again. I'm out of the hospital and staying in a nursing home for a week or so until the doctors think my skin is strong enough to go back to home care. I'm still on the catheter, but drinking a ton of water (per Nurse Estelle) and staying away from coffee. Now, I realize Dr. Oz recommends it, but green tea tastes like boiled forest floor. Sorry, my dear.

I have good news and bad news. The good: I finally came clean with my boss and told him why I've been gone. Instead of canning me for being a useless cripple, they're setting me up with a voice-operated system so I can work from home, plus sending out an assistant once a week to keep me up to date on emails and paperwork.

The bad: I won't be able to send too many emails, if any, until I'm back in my condo. But don't worry about me. It's all uphill from here, baby.

Be good. And if you can't be good, then don't get caught.
-Jack

Chapter 33

Day 1, Week 2

I've lost seven pounds. You'd think Lauren had lost the weight, she was so freaking tweaked. She tousled my hair for God's sake. It was extremely un-British of her. I told her if she slapped me on the ass, I was *going off.*

Still, I smiled a secret smile. Seven pounds. For a few shining moments, I let myself imagine a new, skinny, happy self, all teeth and sun-streaked hair, squeezed into a size eight striped sundress from The Gap. Then I remembered how it always goes. Let's say I become the prettiest little "after" picture anybody ever saw? What happens after that? What happens seven weeks from now when I get off this ship and I'm just me again, a stranger in a strange land with seventeen IHOPs per square mile? Sure, it's easy to be all prudent when you've got the threat of debt, homelessness and possibly even jail time hanging over your head. Sure it's easy to have self control when hundreds of people are watching. What about when I've got money in my pocket and time on my hands? What then?

Lauren wants me to start giving testimonials in her little detox seminars now. She figures Gilligan is paying my room and board, so I might as well start hawking seaweed like a good girl. Still, I'm only one week sober and one week without sugar. God only knows what will come flying out of my mouth in front of a room full of women who look like . . . me.

I wish I could talk to Jack. I'm happy for him, I am. But he's all I've got and now I can't talk to him. I just got him back and now he's gone again.

At the AA meeting, Tweezer noticed my poorly masked malaise. She's the closest thing I have to friendship around here, but her twelve-step enthusiasm can be just a touch nauseating. Still, if someone's going to look me in the eye and tell me "God only dishes out as much as you can handle!" it's best that this person has a silver stud in her tongue and a tattoo of an eyeball with a knife plunged through it on her bicep. I'm a big fan of irony.

"I'm happy for where I'm at today, but worried about the future," I told the group when it was my turn to talk. "I'm a hazard to myself. I heard that in a song once."

"I love that song!" Tweezer interjected.

"No cross-talk in the meetings!" Blender blurted out. I made a mental note to heckle him when it came his turn to talk. "Anyway, Estelle," Blender continued the cross-talk, "Today is all we ever have. That's why they call it the 'present.'"

Seriously? I bet his stand up is *hilarious*.

"Meet me at the coffee bar after," Tweezer whispered in my ear. I winced. "Tea! I mean the tea bar. Later."

"Okay," I said.

I waited at the bar, trying not to stare at the biscotti and reading a cruise ship brochure about day-long snorkeling tours in Belize. I pictured myself in a white bikini, holding hands with James . . . James! Uhg. No, Jack. Or Bill. Anyway I pictured myself tan and trim, swimming along the coral reefs, holding hands with somebody who meets all of my myriad emotional needs . . .

"Hey chicky," Tweezer chirped. "All systems go."

"Eh?" I didn't recall requesting a flight to Mars.

"We're having a good old-fashioned sleepover at my pad. Lauren OK'd it. We got movies, rice cakes, and Diet Snapple."

"A sleepover? Diet Snapple? Holy shit, Tweeze, I'm living the dream!"

"I know, right? Don't let all the decadence go to your head."

"I'll do what I can."

"I'm in number 3402," Tweezer popped a chocolate-covered coffee bean into her mouth as she headed off. "Get your footie-pajamas and meet me in an hour."

**

By the time I got down to Tweezer's room, she had already improvised some party decorations, which included tropical fish string lights, party streamers, and "Gilligan" balloons taped here and there. She had gone to a lot of work. I acted as impressed as I was capable.

Half a dozen glass bottles of Snapple were crammed into two separate ice buckets, and a fruit tray had been added to the menu as well. The mango, pineapple and strawberries looked surprisingly good to me, given that technically, it was all just more of the same colon blow I'd been shoveling in for more than a week. Atmosphere is everything. Even Tweezer seemed decorated for the occasion in her uncharacteristically cutesy "Family Guy" pajama pants and fuzzy red slippers. If not for the "Iron Maiden" t-shirt, I might've thought I was in the wrong room.

I caught myself being tickled, then tried to stifle it.

"Why did you go to all this trouble?" I watched as Tweezer popped *The Big Lebowski* into a DVD player.

"You looked like to needed it," she said, matter-of-factly. "A little chicken soup for the detox guinea pig's soul. That's what's going on here."

It seemed like this was the moment I was supposed to start venting, spewing out all my fears, resentments, and general angst. I was, after all, in the presence of an AA person. My favorite audience: Another female addict, obligated to listen to other alcoholics for fear of the loss of one's own sobriety. Obligated to feel my pain in the name of Bill W. But the very thought of listening to myself complain even one more minute suddenly bored me to the very cockles of my being. What good would it do?

Instead, I speared a strawberry, grabbed a bottle of tea and settled back onto one of the two cots available, staring expectantly at the TV. On cue, Tweezer, reclined on her cot, grabbed the remote and started the movie.

"I've never seen this," I commented.

"Dude!" Tweezer moaned. "It's a cultural experience. You'll thank me."

Jeff Lebowski, aka The Dude, was a middle aged man plopped in the middle of some pretty dangerous, largely avoidable mayhem and foolishness. His reaction to most of this was to spark up a doob and hope for it to blow over.

Mid-movie found The Dude partaking of the weed in the bathtub in the face of grave peril.

"Do you miss smoking pot?" Tweezer asked suddenly, and I immediately knew she'd asked because she wanted me to turn it around on her.

"I never liked the munchies," I shrugged. "It's not like I need help getting hungry, right?" Tweezer smiled and sat up, waiting. "Do you miss it?" I asked her.

"Every day," she sighed. "Every single day."

"Was that your 'drug of choice' as they say?"

"That, and heroin."

"I tried heroin once," I recalled. "You know what a speedball is?"

"Coke and heroin together," Tweezer said, suddenly hanging on my every word. "You shot a speedball? You vixen, you."

"Oh, there was nothing vixen about it. I'm pretty sure the 'speed' part has to do with how fast your Frosted Mini-Wheats come up after you shoot it."

"Yeah," Tweeze whispered, but she wasn't disgusted by my little story. Instead she seemed lost in a memory, a fantasy perhaps. Abruptly, she seemed to wake up. "We should stop talking about it."

"Okay," I shrugged. I'm not the one who brought it up.

"I wish I was a sugar addict like you," she said after a long silence. "A little sugar never really hurt anybody, you know? Not like some things."

"Like what?" I asked.

"My dad was an alcoholic." Tweezer finished off her Snapple like it was something much stronger and grabbed for another one. "He was all about the hurting. Sugar doesn't make you hurt people. I used to think pot didn't hurt people."

Tweezer seemed not so much to be talking to me, but to be sending something awful out into a void, hoping it didn't return. I didn't know what to say. Then after a long awkward pause, she let me off the hook.

"Anyway," she said, levity returning to her tone. "Anyway, I frickin' love this movie. The Dude abides." She toasted her tiny little TV set.

"The Dude abides," I echoed, wondering if Tweezer should be watching a movie whose central character was a marijuana addict. I grabbed for another hit of pineapple. Fruit sugar was the closest I'd be getting to heaven any time soon.

"Why are you so addicted to sugar, anyway?" Tweezer's eyes suddenly appeared red and tired, and I figured our little party was coming to a close.

"I don't know," I laid back, pulling a blanket to my chin. "Maybe because it's so . . . harmless."

She chuckled.

"Thank you for this," I said after a moment.

"For what?" Tweezer yawned.

"I don't know." I yawned in reaction to hers. "Just . . . thanks."

"Don't get all *after school special* on me," Tweezer snorted. "I needed some girl time, too. Pretty damn bad."

I put my head down and lowered my eyelids, expecting that she was doing the same, or watching the movie again.

I kept my eyes shut for about ten minutes, but never got over the feeling of Tweezer's presence. Finally, I opened them again. Sure enough, she was wide awake, and looking at me expectantly.

"Can't sleep?" I propped myself up slightly with an elbow.

"No," Tweezer said calmly. "I don't ever sleep."

"Ever?"

"Hardly."

"I think about things all night," she sighed. "I can't shut it off. I worry."

"What do you worry about?"

Tweezer grimaced a little, like I was asking her for the key to a giant floodgate.

"Like . . . what is tomorrow going to be like? Am I going to say the right things? Am I going to fuck up somebody's caramel latte and end up homeless? Is Blender going to get into another fight tomorrow and get himself fired? I worry about you. Are you going to be okay? Are you going to get yourself fired? Are you ever going to call Gloria?"

"Whoa, whoa, whoa!" I sat up, startled. "You don't have control over any of that."

"I know, but it doesn't seem to matter. The voices just don't stop. I wish I could make them stop. That's not even half of what they say."

I suddenly felt under-qualified for this sleepover. For the first time in weeks, I would've given anything to be able to beam Bea right to where I was so this situation could be properly twelve-stepped into submission. I searched her toolbox of wisdom for the right thing to say. Ah, ha!

"You have to let that go," I said with grave certainty, immediately aware, however, of what a lame-ass thing it was to say.

"God. You probably think I'm a freak," Tweezer covered her face with one bent arm. "Please. Please! Forget I said anything."

"No! It's okay." I said. "It's fine. It's cool. We're cool."

"I just get so tired," she said after a long pause. "So tired of *never not wanting.*"

Never not wanting: my permanent address. I turned to say something in agreement, but Tweezer was focused again on the movie and it seemed quite intentional. I let it slide.

***

When I woke up, it was a quarter-past Pilates, and I was alone in Tweezer's state room. I didn't think anything of her absence, really. I figured anyone who worked at a coffee shop was, by necessity, an early riser.

In the semi-daylight that peeked through her tiny window, I noticed that Tweezer was a bit of a minimalist. As far as I knew, this was her semi-permanent residence, yet she didn't seem to own anything. She once told me she had been homeless until she landed the big cruise ship gig. It was the promise of a reliable place to crash that had attracted her more than anything else. Certainly, it wasn't the opportunity to shuck coffee drinks to overweight Midwesterners who routinely called it "expresso" and certainly it wasn't so she could be the only chick within a thousand nautical miles with an eyebrow ring.

I snuck a peak into her medicine chest, which, by contrast, was overflowing. There were prescription bottles of every imaginable size: Zoloft. Prozac. Trazodone. Antabuse. Metamucil. Ambien. Cough syrup with codeine. Those are just the ones I'd heard of.

205

For a recovering drug addict, she sure kept a lot of chemicals on board.

The knock at the door made me gasp loudly, and brought me sharply back to the reality that I was, in fact, snooping in someone else's shit and didn't belong there.

"Who is it?" I asked after a moment, figuring Tweezer wouldn't knock on her own door.

"It's Lauren. Let me in."

She sounded upset; I figured it was Pilates-related.

"Thank God you're here!" She rushed to me, grabbing both my shoulders in an awkward half-hug. "Well," she shrugged, releasing me quickly. "It wasn't you, then. Thank God."

"Wasn't me, what?"

"We had a jumper. They caught it on the security camera a few hours after it happened. Probably a passenger. They're trying to do a head count now."

"A jumper, like a rabbit? I don't get it."

"A jumper!" Lauren said, exasperated. "A suicide. Somebody jumped off the *bloody boat.*"

My mind returned to Tweezer's medicine chest, her absence. I'm not quick, but I'm not completely stupid.

"Take me to see the video," I said, feeling the acidic taste of the previous night's fruit-fest rising in my gut. Lauren glanced around at the room, which suddenly seemed so much more empty than it had just a moment earlier.

"Come on."

The video was on pause when we arrived, and the same three security guards who I'd wrestled, the same guys who'd bathed in mace with me just a couple of weeks before, sat waiting for me with anxious faces. I wondered why the police weren't there, then remembered: We're at sea. The person in the video was frozen in a stride on the lower left corner of the screen. It was hard to make out unless you knew what to look for; I could understand why Lauren hadn't recognized her.

Then came this surreal, strange feeling; it was as if I'd reached the end of a movie and realized I'd seen the ending before, but forgotten somehow. It was *like* that, only it wasn't just a movie, no matter how much I wished it was.

"The Dude abides," Tweezer had said. I didn't get it then, I don't get it now. Story of my fucking life. Just when I let my guard down a little . . . just when I think I'm just about to be let in on some grand inside joke, some girl I barely know quotes *The Big Lebowski* to me, throws me a party, then takes a long walk off a short boat.

The short Asian security guard pressed "play."

She entered camera range from the bottom left, shuffling. There was a slight pause at the metal railing as she scanned the dark void below her, but not much of one. Not the kind of pause that you'd expect over such a decision. Then I watched in horror as the girl with "Family Guy" pajama pants and Iron Maiden t-shirt kicked off her fuzzy red slippers and slipped out of site.

Chapter 34

Once security had a name, there was the matter of reporting Tweezer's death to the police. Because "the incident" happened while we were still in American waters, the Coast Guard was dispatched and the boat had to stop moving toward Cozumel until they got everything sorted out.

Lauren, bless her cockney heart, took pity on me and let me go back to our state room for a good private cry and a long nap. I'd never lost anyone to suicide. It seemed selfish to say I'd "lost" Tweezer; I barely knew her. But whatever she was to me, I knew watching her end her own life would haunt me for a very long time. More than that, I felt somehow responsible. The voices in *my* head bounced that idea back and forth continually, relentlessly. I had walked in on the very end of Tweezer's long history of drugs and pills and coffee and cult movies and general angst, said one voice. Still, I hadn't done anything to steer her away from what she did, said another. And I hadn't been surprised. If I wasn't the slightest bit responsible for her death, wouldn't I have at least been more surprised by it? She was an addict; I'm an addict. We should have been mates. Brothers in arms.

"I'll come find you at dinner time, alright?" Lauren said softly as I crawled under the covers. "There are going to be staff briefings and all sorts of bustle about this for a couple of days. Far as I'm concerned, you can have all of tomorrow off from detoxing if you want, Estelle. I'm tired of being the sugar bobby, as I'm sure you're right tired of me," she chuckled dryly.

Sugar bobby. That's funny. Wait. Day off? Back the truck up.

I sat back up on my cot to look straight at her. "Did you just give me a free pass?"

209

"Yes indeed. I did. But remember that you just lost seven pounds, eh? Think about how good that feels."

Oh, normal people are just so . . . I don't know . . . adorable. As Lauren began to shut the door behind her, the old wheels started to turn.

"But what about all the wait-staff and everybody who won't serve me?"

"I'll send out an e-mail," Lauren sighed, disappointed but not surprised. "Batten down the hatches. Estelle's on furlough."

Freedom.

Sugar.

Pasta.

Sugary drinks.

Waffles with syrup.

Coffee drinks with alcohol.

Chocolate. Any kind of chocolate at all.

I checked the clock. Too late for the waffle bar, by a long shot. Lunch options were plenty. There were burger bars, international buffets, basically everything. Or should I skip all that and head straight to the ice cream parlor? Or should I head straight to the Starlight and get my drink on? Huh? Two birds with one stone type of deal?

My thoughts were interrupted by the giant, swirling chaos of a Coast Guard helicopter, followed shortly by what sounded like a small plane passing over the ship. They were searching for a body.

I followed the sounds up several floors of stairs to the pool deck. Some passengers were huddled in the twin hot-tubs, others lounged by the pool. Patrons at the bar seemed subdued, speaking in hushed tones. Word had gotten out.

I took a stool at the bar and waited. Out of the corner of my eye, the helicopter hovered over one particular spot on the ocean. Some passengers gathered at the railing to see if it meant something.

"You hear we're gonna miss Cozumel because of that girl?" said a middle-aged man next to me with matching ring and watch tan-lines. He glared angrily at his bottle of Corona.

I examined us in the mirror across the bar. Me, twenty-five going on ten, he, forty-eight going on twenty-two. The helicopter made one last quick circle, then lifted and continued the search. Nothing.

"Well, aren't we a couple of swells," I said to his reflection. "Tweezer's life is over, and all you can think about is how you're going miss Lady's Night at Senior Frog's. And me? She was my friend! And all I can think about is what I'm gonna *eat*. That's right. I've skipped the funeral and gone straight to the church basement for marshmallow salad and brownies."

Mr. Corona sat up.

"Sorry. Didn't realize you knew her." He sized me up and sucked his gut in a bit. "Nothing wrong with a little toast in memory of a loved one, though, eh? Let me buy you something."

Right on cue, the bartender appeared.

"Get the lady a . . ." Mr. Corona leaned in on me a bit with an expectant look.

The bartender shook his head side to side and muttered something about "Cannot be serving Miss Estelle." Corona said "What the hell are you talking about?" Then a waitress stepped in and started talking about an email. A bit of a three-way verbal donnybrook broke out between these three folks who I assumed were from three different countries with three different first languages. All the while, I examined myself in the mirror.

I am twenty-five years old. I'm addicted to . . . everything. A friend just died; she was an addict like me. I don't want to die; more than that, I don't want to be forty-eight and looking like this dude to my right. I don't know what the right way is, I just know I haven't found it yet. And that I won't find it like this.

I hopped off the bar stool and turned to the waitress.

"You can drink, lady," she said matter-of-factly. "I got the email."

"I know," I said triumphantly. "I can drink like a motherfucker. But I really don't want to. Do you know Lauren, the email lady? Where's she right now?"

"Maybe she at the manager meeting upper deck," she said casually. "She said in the email you'd want a drink. She gonna be surprised."

"No more than me, lady," I told her as I walked away. "No more than me."

***

Dear Gloria,

There's a song I used to listen to all the time when I was a melodramatic teenager, running around taking off my training bra for every asshole that held the door for me and trying to drink or smoke everything that wasn't tied down or locked up. I know all the words; I was obsessed with this song, called "Brothers in Arms" by Dire Straits. It's about Vietnam vets. Has absolutely nothing to do with me, according to James. He was right, but still. Remember James? One of about a thousand guys I liked to use as tools to beat myself with about the head and shoulders?

Anyway, I played Brothers in Arms for James during one of our marathon late-night flogging sessions and he more or less laughed at me for feeling this connection, and I was deeply pissed off, but couldn't defend my position in the least; I'm not a Vietnam vet. (It's worth noting, however, that Mark Knopfler isn't either.)

I digress.

Some shit has happened, Gloria, some pretty crazy shit. So, I had to make a decision. I realized there are only two options for somebody like me: try to live or try to die.

I also realized how much I miss you. I don't blame you for leaving; I was acting like your mother and I had no right. I always thought I was so superior, so enlightened with all my twelve-step meetings and my self-help books. Like I was going to help you somehow. Hah! I'm always searching for a cure. You never were. Yet you found something anyway, something to make a life around, and I scoffed at it!

I was wrong.

And I'm here to say for good and all that I don't know anything now. I don't. Well, I guess I know one thing: that I'm an addict, and that addicts sometimes die.

I hope you'll forgive me . . . and I hope you'll write me again. I just lost a friend; I can't afford to lose any more. We could be brothers in arms, you and me. I really think we are.

Estelle

There was a funeral for Tweezer, of sorts. A memorial service in the chapel, attended mostly by employees and a few stray passengers who said she had been very polite to them when she'd served their cappuccinos.

The Coast Guard never found her body. The more I learned about her from my fellow employees, the more I don't know what they would have done if they *had* found a body. She had no family that she kept in touch with, and few friends. On her employee paperwork, she had listed her emergency contact as "Jeff Lebowski."

I found Blender sitting in the back row and took the empty seat next to him.

"You were a good friend to her," he said lamely.

"No." I shook my head. "I really wasn't. Not great. But you were, weren't you? You two pretty much owned that meeting. You made everybody feel welcome."

Blender smiled.

"As a standup comic, I make a pretty good AA greeter."

"That's what I hear," I nodded.

"You gonna keep coming?"

"Yep. I'll keep coming."

Blender sat back, satisfied.

From behind me came Lauren's brisk cockney. "There you are, darling. You've been requesting me?"

I gave Blender an awkward pat on the shoulder, then moved behind the row of chairs to get close enough to Lauren for a whisper.

"I made up my mind. I don't want to go crazy," I said sheepishly into the side of her head.

"What d'you mean?"

"I don't want to eat everything, get drunk, all that," I sighed, embarrassed. "I'm tired of it and I don't want to do it because it won't end tomorrow. Once it starts it never stops. But I need your help. I need you to *keep after me*, as you'd say."

"Now, Es." Lauren paused a moment. "This is all very noble. I'll give you that. But when I said you'd have the day off, I meant me as well. I mean to take a break. It's been a hard time. I'm sure you understand."

I did, and I felt foolish. But I knew what I needed, and I'd gone too long not making sure I got what I needed. Bea's voice boomed in my head: *"If nothing changes, nothing changes."*

"Can somebody else babysit me? Just 'til you're ready again?"

"You're serious!"

"As a cheesecake-induced heart attack."

Lauren scanned the room, landing immediately on Blender.

"No!" I said too loudly for the occasion. "I mean, last resort. Kay? It should probably be a woman."

"Okay, Miss Fussy." Lauren took another minute to scan. Shortly, her eyes brightened, and I prayed I wouldn't hate her next pick.

"Heni," Lauren announced with British certainty.

"Eh?"

Lauren strode across the room without me, engaging Heni with a secretive look on her face. As Lauren spoke, Heni's expression changed from mild horror to grave irritation, to grudging acceptance. She glanced at me with one raised eyebrow. I'm pretty sure I read the words, "You'll owe me, lady" on her lips.

Lauren crossed her arms, smiled and made her way back across the room to where I still sat.

"Go get some things for overnight and Heni will meet you in twenty minutes at your room," she said, quite satisfied with herself. "Can you handle yourself for twenty minutes?"

"That depends on whether the Chocoholics Buffet is underway," I snorted.

"You can do it, Estelle. You're stronger than you think."

"Nope. No I'm pretty much about as strong as it appears I am. But you're a swell gal, anyway."

I hustled my butt downstairs, packed a few essentials into a gift-shop bag, and waited for my nanny, who finally came knocking after more than an hour.

"Where've you been?" I shrieked, opening the door to a nonchalant Heni.

"I been at the funeral of a dear friend," she said calmly. "Now here I am, and here you are, and everybody okay."

"I'm pretty fucking far from okay," I sighed. Pretty sure I heard that line in a movie once too, and that I should get out more. The wait had made me anxious, got me questioning things again. The cravings were back. I needed backup.

"Well, now. Miss Estelle don' want to go crazy. Miss Estelle want to be like Valerie Bertinelli now!" Heni chuckled as we made our way to her state room, which was even smaller than mine, and which she shared with a housekeeper from Guatemala. The room smelled of lavender oil and cayenne pepper.

"I don't know," I shrugged. If there was a snide comment in me somewhere, I couldn't seem to locate the thing. Mostly, I was just tired.

"You okay to sleep on the floor, Miss Estelle?" Heni laid down a large blanket and pillow between the two single beds. "It's all I got."

"It's fine," I told her. Though I'd slept a large part of the day, I felt ready for another ten hours at least. Funerals, life-changing revelations, and their subsequent panic attacks can be really exhausting.

"Tomorrow be better day," Heni said, her tone softer than before. "Tomorrow we take a trip. You meet my family; see my home."

"What? Really?"

"Yes," Heni said, pulling a thin blanket up to her shoulders. "Tomorrow we get off at Belize. Tomorrow, I show you how to *go slow*."

***

Dear Estelle,

You're such a tool. Of course I forgive you. If Jesus can forgive . . . I don't know . . . all those people he forgave, then I guess I can forgive you.

Anyway, I'm not so perfect either. Zeke is gone; he's back out there drinking and drugging and being crazy. So, here I am living with his parents with no job and no skills to get one. But I'm not going to lose faith in myself, and I'm not going to eat seventeen sticks of butter or go off and start drinking again.

You're right; we're brothers in arms. But let's change it to sisters, okay? I'm not too thrilled with men right now.

Your sister in arms,

Gloria

So, by *go slow* Heni meant that she was going to wake me up at 5:30 a.m., drag me to the main kitchen, put me to work chopping vegetables, boning chickens (that's what *I* said), washing a thousand dinner plates, and finally moving about a hundred five-gallon tubs of ice cream from one freezer to another. Don't think the cruelty of that last task was lost on me.

I'd have been really pissed off, except for the fact that Heni did about twice as much work as I did. And this was all on her alleged day off.

When we'd finally moved the last bucket of strawberry cream cheese frozen yogurt to its new home, she at last turned to me and said, "Okay, den. Let's eat." I could have kissed her.

We ate our oatmeal and fresh strawberries while the sunburned masses made their way down the gang planks to the tender boats that would take them to Belize City and to fun-filled excursions and beyond. We took our seats on the very last boat; employees always had to wait, Heni explained to me.

"Did you bring swimming gears?" Heni said, distracted.

"Gears?" I stuttered. "I, uh, I brought a suit if that's what you mean."

One of the tender boat workers, also a disciple of Bob Marley, seemed to know Heni. Loud enough for me to hear, he asked Heni, "Who dis?"

He wore dreadlocks pulled back with a navy blue dew rag, baggy jeans, and a Kevin Garnett jersey from when he played for the Timberwolves. When Heni spoke to him, it was still in English, but her accent was off the charts.

"Dis Estelle. She wit me. She need a friend today."

"I be her friend," said Kevin Garnett, winking.

"No you don't. You drive de boat, Justin Timberlake. Jes drive de boat."

Heni sat next to me protectively.

"Belizeans like their women a little on the Kirstie Alley side then?" I quipped.

"Dat Markus. He like his women a leetle on de *American* side. He tink you rich. He tink he gonna make little salt 'n peppa babies wit you and you gonna buy him a new boat."

"Does he know about my financial situation? Never mind, don't tell him. I do have good hips for birthing."

Heni stiffened.

"I'm kidding, Heni! I'm mostly kidding."

"Yah, yah, funny girl," she muttered, staring out onto the turquoise water. Suddenly, she pointed west and jabbed me in the elbow.

"Oh my God!" was about all I could think to say. About twenty feet from us were four dolphins swimming alongside, racing the tender boat playfully.

"Where exactly are we going?" I suddenly realized I had no idea, and that I should. A gal who doesn't want to keep making the same mistakes again and again should at least make an attempt to know just exactly where the hell she's going at all times, even if there are four happy dolphins escorting her there.

"Caye Caulker," Heni said proudly. That cleared everything right up.

As we approached the island, Heni stood anxiously. By the time the captain had snugged the side of the boat up against the long wooden dock, she looked about ready to fly.

Just then, two small boys, the taller one bouncing what looked to be a large baby-doll on his hip, came bounding in our direction sounding like midget buffalo and looking vaguely like my three Asian security guards, only much cuter.

Heni squealed like she'd just won the biggest stuffed animal at the fair. She was off the boat and holding all three children (the doll was breathing and cooing) before Markus even had us tied to the dock.

I stood there for several minutes while she showered them with kisses, nuzzled the baby, re-nuzzled the baby, tugged her boys' ears, re-kissed their cheeks, and generally made a Belizean *scene* on the taxi dock. It was gorgeous to behold. I've never wanted children, but after all that, I sure wouldn't mind renting one for a nuzzle every so often.

Heni finally came up for air.

"Estelle, dees my children," she sighed happily.

"What? You're *kidding* me."

"Marvin, Recardo, and Analise, dis Estelle. She smart girl with a joke for every-ting."

Then I noticed tear streaks on Heni's face, then more of the same on the oldest boy's face.

"It's so nice to meet you all," I said awkwardly, suddenly wanting to tie an anchor to my own neck and jump off the dock.

Something horrible had occurred to me. This was Heni's day off. Her one day with her family. *Less* than one day, really. A matter of hours. And because I couldn't trust myself for one lousy day, she was forced to let me interlope on that.

"Can I talk to you?" I said secretively.

"Well, sure," Heni said, making no attempt to free herself of all three children, who were hanging on her like cats on a carpet tree.

"You can leave me here," I said. "You can just go have your day and I'll wait for you. I didn't realize . . ."

"Oh, no!" Heni interrupted. "I told Miss Lauren . . ."

"It was my idea," I said sheepishly. "I told her I needed babysitting. I didn't trust myself not to binge, and now I feel like a first-class asshole."

Heni covered her baby's ears.

"No," she said after a long moment. "I want you spend the day wit us. You get da lobster with Markus and Recardo.

You help my sister wit suppa. You change da baby's diaper. Make yourself useful. See how de udder half lives, yah?"

"Did you say diapers?"

"Yah, yah. Come on."

Heni's island was about the size of a large shopping mall, with only three actual streets: Front Street, Middle Street and Back Street. You could walk it from end to end in about twenty minutes, five if you're Lauren. The house she lived in, which she rented from a friend, was about the size of a small boutique in a mall, but much less fancy. The living room was the dining room was the kitchen. Two small bedrooms and a closet-sized bathroom had been added to the structure at some point, but the lack of a hallway connecting them made them look like the afterthoughts they likely were. The most expensive looking features of the house were the heavy-duty hurricane shades, made of rusty white metal. Heni's three children, her adult brother and sister, and three children lived there.

Heni's sister Leelee hugged me on site.

"Aren't you pretty! So pretty. Look at you blond pretty hair." She scrunched my windblown mop into her fingers and watched it fall onto my shoulders.

"Leelee want to be American," Heni said solemnly, as though much effort had been expended getting Leelee to *not* want that.

"And then, of course, you know Markus," Heni sighed.

Behind me, the man from the boat beamed a toothy smile. I hadn't even noticed him walking with us.

"He's your brother?" I squirmed.

"Dat my broda," Heni nodded.

"Helloooo, Beautiful," Markus cooed. "You gonna dive with us? You gonna catch de lobster?"

"Oh, me?" I shook my head. "No, I don't think . . ."

"Oh, yah," Heni broke in. "Yah. You want to give me some time alone? You go get de lobster wit Markus. Jes don't

222

sleep wit him if you can manage it."

"What?"

"She said don't sleep wit me. But don't listen to dat."

"I'm going to *go get lobster?*"

"Yes. You get lobster so Recardo can stay and be with me for a while. Here's your gears," Heni said, handing me a black plastic snorkel and mask. "You put dis on your face, you put dis in your mouth, and you breathe out your mouth. *So* easy. You be an island girl in no time."

"I've never snorkeled before," I said pitifully.

"You have any questions, jes ask Markus," Heni said, shuffling me out the door. "If he know, he tell you. If he don't know, he'll tell you a lie so sweet, you won't know da difference."

***

Dear Gloria,

Who's an adventure girl? Well, that would be me.

Today, I looked a lobster in the eye, hooked the little sucker by the tail, swam him to the boat, named him James, spoke to him at length about the state of our relationship, brought him to shore, then grilled him and ate him.

James was delicious.

I learned so much today! Did you know that there are people out there who actually just eat to live? They go out, gather up what they can to support their families, bring it home, share it, and thank God for it. It's this other planet called Caye Caulker. Interestingly, the inhabitants of Caye Caulker insist that there are many more like them out in the world and that I am the freak who just never noticed.

I also learned that it's much easier to hear painful truths about oneself when they're spoken in a Creole accent and served with a side of grilled greens and garlic mashed potatoes.

Another important thing happened today. A man . . . a rather attractive man who looked a little like a pro-basketball player but with a Creole accent . . . tried to make me feel beautiful for the express purpose of getting me to have wild Caribbean lobster-boat sex with him, but I didn't fall for it. Not even close. And I didn't apologize.

Now *that* is growth. And that, my sister, is one helluva good day.

I'm very sorry to hear about Zeke. But trust me: if your home girl Estelle can go one full day without wanting to binge, starve, drink, or have sex with the wrong guy, then anything is possible.

Tawanda!

-Estelle

Chapter 37

"Good evening Gilligan cruisers, dis is your shipboard meal planner, Heni. I hope you had a wahnderful day on beautiful Belize. I certainly did. Don't forget dat tonight is all-you-can-eat lobster on the main deck. Bring your appetites, we'll bring da bibs! Heni over and out."

The rest of the week I spent basically doing what I was told. Lauren says let's go to Yoga; I go. Heni says eat this: I eat. It's not bad. They mean well; plus I've lost another three pounds.

And because Heni doesn't seem to mind having me as a tagalong, I've started hanging out with her in the kitchen while she's cooking. Heni's an expert in three things: mothering, food, and Hollywood trivia.

So, maybe I'll be chopping the onions and the peppers, while Heni drains the rice, and she'll be telling me all about how misunderstood Brad and Angelina are and how wonderful it is that they've never met a starving child they didn't adopt.

"People always say they marriage is break up," Heni sighed while cutting onions. "Ugliness. Jealousy. That where it come from. Brad and Angie above all dat."

"I hate to break it to you, but that girl's got some kind of eating disorder," I said. "She's way too tiny. She needs to go on a cruise. Eat a waffle and wash it down with five to seventeen pineapple smoothies."

"Yah, you tink everybody like you, den? Everybody have a problem?"

"Not everybody, Heni. Just almost everybody. And especially actresses whose lips are bigger than their thighs."

"Really." Heni shook her head.

"Really," I said. "Look at all the women who show up to Lauren's Seaweed Extravaganza? Look at what they spend on that shit. Ninety bucks for a bottle of sludge somebody scraped off the bottom of the ship! Ninety bucks for a magic pill that ain't. You think I'm losing weight because of that crap? I'm losing weight because of you, Heni. I'm losing weight because you're the freaking *Veggie Whisperer.* I'm losing weight because of good, healthy food. I'm certainly not losing weight because of some bullshit *detox pills.*"

Heni chuckled and shook her head.

"Why everybody so fat?"

"I don't know. All I can say is that I'm addicted to crap that makes me fat," I said. "And in my country, crap is everywhere, and it's cheap and it's usually wrapped in pretty paper with cartoon characters from my childhood. But I have no idea why I would be addicted to it. It makes me happy for a minute; miserable the rest of the day."

"Well, I hope we don't catch the fat bug on Caye Caulker," Heni groaned. "Seem like whenever America sneeze, everybody catch a cold."

"Just don't let Krispy Kreme put a drive-thru on Caye Caulker and I think everybody will be okay."

"No worries," Heni shrugged. "We got no cars."

"Well, there you go."

Heni placed our lunch -- grouper with peppers, onions, tomatoes, and cilantro in a large tinfoil pouch – on a grill and set a timer.

"You really like my cooking?"

"Duh."

"Does dat mean yes, smart girl?"

"Yes, I like your cooking, Heni. I love it. I want to marry it and adopt third world babies with it."

"Good girl."

"You like cooking for me?"

"Rather cook for my kids," Heni sighed.

"Oh course you would," I said, remembering what it was like watching her say goodbye to her two sons and her infant daughter at the end of our day on Caye Caulker. "I can't compete with that kind of cuteness."

"No, ma'am." Heni snapped to. "No, but Markus tink you plenty cute." Then a wicked little smile appeared across her normally sincere face. "Why don't you come next week too, take Recardo's place on de boat again?"

"Because Markus tink I'm plenty cute."

"I make him be good," Heni promised. "I tell him you have crabs."

"Nice. What if *I* can't be good?"

"Nah, you be good. What you say? Come home wit me again. You have fun. Recardo see his mama. Everybody happy."

What can I say? It felt good to be needed.

***

The end of week two came fast. For the second time, I watched the passengers disembark with their over-stuffed bags, their forlorn faces, and their unfortunate tan lines. For the first time, I knew a couple of them.

I waved goodbye to Denise, a 911 dispatcher who was a mean kick boxer and a bit of a crepe addict.

I wished Mike the locksmith a safe flight home to Cleveland. Mike had bought three bottles of seaweed supplements at the low, low price of $270. I'm pretty sure that had more to do with the way Lauren's sports bra aggressively pushes her tits toward the heavens than any real hope that seaweed was going to help Mike with his Burger King gut.

A fool and his money.

The thought of that brought forth a rather icky piece of reality I'd been actively avoiding. Starting with the next cruise, Lauren was going to make me start speaking at the detox hodowns. It was time. I'd lost enough weight to make a decent looking "after" and I'd freeloaded for two full weeks without paying my Gilligan dues.

What would I say and how would I say it with a straight face?

Then I saw Bill and forgot all about it.

It wasn't a shock. I mean, I knew he'd be there. He said he'd be there. And there he was, looking all dapper and shaved and smelling like Walgreens.

"Wow," he said, holding his arms out toward me. "You look different. Great. Gorgeous."

"All three of those? Golly."

"Yeah . . . all three times ten," Bill laughed.

"Well, swell. You look good too."

"I heard what happened to that girl," Bill said. Of course, he would have. He probably knew more about it than I did.

"Tweezer," I said.

"You okay?"

"Yeah," I said, but suddenly felt see-through.

"There was an hour or thereabouts when I didn't know whether it was you," Bill said morosely. "It was awful," he added, then grabbed my hand to emphasize the point. I pulled slowly out of his grasp until he was just awkwardly holding the tip of my pinky finger. He didn't let go. This bugged me. Really, really bugged me. Why didn't I sleep with Markus, anyway? Was I holding out for Bill? Was he my (gag) boyfriend now? Why was he meeting me here on this dock for the second week in a row? I wasn't ready for it. I'd found some clarity on Caye Caulker that day . . . maybe for the first time in my life. I wasn't ready to share it with Ranger Rick, or worse, let him take it away.

"Listen," I said, reclaiming all five of my digits. "You don't need to keep coming here. I'm fine. I'm different, I'm great and I'm gorgeous. And I'm single. And that's for the best, trust me."

"I didn't mean anything by it," Bill said, smiling of course. Jesus Jumped-up Christ that guy pisses me off routinely.

"Why do I always want to Tae Bo that friggin smile off your gob?" I demanded.

"I don't know," he kept on grinning like a true ass-hat. "But, here." He reached into his back pocket and produced a card with his name and badge number: 381. "Here are my numbers and my email. When you get done with this detox thing, you need to call me. I've got a surprise for you, but you don't need it right now."

"Surprise?" I straightened my Gilligan-issue khaki shorts and shifted my stance to emphasize my attitude. "Why don't you just tell me now?"

"Because I want you to have to see me again."

Effing longhorn.

"Do they have stalking laws here in Bush country?"

"Yes, ma'am."

"Maybe you should arrest yourself."

"Maybe so. See you in six weeks."

Chapter 38

Dear Estelle,

I'm home. I always thought I hated this place. Not so. I'm happy as hell to be back. Yet, now I know I have to get off my butt (figuratively speaking) and start making some changes. If nothing changes, nothing changes . . . isn't that what Bea used to tell you? Anyway, I'm getting myself out of here. Cue the theme from *St. Elmo's Fire* . . .

Absolute got Rock back for me, part time at least. I realize he's the dude who helped get me into this predicament to begin with, but when you think about it, he's the least likely person to ever make *that* mistake again. Plus, it's much less likely that I would find myself falling in love with him anytime soon. He looks terrible in a sports bra.

I've started working again, which is also very satisfying. Kia from Projects comes by every Tuesday to give me new assignments and update me on the current ones. I can't tell you how good it is to be back with all you "normal people." As my ass continues to heal, the doc says I can start going in for four-hour work-days, then six, then eight. Booya!

Speaking of work, I want you to know that when you get done doing your thing down there, and if I have an opening, you're welcome to come back to work for me part time. I quit smoking pot in the hospital, just so you know. Also, I promise to keep my paws to myself . . . if you can.

Your friend,
Jack

***

"My name is Estelle and I'm *multi-super-duper-addicted.*"

"Hi, Estelle," said Blender, Paulo, Marie the Chemical Engineer from Manchester and Bernard the over-the-road-trucker from Chicago.

"Today was good. I made it through another day sober, plus no compulsive eating." Enthusiastic head-bobbing all around.

"I miss my parents today. I've done a few things I'm actually proud of lately, and I wish I had some way to share it with them. They don't have email, though, so . . .

"Anyway, I was thinking about the first step today, the part about powerlessness. I've known for a long time that I'm powerless over all the stuff I'm addicted to. But the tough part, especially for a woman, is knowing where power is needed and where it isn't. When am I using my powers for good and when am I using them for evil? When am I being compulsive and when am I just being me? And what's the difference? That's what trips me up. But I must be getting better at it, because lately I feel less and less like I'm going to have a seizure when I pass by the waffle station. And yesterday at the salad bar, some skinny girl spilled her strawberry mousse on my favorite Caye Caulker T-shirt and I didn't grab her by the hair and bounce her head off the ice machine. Nor did I fantasize about it for much longer than fifteen to twenty minutes. Progress, not perfection, eh?"

"Thanks, Estelle," said the group.

It's been five weeks and three days since I drank or ate compulsively. I've had some sugar, but not much, and not like a maniac. Lauren's so proud her lisp has developed a lisp. Heni smiles at me all the time and calls me her "island girl," and it's not just because I've become her son's steady stand-in on the lobster boat every Wednesday. Blender gave me a special, shiny pink and green medallion on my thirty-day anniversary and told me and everybody else that he hadn't seen that kind of personal growth "since they raided Woody Harrelson's private stash."

Rim shot, please.

Bea always said, "Yesterday's history and tomorrow's a mystery, but today is a gift. That's why they call it the 'present.'" It still makes me want to spew chunks, but I have to admit it's more or less true.

***

Dear Estelle,

I'm pregnant.

Any thoughts? I've talked to God a lot about this, but no answer. I hope you don't judge me. I haven't heard from Zeke in three weeks, and his parents are starting to treat me like the stray dog they wished they hadn't given their leftovers to. Or maybe they're just worried about Zeke. I'm not the best at reading people.

Your friend in Christ and California,

Gloria

***

Hi everybody. My name is Estelle. Five weeks ago, I was chunky, unhappy, and undernourished. Then I met Lauren. You could say we didn't get along so great at first.

(Cue the video of me being dragged out of my first detox seminar, drunk and disheveled, alternately spewing vitriol at Lauren and hitting on the hot Latino paramedic.)

But after the sedatives and the triple-vodka smoothies wore off, I realized that what Lauren was offering me, and what she's offering you, is a second chance.

(Cue photo of me looking dumpy and hung over in an oversized pair of running shorts and baggy t-shirt. My shirt says "Cleverly disguised as an adult." My eyes say, "Kill me.")

233

Do you feel sluggish, but can't sleep? Do you feel bloated even when you think you're eating healthy? Do you exercise your butt off without ever exercising your butt off? You can get off the roller coaster; I did five weeks ago and I've never felt better.

(Cue photo of me, tanned and smiling, in a flowing blue sundress with an island print and tie-straps at the shoulders. Make-up and hair compliments of the ship-board spa; flawless skin and unusually narrow waist compliments of Photoshop.)

Neptune's Trident has changed my life. I simply take one easy-to-swallow fortified seaweed tablet before each meal, then follow the Neptune's Trident Meal Plan and exercise three to four times a week. I've lost 19 pounds and never felt better because now I'm changing from the inside out.

(Cue photos of my sparkling clean, super-healthy lower colon. Kidding! I jest.)

At this point, a beaming Lauren usually takes over our little presentation with the nitty gritty details of the detox diet. She tells the ninety-five percent female audience about all the goo we collect in our various organs and how it keeps us from losing weight, feeling great, and basically living full and satisfying lives. When she's done, she sets up individual appointments with people who need that one last one-on-one nudge before jumping off the seaweed cliff, while I ring up the ninety-dollar bottles of pills and the fifty-dollar "detox diet" books with more than two hundred delicious recipes which mostly taste like pine cones and crepe paper.

Every so often, one of the older broads will tell me I'm an "inspiration" and try to hug me or otherwise touch my person. I resist the urge to bust out a facial tick and/or scratch my privates. For all she knows, I could have been snorting cocaine off her husband's belly while she was at a wine tasting yesterday, and *that's* how I'm losing the weight. What is it about having a slim body that makes everyone think you've got your shit together?

After all the ladies have put their MasterCard's back in their Coach purses and headed back out to their various shipboard activities, Lauren wipes her brow like Jimmy Swaggart, hugs me and tells me what a great job I'm doing for the company. By the time I'm done counting the bottles and sorting the credit card receipts, I usually feel about half past icky.

Anyway, it's a living.

Chapter 39

The day started like any other, as they say.

0600: I got up and headed to the deck with Lauren for a two-mile walk. I'd been learning little tidbits about Lauren day after day, such as: her father owns several Lifetime Fitness clubs. She barely speaks to him for reasons including but not limited to the fact that she doesn't get a free membership or even a discount. I also learned that *she* proposed to her fiancé because she knew he was waiting for her permission to take things to the next level. After five weeks only pissing on her say-so, this surprised me not.

0730: Blueberry-oat pancakes and honey with Heni. We were experimenting with different flours, since white flour is off limits. We had the best luck with the spelt and whole wheat. Buck wheat tastes like cat litter to me. I've never really tasted cat litter, but I'm still pretty sure.

0830: Yoga. Warrior 2 is my favorite pose, and Savasana of course. Savasana is also called "corpse pose." We basically lay there like dead people and call it exercise, which rocks. Thanks to the breathing exercises, I'd been learning a little bit about meditation. It's a good way to silence all the voices in my head that used to say things like "eat that" or "drink that" or "take your ping pong paddle and beat that redhead in the yellow thong to death with it." Things like that.

1000: Sitting the seaweed kiosk. *Hey Gilligan cruisers! Just in case you missed the opportunity to get your pockets picked at yesterday's seminar, your detox consultants Lauren and Estelle will be available in the fourth floor lobby across from the Dramamine Booth. Hurry! Today's your last day to purchase before the end of your stay. Bring your husband's money and leave your common sense in your state room!*

1200: Curry lentil squash soup. It looks like something the cat dragged in and horked up on the rug, but tastes like heaven. For dessert, yogurt mango parfait. Heni says I'm easier to be around if she gives me something sweet at the end of each meal and calls it something fancy. I beg her daily to adopt me; she refuses.

1400: Detox seminar. Second verse, same as the first.

1530: Nappy time. Selling sea sludge to the pudgy masses is mega-exhausting, so I was really looking forward to the stewed chicken and brown rice with portabellas Heni I had planned for dinner. I fell asleep and dreamt that I was playing shuffle-board in a white bikini and looking amazing. A large crowd gathered to take in my fabulousness. Suddenly, I noticed James standing by the life boats. I sauntered over to him; he took me in his arms.

He said, "You look so much better than that one time at the grocery store."

I said, "You look about the same."

He said, "I want you now. I didn't before."

I said, "That's a shame. I don't generally like men who want me."

1555: I awakened to a very loud knock at the door. I didn't answer right away. Based on past experiences, it is my persistent hope that people who seek me out are somehow mistaken and will realize it eventually. They never do.

Knock knock knock.

"Heni?" I inquired, hopeful. *Maybe it's time for din din.*

"Security!"

Eh?

"Okay," I muttered, confused. What business could I possibly have with the Three Hmong-migos?

"Hold on." I hastily pulled a brush through my hair, remembering my previous encounters with the ship's extremely ambitious security guards. They basically pepper-sprayed me like a slab of beef jerky the first time we met. The second time we met, it was to identify Tweezer as the girl who jumped off the boat. I searched my memory for something I might have done wrong since then. Amazingly, I could find nothing. I'd been sickeningly good. In fact, I'd even exchanged pleasantries once or twice with the shorter one with the dimples.

"Uh, what can I do for you guys?" I said, opening the door to them.

They filed in without waiting for an invitation. They scanned the room as if looking for drug paraphernalia or perhaps peanut M&Ms. Dimples had a look of grave national security on his face; he was at a level red, or at least orange. His hand rested on his mace holster.

"Why don't you come with us?" he said.

I could think of many good reasons, plus a few subcategories to the primary reasons, but I figured this was probably one of those rhetorical deals. They took my arms on either side and we all filed down to the security offices like we were marching down the yellow brick road.

The boys ushered me into a conference room which I'd seen twice before and sat me down like a true flight risk, seating themselves right next to me. Then a man entered who looked like a Philippine George Clooney. He sat across from me, taking great pains to straighten the padded shoulders of his captain's uniform.

"Yes," he said, looking intently at some paperwork that I assumed was about me. "Yes. Miss . . . Brown? Is it?"

"Yes. It is. I am."

What. The. Fuck?

"I'm Captain Longerbone," he said with a perfectly straight face.

"Really?"

"Yes." Small invisible devils cackled loudly inside my head, but I kept my Beavis and Butthead moment to myself.

Captain Longerbone took off his glasses and placed them in a crisp front blazer pocket. "I'm sorry to say, we're going to have to let you go," he said, emoting almost not at all.

"Why?" A hot flash of anxiety pulsed through my body.

"Basically," he said, "because of this."

He slid an eight by ten photocopy across the table to me. It was an image of my passport. Circled in red was the expiration date I'd fudged with permanent marker. It seemed like a lifetime ago that I'd done that.

"Our HR people found this when they were checking your documentation."

"What . . . what can I do?" I sputtered. "I don't want to leave." I couldn't believe the words even as I said them.

"Nothing we can do. You need a valid passport to work on this ship, and we need honest employees who don't commit international fraud. It's too bad. I hear you're selling the hell out of those diet pills."

"Seaweed supplements."

Captain Longerbone ignored that and rose to leave. His name was no longer funny to me, not even when I caught a glimpse of his first name: Dick.

***

Even Lauren's *knock* has a cockney accent.

"You decent, Es?"

"Come in," I said, opening the door to my state room. Since it would be uncivilized to just throw me overboard, the ship's crack security team had instead been ordered to keep me on house arrest for the remainder of the cruise, which was one more day. Upon arrival in Houston, I would be sent on my way. No car, no money, no job.

"Are those arseholes going to shadow you all the way to Texas?"

240

"So it seems," I said. Lauren's expression was a cross between anger and grief. We weren't best buddies, but she was a good teacher. I would miss her, much the same way that you miss the first Algebra teacher who ever explains polynomials in a way that doesn't make you want to go all *unabomber* on your junior high.

"What are you going to do?"

"I don't know," I sighed. "They're telling me they're not going to pay me anything because I didn't fulfill my end of the contract. The most they'll do for me is just not report me to the Feds for defacing my passport."

"Who says that?" Lauren demanded.

"Longerbone," I said, finally able to let out the full-throated snicker that name deserved.

"Well, we'll see about that," Lauren said, grabbing for the door. "Don't go anywhere."

I gestured to the three stooges camped outside my door. "As if."

"Right," Lauren said. "I'll be back."

"Yes, ma'am."

Alone, I rummaged the drawers, searching for the remote control. I found it at last in a bedside drawer, next to a couple of Gloria's letters. *Well, aren't we just a couple of twelve step success stories? Gloria: relapsed a million times, pregnant twice since treatment, and homeless. Me: relapsed a million times, jobless, homeless, hopeless.*

On Shipboard Channel Six, I was alarmed to see none other than *me* at yesterday's detox seminar, touting the virtues of proper colon maintenance and better living through seaweed. "I've changed inside and out," said Gilligan Cruise Line Drone Estelle Brown, blinking innocently. All I could do was throw up in my mouth a little. Seeing oneself on TV is like surprising your parents in the middle of sex. You knew it would be bad, you just didn't realize it would be *a horror show.*

241

It occurred to me to pack, but I had nothing to pack my things into.

It occurred to me head to the buffet and have my way with it at last. Why not? There was nothing stopping me, except perhaps the three security guards camped outside my door. But they could be reasoned with. A girl's got to eat, right?

I swung the door open with nothing but debauchery on my mind. Deep fried, batter-dipped debauchery with whipped cream, hot fudge and a cherry on top. Instead, I came face to face with Heni.

"Gah!"

Heni held a plate with a room-service-style plastic cover, but her expression was less than hospitable.

"When were ya gowan ta tell me, den? Were ya gowan ta leave with not even sayin' 'goodbye?'"

"Okay, you *did* notice Larry, Daryl and his other brother Daryl outside my door, right?"

"Yah got a phone?" She had a point.

"I'm not exactly proud of myself, okay?"

"I'm not exactly proud of you eeder, but that don't mean we're not family."

I sat down on the bed, defeated. "What?"

"Yah like a daughter."

"Oh," I breathed in. "That's fucking *it.*" Then the tears started and I had no strength left to stop them. I felt Heni's warm hand on my shoulder as I let it out.

"Why you cry? Huh? Why you cry? Oh. Okay den," Heni sighed. "Go on and cry."

***

The next morning, I was up, packed and ready to go at 6:30. Lauren came through for me, sort of. She had tallied up her sales before I began giving testimonials versus her sales after, and presented those figures to the bean counters at Gilligan. Basically, I'd sold enough Neptune's Bullshit to pay off my credit card three times over. They wouldn't agree to pay off my credit card three times over, but were at least able to wrap their heads around *once.*

So, I didn't have any money, but I had a credit card with a shiny new zero balance and a newly-expanded five-thousand-dollar limit (because I was such a good customer). The American dream, alive and well.

"It's been lovely working with you," Lauren said. "I shall miss you." Then we did one of those awkward deals where you think you're going to get a hug, so you put your arms out, then you realize you were just going to get a warm handshake, but then she realizes you thought you were going to hug, and so she tries to readjust for a hug when you've already self-adjusted for a warm handshake. Anyway, it was an amicable parting and both parties meant well.

Saying goodbye to Blender went quickly. For someone who makes his living trying to make people laugh, he sure is a downer. But he left me with one gem that I won't soon forget. He said, "Estelle, try not to fuck up your whole life."

Aye, Captain.

It would not be so easy with Heni. I would hug her whether she was willing or not. I would hold her for an uncomfortably long time, thank her for teaching me how to eat like a human, how to appreciate what you have, how to give without asking for anything in return, and how to make a mango-walnut dressing that makes grown men weep with joy.

I would cry enormous tear blobs all over her white coveralls.

Then, I would ask her for one . . . last . . . itty bitty favor and promise it wouldn't get her fired.

Ahoy, Gilligan Cruisers! And . . . er . . . shiver me timbers. This is Estelle Brown, former Neptune's Trident consultant and current homeless ne'er-do-well. I want to wish you safe passage to your respective homes and lives. You came here looking for rest and rejuvenation without judgment, and I hope that's what you found.

But before you go, I want you to know that whatever you ate this week, and whatever you drank, it's okay. I mean it's okay in that you should just forgive yourself and move on. It's not okay, of course, if you think you're going to take one of those bullshit seaweed pills and make all your troubles go away. You have to know that, right? Deep down? You have to know those pills are bullshit. I didn't lose weight because of those, I lost weight because I got sick and tired of feeling like crap, and when somebody put healthy food in front of me, I decided to go ahead and eat it. It's not a perfect system, but it works most days. Anyone who tells you they have the answer is telling a big fat Splenda-coated lie.

Outside Heni's tiny office, I heard the pitter patter of the Mace Patrol, then finally saw them each through Heni's small window, but I clutched the microphone on Heni's primitive-looking PA system and worried not. I had pocketed the office key so Heni could say later that I had stolen it and locked her out. Tweedle One began pounding on the door.

Anyway, folks, my ride's here, so I just want to leave you with one last piece of advice. The only piece of advice on the subject, if you ask me . . .

Pound. Pound. Pound.

Tweedle Two withdrew what I assume was some sort of master set of keys and began trying each one in the office door.

One last thought.

Crap. I hadn't really thought this *thought* thing through. When a person announces "one last thought" it oughta be something decently profound. And especially, if you're broadcasting that one last thought to something like three thousand people, it should *really* kick ass.

Still, all I could think of, before Tweedle Three came barging in with pepper spray a-blazing, was Jack's sweet face. And all I could think to say was:

Just eat until you're full, then stop, okay? According to Denise Austin and er, other people who know these things, your stomach's only about the size of your fist, okay? It's not the black hole. It's not connected to your heart or anything. And if you find somebody who loves you, put the brownie down and just love him the hell back.

Chapter 40

The best thing about getting maced the second time is that the aforementioned "when one gets maced everybody gets maced" rule is even more applicable when all parties are in an enclosed space about the size of a handicap-accessible bathroom stall. You'd think they'd have learned.

By the time the police arrived, we were like one big pissed off octopus with all arms flailing and all heads spitting and cursing. Despite the excruciating burning sensation being visited upon my eyes, mouth and nose, I was actually feeling pretty pleased with myself. And then I heard his voice.

"Well, lookie who we have here," said Officer Shock and Y'all.

"Bill!" I said between debilitating coughing fits and spitting large amounts of drool on the floor. "Come here and give mamma a kiss."

By the time he got me cuffed and stuffed into the back of his squad car, he seemed amused, mostly.

"Couldn't just go quietly, could you?"

"No, officer," I sputtered, reclining lengthwise on the hard pleather bench seat. "*Hell* to the *no*."

I detected a bit of a chuckle, but it also could have been a rattling within my own lungs.

"When I get you to where we're going, you're cleaning the back of this pig rig."

"Roger dodger. By the way, what am I under arrest for?"

"I haven't decided yet. Don't really know what to charge you with. Mostly, those poor people just wanted you off their boat."

Not entirely true, I thought. Heni had promised to miss me.

Apart from my wheezing, we drove in silence for several minutes. I focused on my breathing, as I'd learned in *yoga on the high seas*, and stared at the ceiling of the Crown Victoria. Someone had spit up there and made it stick, but I'll be damned if I know how they did it.

Suddenly, it was as if lying on Bill's vast back seat brought me back somewhere I hadn't been in forever, or maybe never. I felt ten years old again, and I was in my parents' Grand Prix on the way up to Gramma's house. I'd given up on stopping at the pancake house; I'd stopped begging and wanting and craving. Instead, I'd just shut up and let the rhythm of the tires lull me for miles and miles. Dad drove, Mom navigated, and I slept, never questioning whether I was traveling in the right direction, only trusting that somebody smarter than me knew where we were heading.

That's how I felt, even though, wherever we were headed, it sure wasn't my Gramma's house. Yet I felt carried by a higher being, and it wasn't Bill. I suddenly knew it was going to be okay. I had no evidence to support that. Yet it was as real as the big gob of spit on the ceiling of Bill's squad.

One other thing: I was not hungry.

I was fed. I was full.

I could hear Gloria's voice: "Yeah, you're full of *something.*"

And I could hear Jack: "Atta girl. Come over here and sit on my lap."

Oh, and I could just hear Bea in my damn ear telling me what this was. "You had a spiritual awakening," she would say, all self-righteous and twelve-steppy. "You had a lightning bolt!"

A finger snapped in my ear, waking me from my lightning bolt.

"Estelle? Wake up, now."

I opened my eyes to Bill's scrunched eyebrows over two worried eyes.

"Let me get those off of you," he said, reaching for a set of keys on his big black cop belt. I'd forgotten I was even cuffed.

"Where'd you travel off to?" Bill queried.

"Was I asleep?"

"I don't know, were you?"

I shook out my arms a bit. "No. Just letting somebody else drive."

Bill took in the freakishly large smile on my face with some surprise.

"You go to heaven and back?" he laughed.

"A little."

Then I noticed where we were, or rather, where we *weren't*. This was not a police department, it was a residential street lined with small old houses. We were parked in front of a white one-and-a-half story bungalow with blue shutters and a one-car garage. Bill gave a casual nod of his head to a middle-aged man across the street as he checked his mailbox.

"Is this your house?" I stretched. "Uh oh. I think I saw a porno once that started this way."

Bill shook his head. "If I was going *that* route, I'd have left my cuffs on you."

"Awe," I sighed.

"Don't be a tease, now," Bill said, taking my hand and walking me toward the garage. "I told you I had something for you. Well, here you go."

He pulled the door up slowly. It took my eyes a moment to adjust to the darkness of the garage.

"Oh my God!" I sputtered. "It's . . . is it? Where did you find it?"

There sat my Neon in all its gorgeous four-door, five-speed glory. There sat my freedom.

"Your friends left it stalled at a rest stop just south of the state line," Bill said. "Troopers towed it eventually, and I found it a few days later in the impound lot."

"Does it still run?"

"Oh, yeah. They got a flat tire, parked it, then probably hitched a ride north with some truck-driver." I envisioned the two of them schmoozing some poor bastard in a Peterbilt, telling him all about their exotic cruise on the Titanic Ocean.

Bill produced a set of keys from behind a peg-board on the wall, but kept them in his grasp; his hands resting on his waistline. "What are you going to do?" he said in a way that betrayed his feelings on the subject.

"I'm going to get in and drive," I said. "What do I owe you for getting it out of impound? For the new tire and all that?" I don't know what I thought I could pay him with; I had only a credit card on me. Still, it seemed like a polite, southern thing to say.

"Nothing," Bill said smiling sadly and glancing at his house. A big part of me wanted to let him take me in there, but not the right part, it seemed. I took a step out of the garage and let the sun beat hot on my face.

"Well," Bill sighed. "You know what they say: 'If you love someone, sooner or later, you have to give her the keys to a crappy Dodge Neon.'"

"You love me?"

Bill put his hands on my waist. "I'm a guy who knows what he wants."

I put my hands up on Bill's shoulders and buried my face in his chest for a long moment. I took the keys from his closed hand, kissed him on the cheek and smiled.

"Lucky you."

Chapter 41

Dear Estelle,

Haven't heard from you since my last note. Hope everything's okay. I have some exciting news for you, but I'd rather tell you on the phone or something. Why don't you call me next time you're in Houston? Go ahead and call collect. I can't wait to talk to you. That's all I'm going to say.

I will give you one hint, though: Yesterday, we took all my girls off the bedroom walls and packed them away.

Call me, woman!

Jack

***

A thousand questions ping-ponged in my head as I pulled out of Bill's driveway, not even knowing whether to turn right or left at the end of the street.

I pulled over two blocks away to collect myself, slow down my breathing. I prayed that Bill wasn't following me, then I prayed that he was.

Confused! Confused. Scared. Pissed off. *Bill needs to get his stupid, shit-kicking, dumb hick ass out of my head. I know what I want. I know who I love. I know where I'm going.*

My head slightly clearer, I resumed driving, then pulled into the first gas station I saw. It was time to focus, and to wash the mace out of my hair. I would need gas and provisions, I figured. It wasn't easy finding anything even resembling healthy grub at the local convenient store, but I made due with large amounts of trail mix, bananas, and apple juice. (Heni would have been proud. Lauren would have been proud also, but when I think along those lines, it makes me want to load up on chocolate Zingers and Rock Stars.) I also invested in a good map this time so as to avoid waking up in strange mobile homes and embarking on half-baked vacation plans with devious twin truck-stop waitresses.

Thirty-five dollars and sixty-three cents on the good old MasterCard at something like 33 percent interest. Couldn't be helped. It was going to be a long haul. I was making my way back to Minnesota, and to Jack. But first, a slight detour west to pick up a friend.

***

Dear Gloria,

Is that invitation to come see you still open? I don't know if I'm coming for a day or what. I just know I'm not ready to go back to Minnesota, I'm adrift, and you're pregnant, so I'm headin' west.

If you don't want me to come, let me know soon. Otherwise, I'm sleeping in this fleabag hotel tonight and I'm on my way in the morning. I hope you're okay. Same goes for Zeke, even though, frankly, he sounds like kind of a putz.

Love-
Estelle

***

San Diego took me two long days on the road, and to my surprise, mostly looked dirty and hot from the freeway. Then I realized that was just how *I* felt and was projecting that onto an entire city. I felt dirty, hot and hungry. Gloria's husband's parents' house was actually in La Jolla, a well-to-do suburb absolutely packed with cream colored townhomes with red adobe roofs. Palm trees. I'd never seen so many palm trees. Women in jog bras and men in camouflage Bermuda shorts with baseball caps and tribal tattoos around their insane bulging biceps.

I stopped at a Whole Foods to stock up. I craved fruit and meat. Twenty-seven bucks later, I had a bag of apples, half a dozen bananas, a chicken spinach rap, and a six-pack of mineral water. I'd forgotten about that aspect of the real world: nutritional food tends to cost twice as much as crap.

I sat in the Neon and munched on my wrap. Before my eyes walked some of the most beautiful human specimens I'd ever seen. I'd once heard some commentator from a fashion show on E! describe Minnesotans as "small houses." She must be from California. Of course, heavy Californians must exist, I surmised. Perhaps they aren't allowed to walk on this particular sidewalk in front of Whole Foods. Perhaps there is an alternate path for "big girls."

A blond gal and her blond dog both glanced at me as I stared longingly at them. They both picked up their pace. Apparently, I was frightening the natives. I popped my visor mirror down in front of my face. Comparing myself to these women was making me hungry. I glanced at my open hands. The chicken wrap was completely gone. I didn't remember eating it, or even whether it was good. I felt like I could eat another three of them.

Then it occurred to me to be nervous, so suddenly, I was. Gloria had never answered my note. Would she want to see me? I was finally in California. It felt like I'd been trying to get there for years, but I couldn't remember why. I didn't seem to belong.

See, that's what's so terrifying about being sober. There's nothing funny about it, most days. There are just all these feelings. Feelings and fears. Shit. I needed a meeting. I wondered what the meetings were like there. A big circle of addicted Barbie dolls with Coach purses and French manicures? *Hi, I'm Tempest and I'm a drug addict. Yesterday, my Shi Tzu got a hang*

nail and I almost had to take seventeen Oxycontin just to cope
with the stress of it.

Bad vibes here. Danger. I thought about getting back on the freeway.

Then, across the street, between a Kinko's and a Jimmy John's, I saw it. Cold Stone Creamery. Agony. Sheer temptation, agony and longing crept all over me like . . . like caramel syrup on a turtle sundae.

I wanted not to want it, but there it was. Not wanting it was not an option. It was distraction. Love. Escape. Hope. Sugar.

The ice cream was in my mouth before I even knew what I was doing. Supermodel Kate Moss once said that "Nothing tastes as good as skinny feels." She's probably never had cake-batter flavored ice cream with cookie-dough chunks.

By the time I got back on the road, I felt like the Amazing Imploding Girl. It had been a long time since I'd had *binge-belly*. My abdomen felt like a hundred marshmallow-shaped gremlins were fighting to exit my body through the navel. I had a pooch, like a kitten with a tape worm.

For one lousy burp, I would have happily killed a puppy. For the ability to vomit, I'd have stolen a wheelchair from one of Jerry's kids. How did I live like this before? And was I going back to that?

Shit.

Double shit. I'd found the house.

I remained parked in front for the longest time. So long, that I lost track of time. So long, that I fell asleep. I awoke to a tap tap tap on my half-open window.

"Ma'am?"

Tall. Shades. Buzz cut. Badge.

"Bill?"

"No, ma'am."

"Then, uh, what?"

"Do you live around here, or are you visiting somebody in this neighborhood, ma'am?" The officer glanced at my back seat, probably looking for drug paraphernalia but only seeing an empty Cold Stone bag. "The neighbors are getting concerned. They say you've been here for . . . quite a while."

Just then, a bob-haired brunette wearing a white t-shirt and a brown tie-died skirt walked up to the passenger side of my car. It took several seconds to realize that it was Gloria.

"Is everything okay, officer?"

She was barefoot and tan; I'd never seen her so pretty, or so shaggy.

"Do you know this lady?"

Gloria leaned into the passenger window of my car and smiled. What had I been so worried about? She didn't even seem surprised to see me.

"Yes, officer," we both said.

"Good enough for me," he snorted, adjusting his mirrored shades and walking back to his squad.

"Those dudes sure don't try too hard to fight the clichés, do they?"

Gloria shook her head and giggled. I'd never heard her giggle. I didn't know she had one.

She smoothed one hand over her baby bump.

"Come inside. You're ruining the neighborhood."

***

We talked and talked, at first. It was just like old times, minus one large empty White Castle bag and thirty-two Three Musketeers wrappers.

It was lucky that Gloria was even home when the officer pulled up. Normally, she spent her days as a volunteer waitress at Zeke's parents' restaurant, where all tips and profits went toward staffing a local homeless shelter. She had thrown up her breakfast and decided to take a sick day.

Gloria was a little more than two months along, so she figured it happened some time while they were on the road. Zeke had been gone two weeks. He had called once to tell her he was at the dentist getting "root work" done and might be a while. That was five days before. His parents were a mess, and didn't even know about the baby yet.

"You're different," I finally said. It was the elephant in the room. She was wearing Birkenstocks for shit's sake.

"I know," she shrugged. "It's Jesus in my life. In my heart."

I squirmed. That again. But it was hard to deny. She had a certain Mackenzie Phillips quality about her. She was all *Zen*. Setting aside all the flowery Jesus talk, I was jealous. But hadn't I grown? Hadn't I changed? And how could I even think that, with half a quart of Cold Stone burning a hole in my gut? I hadn't changed. Maybe I never would.

"What's wrong?" Gloria leaned in on me.

"I fucked up," I whispered. "I was doing so well. But I should have known. Leave me to my own devices, and it's only a matter of time."

"No!" Gloria announced. "That's not true. You can get back on track. You're strong. I'll pray for you."

I recoiled a little. This was just too much. She was sweet, she was serene, and she was . . . praying for me? All this change for the better was making me desperately uncomfortable.

Just then, a door opened from the back of the house and we heard the jingle of keys being set on Formica. Gloria listened intently to the sounds, smoothing her hands on her legs.

"I'm sure it's okay that you're here," she reassured me.

"Oh, well, good."

A small, round woman in her mid-fifties shuffled in, and Gloria stood up. She wore clothes that looked to have been purchased for "business casual" purposes about ten years ago.

She looked as tired as her sweater vest.

"This is Estelle, Lana," Gloria said. "She came all the way from Texas to see me."

"Nice to meet you, honey," Lana sighed. "Will you girls be eating with us tonight?"

"If that's okay." I'd never seen Gloria so polite, eager to please. I stared at my feet.

"Sure. Sure," Lana said.

"Let me know what I can do to help," Gloria said.

"Okay, dear. Actually, just wash and peel some potatoes. I'm going upstairs for a little nap." She paused at the foot of the stairs. "Hear anything today?"

Gloria shook her head and the woman trudged upward, slouching.

Gloria paced to the front window, her hand returning to her back. She looked right and left. "I don't think he's coming back," she said matter-of-factly.

She looked at me. My face said "duh."

She turned to face me. "What did you come here for?"

"I just . . ."

"What?"

"Thought you might need a ride back to Minnesota?"

"You came here to save me."

"A little."

"You came here to save me, but you're the one who shows up all stressed out. Come here to see me. Come here to be with me. Don't come here thinking you can save me from something. I *am* saved."

"Jesus."

"Exactly."

"You don't even know where you're going to live."

"Jesus provides."

"Right. I got that part. What's his cell? I'm just wondering if he delivers in thirty minutes or less."

A phone rang from the adjacent dining room and Gloria quickly bolted from the window to the kitchen.

Both women yelled "I got it!" and from what I could tell, both women picked up different extensions at the same time. Gloria stood silently with the receiver to her ear, suddenly looking angry. After a long moment, she said, "How can you be sure it's him then? You guys don't know what the fuck . . . I'm sorry. I'm sorry for swearing. But I just don't think . . ."

From upstairs, I heard something crash onto a hardwood floor, then a loud, "Oh, no! Oh, no, no no no, Jesus, no."

Gloria was right about Zeke, the not coming back part.

I closed my eyes and imagined I was wearing flip flops and a flowing sundress with Paris Hilton sunglasses, standing in the sun on the deck of a giant cruise ship. Feeling skinny.

***

People came from everywhere. Church people. Neighbors. Family from all over the state. They weren't there in Zeke's memory so much as they were there for his parents, who, between the restaurant and the church, were extremely popular with a wide range of types. Hippies, ex-junkies, city council members, even a bishop showed up at the house with potato salad, apologizing for the fact that it was store-bought.

Little was said about the fact that Zeke had died of a heroin overdose. I registered only small amounts of surprise about that from the beginning. Except from Gloria. Gloria walked around in a barefoot daze. When she tired of walking around, she *sat* in a daze.

Two days before the funeral and on the day of, there was nothing but food and people in a steady stream hour after hour. Blacks, whites, Asians, Hispanics, Indians. Bean casseroles, lemon bars, cream cheese tortilla wraps. I've never seen so much booty in all my life.

Lana turned nothing away, but stopped dealing with any of it after the first day. As the sun began to set and the people started taking their shoes, repeating how sorry they were, and filing out the door, I started to see it. I started to see why I was there.

For the food.

Not to *eat* the food, but to manage it. Every day, I made it my duty to heat and cut and serve the food to all the visitors, package all the leftovers, freeze what needed freezing, divide what needed dividing, and wash what needed washing.

I kept the coffee flowing and the cups clean. I cleaned up the floor when the mayor's granddaughter spilled Jell-O salad all over Lana's sisal rug. I threw out some deviled eggs that smelled less than Kosher, then realized that's actually how they always smell.

I made sure Gloria ate something.

On the evening of funeral day, Zeke's dad finally noticed I'd been crashing at his house for almost a week.

"I'm Richard," he said. He looked as if he'd let a child draw the black circles under his eyes, yet I sensed a glimmer of charisma. "I'm so rude for not having introduced myself before."

"I'm Estelle. And please don't apologize for that."

"You're quite the hostess, I hear. Keeping everything running. Thank you."

"No problem, padre. I live to serve."

"Estelle, have you come to know the Lord our Savior?"

Should have seen that coming. I cocked my head.

"I mean, I think we're friends on Facebook, but you know how *that* goes . . ."

"Well, I'll just say that Jesus loves you, and if you ever have any questions about that, you can ask me."

"Um, all-righty then."

What could I say? His son just died. *I'm sorry for your loss, but would you please stop being all filled with the Holy*

259

Spirit? And besides that, I did. I did have a question.

"Actually, I do have a question."

"Yes? What is it?"

"Am I . . ." As I began to speak, the weight of all my searching seemed to rush straight to my forehead. Even though I'd never thought to ask it, suddenly I felt that if this man, who claimed to have answers, didn't actually have one, well, I was going to have to hurl myself off the Golden Gate Bridge. That is, if I didn't accidentally book a cruise somewhere along the way.

"Am I ever going to be normal? Thin? Happy?"

"Well, that's three different questions, now isn't it?"

"Not in my mind, no."

"In God's mind it is. Do you pray for those things?"

"No. I just wish for them really, super hard."

"Pray for acceptance. You don't have to be ashamed of who you are, Estelle. God made you and is proud of you." His smile was heavenly; his tone soothing. I felt that if he'd have put his hand on my forehead, a demon might have flown out and I would have said a few words in Latin.

"Did God mean to make me a sugar addict? Because if he did, that wasn't very nice."

"God has a plan for you, Estelle."

Crap. He lost me at "plan." The priest at the Catholic church my parents go to used to always say that. What does that even mean? We attribute plans to all our bigwigs, in the hopes that they actually have their shit together so we don't have to. God has a plan. The president has an agenda. Santa Claus has a list. I submit they're all just winging it – especially The Big Guy. If not, then explain the second Bush Administration.

"I think I better go catch up on the dessert plates," I sighed. "That cheesecake is a real barn-burner with the evangelicals."

The pastor scratched his head. "Uh, did you say, you were a *sugar* addict?"

"Yes, indeed."

"What do you do when you crave sugar?"

"Oh, you know, the standard addict stuff. Sometimes I go crazy and eat everything sweet within five miles of me. Sometimes I join a support group. Sometimes I actually quit it for a while. But it's always there. It's always just around the corner, and no matter how good I'm trying to be, BAM! I always end up back at square one. We live in a sugary-sweet world, Rev. And I'm a sugarfiend."

"What's your favorite?"

"There's too much to pick from. I couldn't name just one thing."

"Just one thing," he insisted.

"Okay," I said. "Special K bars. They're a killer."

The pastor smiled an unholy smile. "Me, I can't stay away from those Krispy Kremes. God help me! They're so delicious."

"Don't worry, Padre," I said re-tying my apron. "I'll pray for you."

***

The next morning, we all slept late, exhausted from all the funeral traffic. I was up first, and made my way down to the kitchen. I examined the options from the funeral booty. I remembered an egg dish Heni had once made me using Indian spices and spinach. I grabbed some leftover pan masala from the refrigerator and got to work.

By the time Lana, Richard and Gloria had made their way down the stairs, I had a stack of oatmeal pancakes in the oven, eggs almost ready on the stove, and fresh coffee made.

"What's all this?" Lana hugged her bathrobe and breathed in deeply.

"Breakfast," I said. "Take a seat."

Gloria and Richard entered right behind her, sniffing the air like eager puppies.

"Look at you, smarty-pants." Gloria yawned. "Where'd you learn to cook?"

"I cooked at the duplex, didn't I?"

"You baked. Box cake. Cookies. You never cooked."

"Oh. Right."

With everything else ready, I set some jam and honey down for the pancakes.

"Bon Appétit!"

Lana took a bite of the eggs; Richard went straight for the pancakes. Gloria grinned at me like I had schmutz on my shirt. Then the three dug in while I stood there like a moron, glowing. I couldn't help it. I felt like I'd driven to Houston, circled the Caribbean six times, then trekked all the way to the Pacific Ocean for one purpose:

To make a meal for this family.

As if she had also heard the theme from *Chariots of Fire* playing in my head, Gloria set her fork down and stopped chewing.

"Richard and Lana," she said, loudly enough to drown out my inner synthesizer, "Um."

Lana and Richard sat up straight; Lana grabbed Gloria's hand with hers. She said, "Go ahead."

"I'm going to have a baby," Gloria said. "I'm pregnant."

Richard gasped, slamming both hands on the table. Lana burst from her chair with a loud "What?" Gloria looked a tad scared, but still hopeful. Then, the two mourning parents enveloped their grandchild's mom like a big loving Venus Flytrap.

It was time for me to go home.

* * *

I didn't spend a ton of time saying goodbye. Kingdom-Comers like Richard, if they know their time is limited, pull out all the stops to get you to Trip The Lord Fantastic. I barely made it out the door with my poor condemned soul intact.

"Here, take this with you," Richard said, handing me a small tree's worth of glossy color brochures from his church. Guess they don't call it "organized" religion for nothing. I shoved them into a grocery bag Lana had filled with snacks for my trip.

Lana hugged me, thanked me a million times, and made me write down the pancake recipe.

"I want lots of pictures of Gloria Junior," I said, wrapping my arms around Gloria's neck. "And take care of yourself."

"I'm going to be okay," she said, which is really all she'd been trying to tell me for months.

***

Back at Whole Foods, I stocked up for my long trip. Peanut butter, whole wheat bread, kiwis, grapes, crackers, guava juice, Bran/mango muffins. The clerk handed me the receipt, but I just stuffed it in my pocket without looking. Whatever the cost of decent food, I figured I'd spent twice as much every day for booze on the Love Boat.

My car was once again parked facing the sidewalk. I piled my booty into the seat next to me, pulled my keys out of my pocket and hopped in. I busted out the guava juice and took a long swig before putting the cap back in place.

A lithe middle-aged blond stopped just left of my car and waited as her greyhound shat on the grass. She pulled out an adorable pink plastic bag and, as if she was a ballerina stretching at the bar, bent down to pick it up. Geez Louise. And good Lord, the creepy smile on her face, as if she was picking up a downy yellow baby chick off the ground instead of dog excrement. And get a load of those Chiclets. *If I didn't know better, I'd think she was . . .*

She sure was a dead ringer for . . .

Holy Downward Dog.

It was effing Denise Austin.

"Denise Austin!" I blurted out with no preamble. Her smile turned quizzical. "Denise God-damned Austin!" Her smile faded.

"Can I help you?"

"Oh, you've helped me *plenty*, Denise Austin," *Holy Filter. I should probably dial the Jack Nicholson back a bit.* "Er, I mean, you've probably helped *millions.*"

At this, Denise Austin seemed to un-tense a titch.

Truth was, I didn't know how I felt about Denise Austin anymore. I had spent six weeks on a cruise ship with her disciple, Lauren, monitoring my every move, morsel and bowel movement. Had that helped me? Had it hurt? Here before me was the epitome of the California Girl, female perfection. The American Dream in Danskin jog shorts and matching t-back cami. Did I hate her for that? Did I still want to be her? Could I just go ahead and live on the same planet with her? And all her clones?

"Well," Denise Austin's face softened. "I'm glad . . . if I helped you." She didn't move. Perhaps she was activating a silent security alarm for just these types of occasions.

"This is Grommet." Denise Austin gestured to her dog. I knelt down to pet the poor thing and he cringed. "He's a little shy," she said, shrugging. "I just got him from a rescue two weeks ago."

Denise Austin, dog rescuer?

"You both seem nice; you both have really white teeth," I said awkwardly. Perhaps I should just never, ever, speak to anyone but close family and friends from now on. For everybody's sake, really.

Denise Austin laughed and started back down the sidewalk. "Nice talking to you, now . . . what was your name?"

"Estelle," I said. Because that's my name. "Ooh! Could I get you to sign something?"

Denise Austin's matching stretch outfit turned back toward me. Then patiently, she stood and waited while I rummaged through my trunk to find my DVD.

"Here we go," I said, pulling out one of my all-time favorite ass-kickers: *Shrink Your Female Fat Zones!* It was an instant classic from the early turn of the century featuring Denise Austin front and center on the cover in a white tankini and a golden tan across her insane six-pack. The last time I'd attempted this little romp was with a belly full of Special K bars. It made my gut ache to think of it.

"Oh! You like this one, huh?" Denise Austin said.

"It's brought me such joy. I can't describe it."

She examined the cover before signing it with my Sharpie. Then she shook her head, handed it back to me with a pained expression, and shrugged. "Not my favorite picture of me."

"Huh?"

"Anyway, very nice to meet you Estelle," Denise Austin beamed one last thousand-watt smile at me. Then in a super-toned spandex flash, she and Grommet were gone.

***

For probably the first hundred miles, I chewed on those words: "not my favorite picture of me." I thought about the look on her face when she saw that DVD case: like she'd been cleaning her car and found a moldy apple core under the seat. Remarkable. Denise Austin, the face of the fit female, with thighs like a Greek goddess and abdominals that defy reason, had Self Loathing. It flew in the face of logic.

265

I kicked myself for not saying something encouraging, like maybe "Denise Austin, you're the most beautiful middle-aged woman I've ever met!" which would have been true, or perhaps "Denise Austin, everybody has a bad camera day," which I assume is true or "Denise Austin, you totally rocked that tankini!"

But I know from experience that none of that ever works. It never works on *me* anyway. Denise Austin has to believe it for herself, Bea would have told me. You can't make her believe that she's a *freaking goddess.*

Oh, Bea. Would I call her when I got back? Would I ask her to be my sponsor?

Of *course* I would.

The only alternative to that would be run into her at some meeting somewhere and have her kick my ass into submission with those Hitler boots of hers. Would Bea be my sponsor again? It wasn't really a matter of choice; I figured was okay with that.

Which brought me to Jack.

Every mile marker I passed, I was conscious of getting slowly closer and closer to him.

When he saw me, I knew he'd be able to tell me if I'd changed. I needed to know. Going back to him would be a comfort, like relaxing onto a childhood bed in the house you grew up in. I pictured a sliding onto his lap, kissing his face, his lips.

Did I love him? Yes. And I figured in time, I'd also *fall in love.*

On that point, I was pretty sure.

Chapter 42

Dear Jack,

Sorry it took me so long to get back to you. I meant to write or call once I got to Gloria's, but then Zeke died and . . . well, I'll tell you all this when I see you tomorrow.

That's right, tomorrow! I'm coming home. And you're my first stop.

Love-

Estelle

***

Jack

The most ridiculous thing about that big, grandiose cliff-diving dream I always have, in my opinion, are the big brass balls I have when I'm up there staring down at that water, those big fucking rocks. In real life, it wasn't quite like that. I didn't jump willingly; the three times I went up there, I was scared shitless and doing it to impress somebody. That last jump was, of course, meant to impress some girl . . . a girl whose name I would have eventually forgotten if she hadn't been so intricately tied in with the day I dove into the Mississippi River and snapped my neck like a dry twig. Stephanie. In case you're wondering. She never came to see me at the hospital, but she did send a "get well soon" card.

Every once in a while, I hear something on the news about stem cell research and advancements in treatments for spinal cord injuries. Someday, they say there will be no such thing as paralysis caused by trauma, as long as it's treated in time. Someday, they will find a way to bridge the gap between pathways, and a broken neck won't mean life in a wheelchair anymore . . . for some other guy.

Usually, I turn the channel to something else.

Isn't that some shit? I can't quite be happy about it. I can't get myself to go there. Because one thing's for sure: that guy who gets to walk again won't be me. There's no bridge left to be built in my busted body, no pathways to be fixed. Just wheels and tubes and wet dreams about walking.

After my fiancé left me, I crawled into a cocoon and surrounded myself with daily routines and pictures of naked ladies. I figured the naked ladies were always smiling and of course they'd never leave because their parents were uncomfortable with wheelchairs, or because they can't give up their Coach purses. Every morning while some poor nursing student got me ready for work, I'd stare into their vacuous eyes. Miss March looks a lot like Stephanie, the girl who looked so great in a tube top that I broke my whole life to try and win her.

I'll never forget the first time Estelle saw my bedroom walls. That morning and every morning afterward, she looked at those girls the same way I look at a young man playing soccer in the park or some guy taking a woman in his arms on a darkened dance floor. Why can't that be me? That will never *be me. Our sadness made us soul mates. Her longing took the edge off mine.*

***

Back home day one: Déjà vu all over again.

Welcome to Minnesota, sayeth the big wooden sign at the Iowa border. It's always nice to know you're no longer in Iowa.

The last time I returned to Minnesota from being gone, I was leaving Jude, and my life was not unlike the large pile of poop in Denise Austin's little pink plastic bag. The first thing I did when I got to my parents' house was tell them everything. I was a crack addict. I was probably an alcoholic. I'd stolen two-hundred dollars from their dresser drawer right before I'd skipped town, and later I'd pawned the ruby ring they gave me for my grade-school graduation. I was twenty-three. While all my old high school friends were looking at graduating college, I was filling out paperwork for a 28-day spin-dry.

I liked treatment, and I liked getting sober. When you're in treatment, everybody's your cheerleader. All you have to do is not fuck up and the crowd goes wild. "You've been sober five days? Good for you!" "You've been sober 23 days? We always knew you could do it." "You got up and put the right shoes on the right feet again? Here's five dollars!"

Step nine says you're supposed to apologize to anyone you've harmed by all your bad behavior. I never really got past the first two or three. I just rode the wave, hoping my sobriety was apology enough.

But sooner or later, the shine starts to wear off your sobriety and people start expecting good things of you, as a rule instead of as an exception. That gets tricky for me. I could really use a little pocket-sized statue of Benjamin Bratt on my dresser every morning, whose only purpose in life is to tell me how awesome I am.

It's hard coming back to Minnesota like this . . . again. The cheerleaders will be leery. I thought I was going to California to save Gloria from her latest crisis by bringing her home. Now it's obvious I was just hoping to create a diversion. Everybody look at Gloria! She's pregnant again. Isn't that just so much more fucked up than running away and joining the floating circus?

***

So that night, I found myself not at Jack's condo, but in my Mom's kitchen, reunited with Sesame. The cat seemed very happy to see me.

"Would you like some Tabouleh salad?" mom said nervously, rummaging around in her new stainless steel refrigerator. They'd done a bit of a remodel while I was gone. Hey. Life goes on.

"I'd love it," I said enthusiastically.

"Some rice pudding? Er, no. You're not eating sweets, right?"

"No rice pudding, thanks." Sugar or no sugar, rice pudding is just *wrong*.

"Your dad's golfing," she said for the second time. "If he'd have known you were coming today, of course he would be here."

"It's okay, Mom."

Sesame sat on my lap, staring at me intently. His expression was a loving one, but I knew with certainty that there'd be a *where the fuck have you been* turd in my duffle bag in the morning. I scratched between his shoulder blades.

"So tell me all about your cruise," mom said uneasily, placing the salad in front of me. "Cruises, plural?"

"Mom, sit down, would you?"

She took off her apron and sat. She let out an exasperated sigh.

"Okay, what the hell have you been doing for the last six weeks, Estelle? Besides taking five years off my life from worry?"

"*That's* more like it, ma. Good on ya."

"Well?"

I told her everything. I told her about the first time I ever got high, the last time I ever got drunk, and every single bullshit binge in between. I told that I'm addicted to sugar, to men, to meetings, to drama. I told her it's not her fault.

Then my dad got home and I told it all to him.

I told them about the truck stop twins, about the cruise ship, about Heni, about Tweezer. I told them about Bill.

I told them I was sorry not just once, but about seventeen times in seventeen different ways. I ninth-stepped the *stuffing* out of them.

Holy shit. We talked for three hours. When I was finally done talking, we were hungrier than hell, so Mom and I went to the grocery store. I had a kick-ass recipe for herb-crusted lemon chicken and just needed a couple of things.

An hour later, my dad had downed three helpings of string beans with almonds, and the cat had finished up the last of the white meat. Mom poured herself a glass of red wine. Dad rested his hands on his belly, satisfied.

***

The next morning, a Sunday, I popped out of bed jumpy. I showered, borrowed a puff of Avon perfume from my mom, curled my hair, checked my teeth for basil, and even used a little eye liner. In my old bedroom, I found a few of my super-tiny high-school jeans, which, despite Lauren's and my best efforts, still made me look like ten pounds of Jell-O in a five pound sack. *One day at a time,* Bea's voice advised. I opted for some baggier cargo pants and a stretchy black top with a scooped neck.

I checked the mirror one last time and added some hoop earrings to the ensemble. I raised my arms uncomfortably. Sweat was tingling in my pits and I couldn't figure out why. Was this a lover's reunion or a job interview? I guess I'd find out when I got there.

The Neon felt troubled, like I'd run the thing a few too many miles on the same old oil. The half-hour drive to Jack's felt twice that. That's the thing about coming home after you've been gone a while. Deferred maintenance catches up with you.

I pulled into the parking lot of Jack's building. The door to Jack's ground-floor condo was propped wide open, which was unusual, and not generally a good idea in a low income housing complex.

Just then, a short brunette with curly bobbed locks and Susan Sarandon eyes came bounding out with a large cardboard box in her arms. She seemed to be at the end of a pretty good giggle, which basically died the moment she saw me.

"Oh," she said, shifting her weight from one round hip to the other, "are you Estelle? Jack's, um, in there."

"Thanks," I said awkwardly. She was already several steps away from me when my mouth had finally formed words to ask who she was. I watched as she shoved her box into the back seat of a maroon Honda Accord, hopped in and pulled away, just slow enough to steal another look at me.

Oh, never mind, anyway. Jack awaits. I fluffed my hair a bit and crossed the threshold without knocking.

"Jack!"

Away from the office for so long, he had grown a Fu Manchu, and his hair had grown past the collar of his flannel shirt. He smelled freshly showered and familiar. His arms were out, so I dove on in. When I finally pulled my face back to look at him, I was in his lap.

"Atta girl," Jack sighed. "Now tell Santa what a bad girl you've been."

"You look great," I said, and kissed a cheek.

He moved his forehead to meet mine.

"I was afraid I'd lost you forever. Let's never do that again."

"Which part? The part where I ran away to California but wound up in Belize?"

"The part where we let our pride get in the way of our friendship."

"Yeah, that part sucked."

"Good. Now get off my lap before I do something I won't regret."

"You look great," I said, straightening up. He really did.

"By the way, check the fridge," he said proudly. "I had Kia pick up some peach Fresca. You mind grabbing me a Pepsi out of there?"

That reminded me. "Kia?"

Jack pulled up to his dinette table while I cracked open our sodas and dropped a straw into his.

"You saw her on your way in, didn't you? She works with me." Jack glanced at his TV, which was off. "I keep telling her she doesn't need to take so many trips now that I'm in there half the week, but . . ."

"She works on Saturday?" *Ambitious little thing.*

"Not at the office. She's started filling in around here when Absolute can't find anyone on the weekends . . . for extra money."

Like I said.

"Oh," was all I could think to say. That, and, "She sure was cute, in a plus sized model sort of way." (You know, those ones that are supposedly "plus-sized" who are actually somewhere around a curvy size ten, with lips like rose petals and cute Swedish noses.)

Jack just laughed. Then he looked at his TV again. It was still off. Gah! This couldn't be happening. I left a promising career as a homeless panhandler in Houston just so I could come back to Minnesota and reclaim my title as Jack's Queen Crush. This Kia chick was cramping my style.

"Anyway, she's not coming back 'til dinnertime so we can catch up," Jack grinned. "So tell me everything." He took a long draw off his Pepsi. "Are you banned from just one boat, or the whole Caribbean Sea?"

"I think just the entire Gilligan fleet," I said honestly. "But I'm pretty sure Belize is still an option for me if I get the

273

fraud thing straightened out. I'm a hell of a lobster fisherman, you know."

"Fraud? Lobster?" Jack shook his head. "Tell me all about it, my dear."

**

Jack's a good listener. He must have gotten that way from years and years of people telling him what his life is going to be like from day to day. *You're never going to walk again. You're never going to function normally. I'm going to stretch your leg now. I'm going to put this ointment on your skin. The nurse is going to bathe you now. Then you're going to bed.*

I talked and talked at first, but then I started thinking about all the things I didn't know about him, and it started to bug me. I didn't know how he got into programming. I knew he'd been engaged once, but I didn't know what happened that he became *unengaged*. I knew he had family down south, but that was *all* I knew about it.

So, when I got done telling him a very brief version of my Close Encounter with Denise Austin, I started asking him about his life.

"So, she left you because her parents didn't like you?" I asked, sipping on an ice-water.

"I don't know," he shrugged. We had dug out a picture of his ex-fiancé, and were discussing how homely she was, and how nobody liked her.

"I think she was scared," he said finally. "And her parents were a good excuse."

"I'm sorry you had to go through that," I said. "That chick wasn't even fit to empty your leg bag."

Jack got lost in a thought for a moment. Then out of nowhere, he smacked his hand on the table.

"Holy shit! That reminds me," he beamed. "They took the catheter out. I got my dink back!"

"Dude! If I'd known you got your dink back, I'd have baked a cake!"

I jumped up and hugged him again.

"Well, then a toast," I said finally. "To your junk. Live long and . . ." I paused. "Okay, I should probably use that filter thing I keep hearing about."

"Awe," Jack smiled. "You have grown."

I have? Squee!

"Yeah, yeah. So what do you see yourself doing in five years, Jack?"

He chuckled. "Is this a job interview?"

"No! It's just something I've never asked you. And unlike most people, your answer might actually be interesting."

"Well," he said, hooking his elbow around the handle of his wheelchair. It was something he did when he needed to re-straighten himself in the chair, and also something he did when nervous.

"I want kids," he said finally. "I mean, first, I want a house and a good woman. But eventually, I want kids."

"*Really*?"

"My fish still swim," he said sheepishly.

"Lordy."

"Are you looking at my junk?" Jack exclaimed. "You're unbelievable."

"No!"

"You are!"

"Only because you were talking about your fish."

"Pervert!" Jack howled, and we both lost it for a bit.

"You should talk," I said finally. "You with all the naked boobies on your walls."

Jack wiped his eyes with the back of one hand. "I told you, I took the centerfolds down."

I jumped up and walked over to the open door of his room. Sure enough, the walls were bare, but for about a million tape marks and smudges.

"I hope you didn't do that on my account."

"No. Kia doesn't like them either."

Oh, *her*.

"She's one smart lady," Jack sighed, then seemed to be enjoying a memory he didn't plan to share.

That's when I noticed all the U-Haul boxes on the floor.

"You doing some spring cleaning, Jack?"

He wheeled himself into the middle of the bedroom, shrugged his shoulders and said, "I'm moving!"

"What? Where? When?"

"I'm buying a house."

"Whoa. How'd you swing it?"

"I had a lot of down time when I was sick, so I did some research on accessible homes. Then Kia hooked me up with her brother, who's a mortgage broker, and I found out I qualify for some help if I buy an existing house and renovate. The rest is . . ."

Jack's expression changed and his head turned toward the bedroom door.

"History?" I queried.

"Hey, there," Jack said to somebody other than me.

Was it Kia time already? My, how time flies when you're trying to decide whether you're in love with your best friend. I guess that's what I was trying to do. I was trying to decide when was the right time to make a move, or if I should. Right up until the point that I realized it didn't matter half a crap how I felt at all. He was in love with someone else.

How do I say it? The dude was smitten. He couldn't have looked more in love if Kia had come in holding a basket of baby seals. Then Kia blushed. She had changed clothes. Her white pullover fit close to her skin, and her lip-gloss was extra glossy, and the whole affect was -- forgive me – paralyzing for Jack. *Jesus, what a Lifetime Movie this is turning out to be.*

"I brought a take and bake pizza," she said finally. "Are you having dinner, Estelle?" Not really entirely an invitation.

"I could eat," I said. Not entirely an acceptance.

Kia smiled uncomfortably and headed off to the kitchen. I turned to Jack.

"So . . . how long have you two . . ."

"What?"

"You're going to make me say it? You limey bastard."

Jack's face went blank for a second.

"We're not. And don't go getting me all hopeful."

"What . . ." I stammered. "What d'ya mean hopeful? If that chick doesn't dig you then I'm not Estelle Brown, the Scourge of the Western Caribbean."

"Okay, shut up already," Jack hissed. "You're going to embarrass me."

"Is she married?"

"No."

"Gay? Psycho? Mormon?"

"No, no . . ."

"Then you're a punk bitch if you don't do something, like, soon."

"Woman, I will punch you in the . . ."

"Yeah, yeah. Why are you being so shy?"

Jack hesitated. We listened while Kia opened and closed drawers and cabinets in the kitchen, then maneuvered a second chair to Jack's tiny dinette. She was setting a table for three.

Jack sighed. "Last time I told somebody I loved her, it didn't go so hot . . . did it?" he said finally. "I don't want to scare her off."

Well. *Shit.*

"I think it'll go better this time."

"You think so?" Jack said without a big ton of certainty.

"Yes."

"Why?"

"Trust me. It's pretty obvious you two have been up in here acting like a couple of chess club nerds waiting for somebody to make a move. She loves you. She wants to make babies and renovate kitchens and do all that happy shit with *you*. I'd bet my Neon on it. Stop being a schmuck."

When I finally shut my big yap, I noticed that Jack's face was about as red as Kia's, who had been standing behind me for who-knows-how-long. I've never been able to perfect the *silent* diatribe. Kia clutched a pizza cutter. I hoped she wouldn't use it on me.

Jack chuckled nervously; he re-hooked his arm on his chair.

"Pizza's ready," Kia said at last.

We ate in silence for a bit.

Finally, Kia started in with the polite questions.

"So, Estelle, did you like working on the cruise ship?"

"Yeah. I did. There was this cook named Heni . . ."

"And this cop named Bill," Jack broke in.

"And all kinds of wacky characters I won't bore you with," I said.

"She doesn't want to talk about Bill."

"Tell us about Bill," Kia insisted. Of course, she would want to know about Estelle's Other Love Interest.

So I told them all about the old boy, the g-rated parts anyway. I told them about the day we met, his t-shirt fetish, and the way he's always grinning and how mad it makes me. I told them about the day he arrested me and about the epiphany I had in the back of his squad car. I told them how he found my car for me and kept it safe until I could come back for it. I remembered how hard it was to drive away from him, but didn't say that part.

But I could have been telling them I'd fallen in love with Jack the Ripper for all the attention they were paying me.

Somewhere between the first time I snubbed Bill and the second time, they had caught one another's eyes, and they had come to some sort of silent understanding. And it was mutual. And it probably involved K-Y jelly and a Little Bo Peep costume.

Kia started clearing dishes off the table, so I followed suit.

"Do you like strawberry shortcake, Estelle? I could put a dessert together."

"Er . . ." I was feeling vulnerable. Probably not a good time for shortcake-related stress relief.

"I'd have some," she said, "but I'm trying not to eat so much sugar lately."

"Of *course* you're not," I muttered.

"What?"

"I said 'I'd love some strawberries.' Just the berries, please. I'm trying to cut back, myself. A little."

"Well," she said sincerely, "whatever you're doing, you look great."

When Jack wheeled me out to the parking lot to say goodbye, I reminded myself not to hop in his lap again.

"Are you mad at me?" I said, hugging his neck.

"You know I'm not."

"Are you going take Kia for a test drive?" I couldn't help myself.

"Woman!"

"You know you wanna."

"Goodnight, Estelle."

"Goodnight, Jack," I said with an exaggerated wink. "Happy packing."

Chapter 43

Hi Bill,

I just thought you'd like to know where I'd landed, and whether I landed on my head, my ass, or my Converse All Stars.

First off, I've been sober 90 days last week. Also, I haven't eaten compulsively for 56 days. I know what you're thinking: "An alcoholic AND a compulsive overeater? That's insanely hot."

Also, I'm living with my parents again. It's not ideal, but it's amazing how much smarter and more interesting they got while I was gone. We've developed a bit of a routine. Every weekday morning, I toddle off to cooking school (more on that in a bit), I learn a thing or two in class, then I come home and experiment on them at dinnertime.

We had a bit of a scare during "shellfish" week; we learned the hard way that oysters make my dad's windpipe close up tighter than a frog's ass. Bless his allergic heart. There he was with the paramedics trying to shove a tube down his throat so he could breathe, and all he wanted to do was tell me that despite the fact that it was just about killing him, my Bayou Crostini was the best he'd ever tasted. As if he'd ever even had Bayou Crostini before. I swear, man, if you have parents that love you, don't ever take it for granted.

Anywho, you read it right. I'm in culinary school.

About a week after I got home, I got a letter from Lauren at Gilligan of all people, asking me if I wanted my job back! She said they sold more books and seaweed pills that last morning on the ship than they had all month. People wanted to know what all the fuss was about, and they were impressed by my "passion." She said I could come back and say whatever I wanted. She said that Gilligan found my "Dr. Phil" straight-talking style refreshing.

Bea and I agreed whole-heartedly that any boss who wants me to act like that hack-shrink-moron all the time is destined to fire me again eventually, and that returning to that cruise ship is tantamount to living in the proverbial barbershop. Someday, I'll explain that one to you.

Still, I figured, I wouldn't mind being a cook like Heni. Not on a cruise ship, but in a really swank restaurant somewhere in Minneapolis maybe, making wild rice burgers from scratch and sweet potato fries and the like. In case you hadn't noticed, I'm a bit of a Food Person.

I ramble.

The point is, I think about you a lot.

That's actually what this note is about. I didn't really think you needed to know that I'm studying to be a chef or that I love my mom and dad or that Gilligan Cruise Lines will hire anyone with a pulse and a social security number.

I miss you.

See, there was this guy I used to think I needed, but he was in love with a Mills Fleet Farm model or something, and anyway, he only called me when she was on a psych hold and he wanted some pussy, and I of course I don't mean my cat.

I never wanted to feel that way again -- like what I am isn't enough – and I was afraid you had the power to put me back there. So I figured I'd cut you off at the pass. Even if we never get to be together, I think you deserve to know that you're more than enough. You're all that and plus a bag of organic flax corn chips. You're the reason I find myself watching "Cops" reruns every blessed night, and you're why there's now a country music station programmed into the stereo of my Neon.

Cooking school lasts another ten months. After that, I don't know where I'll be, or if I'll ever be anywhere near Texas again. But if you ever want to spend your precious vacation up here in God's Country, southern man, you let me know. The fishing's good, the food is better, and if all three days of summer land on a weekend, we have a picnic. So, mi parents' casa es su casa. That's Spanish for "You'll have to sleep on the couch, but if you can wait 'til the folks go to bed, I'll definitely let you get to second base."

> Love with a capitol L,
> Estelle

***

Oh, *argh.* Putting myself out there like that made me want to change my focus to "cake decorating" then do some seriously intense cream cheese frosting research.

But it's not the "outcome" that matters, Bea reminded me when I told her I was writing to Bill, it's the "effort." Addicts in recovery like to say that when they feel with an almost absolute certainty that the person they're trying to mend the fence with is going to tell them to take all twelve steps and shove them where the sun don't shine.

She also advised me that "God laughs when you make plans." *This* is what addicts in recovery say when you try to accomplish something, you hope for it real hard, and then it all goes to shit anyway. God finds that humorous, apparently.

For four long days, I waited. I didn't just wait; I hung on pins and needles. I pissed vinegar. I shit a brick. I hoped. I meditated. I called Bea three times and went to four meetings. I pictured God throwing his head back and laughing at me with a hearty "bru ha ha ha."

I got a little jolt when I pulled a card out of the mailbox, handwritten, with my name on it. On closer inspection, I realized it was from Jack. The front of the card was a cartoon house with a "handicapped" parking sign in the driveway. Inside, it read: "Join Jack and Kia for a housewarming on July 11th." A side note from Kia said, "We sure hope you can make it!" They had gone from being just "Jack" and just "Kia" to "Jack and Kia."

Heavy sigh. When you're missing somebody, it sure seems like the whole rest of the world walks around in pairs. I was happy for them, but would have been a whole lot more so with Bill's tongue in my ear.

I set the rest of the mail down on the kitchen table, then started thinking about dinner. "Poultry week" at Le Cordon Bleu Cooking School was actually more like three weeks, and my parents were getting the slightest bit tired of being subjected to my various adventures in chicken preparation. *Baked. Fried. Broiled. Grilled.* I leaned into the bump-out window over our kitchen sink so I could see my mother in her herb garden; she was pulling weeds from among her chives.

"Should I just grill some steak tonight, Ma? Maybe toss a salad?" I called. "I think we've probably had enough bird for one week."

She looked up, but didn't answer. Instead she appeared to be trying really hard to make sense of something by the front door through the lens of her tri-focals.

"Excuse me, ma'am," a familiar voice said. "Are you Mrs. Brown?"

He was dressed like a dude on vacation. His knee-length khaki shorts and brown leather flip-flops said "I don't actually know how to fish, but I could learn." His t-shirt said "Sarcasm. Just one of the many services I offer."

I tackled him; there's really no other way to put it. I tackled him like he was Brett Favre on the one-yard line. But he held his own and stayed on his feet.

"How did you find me?" I demanded. "How did you get here so fast? How long are you staying? Does this mean you still want me? I bet it does."

Bill just laughed and held me.

"Never mind," I said after a moment of breathing him in. "I don't need to know everything." God in heaven, he smelled good enough to eat.

.

www.ingramcontent.com/pod-product-compliance
Lightning Source LLC
Chambersburg PA
CBHW030036180626
46810CB00001B/392